TUTEM'S POOL

TUTEM'S POOL

LOCKHART MOON

Library of Congress Control Number:		2014905568
ISBN:	Hardcover	978-1-4931-8941-0
	Softcover	978-1-4931-8940-3
	eBook	978-1-4931-8942-7

This book was printed in the United States of America.

Rev. date: 04/04/2014

To order additional copies of this book, contact:
Xlibris LLC
1-888-795-4274
www.Xlibris.com
Orders@Xlibris.com
553523

For preparation of the typescript and continued encouragement, I shall always be grateful to Theresa. To members of the Upstate Bar Associations, who insisted on anonymity, I acknowledge the drama and vivid struggles of their profession. *Dura lex sed lex.* Hard is the law, but it is the law.

In all my travels in the world, Greenville is my favorite town, the equal to Athens or Rome or even Paris, the city of light.

DEDICATION

Dedication to C., muse, and to swim coaches all over the world who taught us how to swim with the fishes . . . and the sharks.

There have been many pools in my life. Pools of love. Pools of ambition. Latin pools. Risky pools and safe pools. They have all been the same to me. I got ready. I learned to swim in each pool and perfected my strokes. And then I started the first race. Swimmers, to your mark, get set . . . I dove in and swam as hard as I could.

Fred Tutem
Unpublished Journal

PROLOGUE

I have found four realities since this whole process began. One is the reality of the present and its demands to breathe or eat. To put one foot in front of the other. Another reality is the reality of memory where, for moments at a time, you take yourself to some other day or week or month, editing and selecting as you go, magnifying or diminishing. The third is the reality of sleep and dreams— so much like memory but compressed and more vivid, distorted by intensity, beauty, and terror. The fourth is the most subtle reality of all—just after sleep and just before the day begins. What is it then? A dream or a wish or a memory?

What is reality then?

What happened to my life?

Who fed me the strawberry?

I wanted to remember . . .

CHAPTER ONE

Where is she? Where is she? It's so dark here on this damn road! Don't they have street lights out here? Ha! She told me she was a country girl—ridiculous. So many curves. I have been up Highway 25 once. Now what's this? Fields? My lights are disappearing, but the moon might come out. What's this, Cliff Falls Road? I'll turn here. This ol' Porsche still has some muscle. That's why I love it. Whoa! Too many curves. Is somebody following me? Vvvvvrooooommmmmmm. That'll leave 'em behind. Oh no—a tree . . . CRRRRAAAASHH!

Do I smell something? *Do I smell something?* Ke-k-k-k-k-rack.

CHAPTER TWO

Uuuuuuuuuuuuuuuuuuueeeeeiiiiiiiii! Yaaaah!

"Make him shut up!"

"You're the one with the morphine."

"Yeh, but you're the one who wants him to shut up."

Nnnnneeeeeeeeueueueueueuiiiiiiiii.

"He's thrashing now. We've got to cut the dead skin off. They always scream when we do that. We better give him some morphine."

"We'll let the attending worry about that. There, it's done."

Mmmmmmaaaaahhhhhh.

"All right, hurry up. Boy, that's messy. We have to trach him."

SSSSHHHHHH–tck–fffuoh–SSSSHHHHHH–tck–fffuoh–
SSSSHHHHHH–tck–fffuoh–SSSSHHHHHH–tck–fffuoh–
SSSSHHHHHH–tck–fffuoh–SSSSHHHHHH–tck–fffuoh–
SSSSHHHHHH–tck–fffuoh–SSSSHHHHHH–tck–fffuoh–

The ooze from his face looked like Carolina BBQ Sauce, mild to hot, tomato-based. It oozed over the bandages into his ears, down his neck, and onto the sheets of the hospital bed. The interns pulled at him for twenty minutes with forceps, scalpels, and little scissors. His neck was burned too and also his arms and chest.

He had been pitched free of the wreck just as he caught fire, although he was on fire the whole night—chasing her, chasing his dream of her, an image swimming before him, just out of reach in a lake of darkness—until the crash and the fire.

Someone had followed him.

CHAPTER THREE

SSSSHHHHHH–tck–fffuoh–SSSSHHHHHH–tck–fffuoh–
SSSSHHHHHH–tck–fffuoh–SSSSHHHHHH–tck–fffuoh–
SSSSHHHHHH–tck–fffuoh–SSSSHHHHHH–tck–fffuoh–
SSSSHHHHHH–tck–fffuoh–SSSSHHHHHH–tck–fffuoh–
SSSSHHHHHH–tck–fffuoh–SSSSHHHHHH–tck–fffuoh–
SSSSHHHHHH–tck–fffuoh–SSSSHHHHHH–tck–fffuoh–
SSSSHHHHHH–tck–fffuoh–SSSSHHHHHH–tck–fffuoh–
SSSSHHHHHH–tck–fffuoh–SSSSHHHHHH–tck–fffuoh–
SSSSHHHHHH–tck–fffuoh–SSSSHHHHHH–tck–fffuoh–
SSSSHHHHHH–tck–fffuoh–SSSSHHHHHH–tck–fffuoh–
SSSSHHHHHH–tck–fffuoh–SSSSHHHHHH–tck–fffuoh–
SSSSHHHHHH–tck–fffuoh–SSSSHHHHHH–tck–fffuoh–
SSSSHHHHHH–tck–fffuoh–SSSSHHHHHH–tck–fffuoh–
SSSSHHHHHH–tck–fffuoh–SSSSHHHHHH–tck–fffuoh–
SSSSHHHHHH–tck–fffuoh–SSSSHHHHHH–tck–fffuoh–
SSSSHHHHHH–tck–fffuoh–SSSSHHHHHH–tck–fffuoh–
SSSSHHHHHH–tck–fffuoh–SSSSHHHHHH–tck–fffuoh–
SSSSHHHHHH–tck–fffuoh–SSSSHHHHHH–tck–fffuoh–
SSSSHHHHHH–tck–fffuoh–SSSSHHHHHH–tck–fffuoh–
SSSSHHHHHH–tck–fffuoh–SSSSHHHHHH–tck–fffuoh–
SSSSHHHHHH–tck–fffuoh–SSSSHHHHHH–tck–fffuoh–

Suddenly he felt sleepy as the Valium and the narcotics took effect, and he lay there now like a big over-toasted, over-confected dessert. His face caked on dark chocolate, raspberry, and strawberry sauces dried on the crisp chocolate wafers of his skin. His eyes, two cherry-streaked marshmallows. He had been cooked too much in the oven of love, she said.

That was a nice way to think of his pain and the burning that he still felt. At least he wasn't drowning any more as he slid into sleep. He had been in darkness so long.

Now, there was light.

CHAPTER FOUR

Several days flickered by in a morphine haze like a mountain fog. Skin grafts, more debridement, more bandages, more skin grafts. In and out of awake. In and out of aware. In and out of sleep. He was a leaf in the high wind or a branch attached to a tree in a storm, something floating in a strong current.

So I didn't know if I smelled it or not. Sometime, as they waited for me to heal, there it was—a heavy smoldering fragrance, not like a fire but like some bloom full of pheromones and plant musk—a drop of it would fill the room.

I felt myself saying, "What's your name?" and I heard her cry. She was the source of the smell, and I couldn't see her. I felt her take my hand. I felt something soft—that was her skin. Then she moved my hand onto a very soft cloth—she whispered, "This is my dress—we'll get you back, baby." I felt a hug, and then she was gone, but her perfume lingered, and it's the first thing I began to remember day by day. She repeated her name each time she came by—Travis Camelia Boykin. She told me to call her TC and said we had known each other our whole lives. She had been on the swim team with me. If I couldn't remember a detail, she repeated it and repeated it and repeated it until a compelling picture of our chronic romance had formed. She tried to add a new paragraph or two each day, and I tried to remember the story as well as her smells and the way the skin on her face and thigh felt. "I am going to reeducate your senses. Call me TC," TC said. All I could remember was Travis. That's what I'll call her.

Days passed in a fog of pain, painkillers, caresses from Travis, and perfume . . .

Finally, the bandages came off. Travis wasn't there, so now I am looking at a picture of myself—at least I think I am. It's very hard to think. I know I have been burnt by something. Let's call it fire.

In the mirror, scars cover my lips and cheeks but my hair is trying to grow back. My plastic surgeon, Bruce, swears the scarring will go away. "All this is temporary. Just the skin healing. We have done nice split-thickness grafts, and pretty soon we will have you back in the pool once your legs heal up," Bruce said. I wasn't sure exactly what he was talking about. He talked like he knew me very well. Did I help him with his divorce, really? "You really helped me with that divorce, Bubba, and I am going to look after you."

What divorce—who are you? I keep thinking about swimming but in what pool? Who am I? The fire burned me totally—outside to inside, like barbecue ribs.

"Now, Fred, I am giving you this picture just for a keepsake. Don't let it frighten you. Look here in the mirror and you can see that you look nothing like this now. I have done a pretty good job—the least I owed you, Bubba."

The surgeon was snappy in creased whites and immaculate greens. Even his OR cap was spotless, and his cheeks had a new tan. He was lean as a race horse too and looked like the kind of guy who would catch a session in the tanning booth after his workout. He kept a store of nicknames for everybody. He trailed gossip like footprints throughout the hospital.

In the picture, I am a wreck—total. The skin is cracked and oozing, burnt and dried like some evil dessert—chocolate, raspberry, strawberry, barbecue sauce—burnt meat. Cake. The hair frizzled down to charred nubs like melted nylon rope. My left ear is covered up by black ash and soot. My face looks like I used a gasoline mouthwash for a stupid magic trick but swallowed it just when it caught fire. Maybe I had French-kissed a dragon with acid reflux, bad reptile acid reflux. I can't laugh, and I can barely think.

He tapes the picture by the bed, pats my foot as he leaves the room.

I still don't know who I am. I want a caress. I need some perfume. It's about time for Travis to get here.

She was coming by every day, fresh as a flower. This time was a little different. She looked around warily and closed the door. Then she took off her beautiful winter coat and snuggled up to me on the bed. She had put the rail down, and then she stretched her lean leg up on the side, steadying herself with her other foot on the floor. She nuzzled me and hiked up her skirt, putting my hand on the warmth of her thigh. I could see now. They had taken the bandages from my eyes, and now I could see what I had been feeling those long days in darkness. Today, she had on my favorite musky perfume. It was winter—I could tell by her dress, a puffy turtleneck number with a slit down the side. She was like a mink in heat.

Was this the same heat that burned me in the first place? I knew it could have been. It burns everybody—but it was keeping me alive for now.

"I can't wait to get you home, baby," she said.

"Now just where is my home?" I asked.

"You don't remember. I have been telling you day after day your home is with me."

"But, Travis, all I remember is your name now. You've convinced me that you're my girlfriend, but I still don't know where I live—I mean house, street, like that."

"Okay, we'll go over it again. You live at 43 Crescent Avenue—got it. It's a nice big roomy house my mother left me. You've got to remember me by now." She pouted. I was burned, and she was pouting. Go figure.

"Okay, okay." I wasn't sure at all of course, but I went along. I knew she came every day. I knew she called herself Travis, and the nurses called her either Travis or TC. I knew she smelled good and different from all the salves and creams that were slathered on my face. I knew she felt good.

"Listen, Travis, of course I remember you. Who could forget you?"

"Now, that's better." She smiled and kissed my hand. "Bruce said I could take you home at the end of next week maybe. I've got a room all fixed up, and we'll have home health nurses if we need them."

"Whatever you say, honey. I know I can depend on you."

After that, she kissed me a little more then left. Her perfume lingered. I could remember her skin all day. Otherwise, I still remembered nothing except what she had told me over and over. Even that sometimes vanished with a bandage change. But I was getting further away from morphine. The tendrils of fog that wrapped me like a kudzu vine had stopped growing at last.

I think that two days after this—maybe the day before or maybe midnight that day. I had no way of knowing because the light stayed the same in my room. The blinds stayed closed, and I couldn't see daylight or the winter sky. I don't know what time it was, but I think I saw—or I think I know I saw—someone peering into my room. Very carefully. The door eased open, and the silhouette of a rather plump girl appeared in the doorway. I couldn't see her face well, but her body was swollen. She appeared in the doorway. I think she wore some kind of uniform. I saw the reflection of a button or a badge. She came a little closer, and I could see her long hair. Her abdomen protruded. For one instant, I saw her face. I felt sick. I felt frightened, and I wanted to moan in a primal way. I stirred in bed, and she vanished. Was this a dream? I had a troubled sleep. The next time I saw the nurses, they said I had screamed, and they had asked me why I was crying. Something else I didn't know.

CHAPTER FIVE

"Fred, you have been out of it a long time, my man." I heard this through a kind of early haze, that time in the morning when you can't really get up, and you can't go back to sleep.

"I am Craig—maybe you don't remember—Craig Olds. I am a neuropsychologist, and I specialize in head injury. We worked on a case together a couple of years ago—remember the kid with the head injury? The one with the crushed pelvis?"

"I am sorry, uh, Dr. Olds. I really can't remember much of anything right now."

"Well, you always impressed me with your Greek references and the Latin you liked to quote—what was it, *Abyssus Abyssum Invocat*. You said it meant, 'Hell follows hell.' Well now, that might apply in lots of ways," he said and winked.

I didn't know what he was winking about, but there was a friendly conspiratorial quality about it—so I winked back.

"Do you wink like that often?" he asked.

"No, I was winking back at you."

"Oh, oh. Anyway, I am sure your memory isn't working exactly right. Your winker isn't either. Those scars, you know. You took quite a lick on the head, plus we don't know how long you were unconscious from the fire, and you couldn't have been breathing well. Your poor brain has been jerked around a lot in the last month. I am here to try and quantify exactly what's wrong if we can do that. Can you see all right?"

"I think so."

"Good. Now let's start at the very beginning. Your name is Fred Tutem. Do you understand?"

"Okay, thank you. I couldn't remember that either, but it sounds familiar."

"Let's get started on the rest of this."

He then did a brief test to see if I could follow his finger around while he waved it in the air in various directions. He made me touch my nose. He made me grin and stick out my tongue—I felt like a misbehaving kindergarten student making faces, about to be sent to the corner for time out. In a way, this whole thing was time out from something and because of something I did—I just couldn't remember. Maybe time out does follow hell, who knows. What the hell is hell any way?

Dr. Olds talked on and tried to explain what we were going to do. He had a thick sheaf of papers with questions and designs, numbers and rows upon rows upon rows of answers.

"This is a neuropsychological test. It will help us fully see where we need to go with your rehabilitation. It's going to take all day, so go pee right now, and then let's get to work. Want some coffee?"

"No, thank you. I have already had breakfast."

The breakfast was barely palatable—a cup of oatmeal, some fruit, and some watered-down coffee with one of those containers of juice that doesn't open right so you can cut yourself on the foil top. Just what I needed, a paper cut. One more reason to stick out my tongue. I couldn't taste anything with it anyway.

We settled in for the day, and it was boring. I couldn't remember things. I was slow in my reaction time. Dr. Olds just shook his head every few minutes. I couldn't remember three numbers in a row. I couldn't copy a circle right. I don't know what a rolling stone does. Rolls, right? I would love to yell fire in a crowded theater over and over again. I yelled it in my sleep any way, and I smelled it all the time. Lying in bed looking out of my bandages had been better than this test.

By the end of that day, Dr. Olds' chipper manner had become grim.

"Well, I can see we have a lot of work to do, Fred, but I am hanging in there with you."

When he gathered the papers and left the room, his white coat swirled like an opera cape.

Where is the fat lady? I haven't heard her singing yet. But today's opera was finished.

I tried to sleep. None of my dreams were clear, only fragments of test questions. Nothing made sense . . .

CHAPTER SIX

The next few days, I worked with Dr. Olds and also with physical therapy. They stretched me and pulled me like play dough. Everybody seemed to know me, and everyone winked and leered like I was a naked circus freak, a big burn scar we'll mold into something we just don't know what yet.

Finally, I asked Dr. Olds what happened to me.

"Fred, you mean you don't remember any of that?"

"No, I don't. I have told you that now twenty times. Is my memory bad, or is your memory bad?"

"Well, at least your sense of humor is coming back a little. I don't know the full story, but I'll tell you what I know. You got in some kind of trouble at work. There was a girlfriend involved, and then you were found out on Cliff Falls Road, above Travelers Rest, knocked out beside a burning car. You've been here since then. That's all I know, really." He shrugged.

"Why would Travis not tell me any of this?"

"What do you mean?"

"When I asked her, she just patted me on the head and kissed my hand and said, 'That's okay, baby, we are going to make you feel better.'"

"Well, use your thinking skills."

"I don't have any."

"Well, try to use your thinking skills. Either she doesn't know what happened to you, or she just doesn't want to tell you. You're going to have to ask her again." Wink.

Whatever the hell that meant.

Dr. Olds says I have amnesia—as if that cleared things right up. I am walking, and that's some progress, although I have a funny little twitch in my right leg. They assure me it will go away, but I am not sure—I am totally unaware of how it happens. Sometimes a fog comes over me after a strong bout of twitching while I walk. Maybe it's a new dance—let's call it the "Brain Fog Boogie." You do it to beach music, like the shag.

Anyway, when I asked Dr. Olds my diagnosis, he winked (wink, wink) and said, "Amnesia, of course . . . or did I forget to tell you." (Wink, wink, wink.) He is certainly a merry little psychologist.

He did tell me my CAT scan was normal—thank God—and my MRI showed nothing. They couldn't do an EEG because my scalp was still burned—the neurosurgeon had said, "Fred, buddy, I think you are going to live" and chuckled like this macabre sense of humor would cheer me up. "You will be around to help me with my second divorce." (Ha-ha!) I guess I helped him with his divorce too.

I had finally figured out that I used to be a lawyer. Now, with that tidbit of information from Dr. Olds, I wondered whether my neurosurgeon's ex-wife had tracked me down, beat me up, and burned me—that would mean I had been a good divorce lawyer I guess . . . It must have been nasty—or maybe it was my plastic surgeon's ex-wife.

Sometimes it's nice to have amnesia . . .

———+—+—+—+—+—+———

CHAPTER SEVEN

We worked and worked and worked. Every day I did memory drills. I learned words that seemed new to me—like butterfly, flower, the sound of dogs barking. Olds even got a law text brought to me to see if I could still read: "Wherefore, party of the first part Article VII, Paragraph 4, Part III. The proper transfer of assets . . ." and so forth. See section CFR part two, subsection 3A.

He was fond of quoting Latin to me—just as, apparently, I used to quote to him.

"*Fugaces labuntur anni*," he said one morning, looking at himself in the mirror.

"What's that supposed to mean?" I asked.

"You wake up one morning and find you are old. I didn't have this gray hair here yesterday. How the fleeting years glide by. Those Latin scholars really could say it just right."

Suddenly I had a memory from college. It took me under like a wave. I was not in the hospital any longer.

There I was in Professor Labban's class. Captain George Labban who doubled as a Latin scholar and an ROTC instructor at Washington and Lee, my alma mater. It all came back to me suddenly. The drilling, over and over and over again. "Attention, present arms, parade rest." And the Latin verbs. We were the best in the whole school because we had the only course in conversational Latin. The captain prided himself on that and used to boast that there wasn't another course on conversational Latin in the Western Hemisphere, anywhere except the Vatican.

In between ROTC drills, we walked around with pipes and tweeds, pretending we were Romans. We stood vigil on certain nights of the year—the Battle of Fredericksburg, the Battle of Richmond, and of course, Appomattox. One of us was always sent to the chapel to see if Robert E. Lee's tomb shook during our displays of commitment to honor, truth, and duty. We were sure he raised his marble arm to bless us. A polite glass of sherry and a toast to the memory and ideals of Robert E. Lee always followed. The next day, we could be as rowdy as we'd like; but after the Appomattox celebration, we always cried. The whole campus was quiet as a tomb—"The night they drove old Dixie down." Played out from the KA house, repeating all morning.

A whole chunk of my life was restored in that moment. I felt oriented in a strange new way. My leg had been twitching, and I felt as if I was coming to, out of a sleep or a dream.

Olds was shaking me. "Fred, Fred, it's all right."

"I just remembered something, and I wanted to get all the details before I came back to this hospital."

Olds calmed down and looked pensive. I noticed now how properly dressed he was—his white coat pressed, name embroidered on the left hand side with a hospital insignia above it. He always wore striped shirts, buttoned down and starched. His pants were creased like razors. He had shiny loafers. His hair was a little mussed up, and his beard was so light he probably shaved only every other day.

Before his Latin phrase, none of this would have seemed possible. I took a deep breath.

"Craig," I said. "I am going to call you Craig from now on."

"Good, because I told you to do that about a week ago. Maybe you have remembered something . . . What is memory any way?" he mused.

"Now, that is a very interesting question. To be lawyerly, I don't know, or rather, we, psychologists, don't really know. We have ideas about how it happens—bursts of norepinephrine, lying down associative tracks in neuronal pathways. But why, for instance, would you suddenly remember an entire chunk of your own history that up to now you couldn't—simply by the prompting of one phrase—can you follow all of this?"

"Yes, I think I can."

"Well, the study of memory is fraught with all kinds of dynamic possibilities. I have even dabbled a bit in the oriental ideas of yoga and universal consciousness. I believe that Dr. Jung, an associate of Dr. Freud, had some thoughts about these matters as well. For you, however, it's going to be question of repetition, kind of like building muscle. Do you remember how you used to swim all the time?"

"Not really."

"Well, I'll tell you. You used to swim every day. I saw you at the YMCA from time to time, although mostly you came in the middle of the day when I was working. The reason I mention this is the practice you did—stroking over and over and over, up and down the pool—breaststroke, freestyle, backstroke, butterfly—at least an hour every time. Now, this is what it's going to take to get some of your memories back. I don't think you will ever remember the actual events of your accident—but you might. You are making good progress so far. So I would say, *"Persta* atque obdura"—as he said this, his eyes were twinkling.

"Please don't wink," I said.

"Okay, okay, be steadfast and endure." He had me repeat this, and we actually wrote it on a card and taped it to my bed—the same as the other cards that gave the date each day to keep me oriented—my name is Fred. This is December 5. Now *"Persta atque obdura."*

After he left, I was full of questions that hadn't occurred to me before. I even felt a little hope for a moment.

CHAPTER EIGHT

I smelled her before she arrived in my room. Her perfume wafted down the hall like a line of trumpeters playing a flourish for a queen.

In fact, she had become a kind of queen to me. I looked forward to her smells and the fussy little rituals of dependence and sensuality that she performed each visit. The uneasy part of me simply hibernated—"Who am I?"—crawled into a crevice in my injured brain and rested, hidden there.

"Honey, I am taking you home next week."

"Well, I love you, Travis, but this is news to me. Nobody has said a thing."

"Well, I just went over to the doctor's office a minute ago and told him I was ready to look after you, and I can do it by myself."

"Are you talking about the plastic surgeon, the neurosurgeon, or Craig, the psychologist?"

"Well, over the last two days, actually all of them."

"So you have been planning this for some time."

She looked at me directly with her beautiful brown eyes, and her face grew faintly red.

"Yes, I have." And suddenly her eyes were moist, her pupils grew wide, and her lips parted as she whispered, "You are mine now, for good."

My heart started beating faster. I knew this without an electronic monitor—I wanted to push myself up in bed. I couldn't fight, and I couldn't flee. I wasn't ready for love like this.

She pinned me down with perfume, and both of her hands on my unbandaged arm—one in my palm and one in the crease of my elbow, as if she were taking my pulse. Her soft hair fell forward onto our faces as she leaned over and kissed me. Her lipstick was fresh. I was totally overwhelmed.

"Poor darling. You hadn't thought this moment would come, had you?"

"Well, actually, no. There is still so much I don't know about anything, including the exact story of what happened to me, what I was doing, why I was doing it, and what do I plan to do in the future—besides be with you—am I really a lawyer? Can I drive anymore? Travis, I have just begun to walk, but I still get tired, and I have got pains everywhere. Are you sure you want to do this?"

She reared back. She focused her eyes with a determined glow. "Of course, I do. You think you are tired now. You wait till I get you home." She licked her glossy lips.

"Travis, okay, okay."

She relaxed a moment and then leaned over and kissed me again. This time she put her hand on my waist, and I felt her squeeze my side.

"It's time for me to go now. I will be back this afternoon, late, and bring you some home cooking. The stuff they have been feeding you is garbage." With that, she got off the bed and swirled around. Her skirt was fairly long and contrasted with vivid colors. Her blouse was a cream-colored silk, buttoned low at the neck. She wore a strand of pearls. She turned at the door and blew me a kiss again.

I thought—well . . . This is going to be a new adventure—and I haven't really gotten over the first one yet, whatever it was.

Just then, one of the nurses came in and asked if I was all right. She had not done this before that I could remember.

"Yes, we have to check on you after Ms. Travis comes."

She leaned over, looked at me, and whispered, "Please don't forget." She then proceeded to take my pulse at the neck and the wrist. She took my blood pressure in a crisp and efficient manner then smiled and disappeared without a wink—thank goodness.

I could not fathom any of this. Travis had appointed herself my guardian and keeper. The nurse had been conspiratorial.

I felt dizzy all of a sudden.

Craig told me to take deep breaths when I felt like this, so I gave it a try. I wanted my respirator back.

CHAPTER NINE

"Well, you have come far enough to start reexposure therapy," Craig announced as he strode into the room, groomed like a show pony. "I don't know any Latin phrase for that, but maybe you'll remember one as we go along."

"Well, that would be 'Felicitous,'" I said and tried to smile. The smiling hurt my still chapped face.

He chuckled then announced "We are going in the 'OLDS' mobile—my car." So he helped me get dressed, and we checked out at the nurse's station. The nurse who had told me not to forget eyed me warily but said nothing.

The hall smelled like antiseptic mixed with feces—initially unpleasant but after a few moments, not bad. Maybe that's what babies smell at birth. Maybe this was the start of reexposure therapy. Life is part antiseptic and part feces. Sometimes you can't tell the difference. Maybe that's why babies cry when they're born.

It was a chilly gray day. We were in late fall now—late November or early December. The sky was gray and sunless. Workers risked their lives to put up Christmas decorations in the huge hospital lobby. They perched on ladders, dangling chains of lights and special glass ornaments to spangle all over a forty-foot tree. Two sub-sub managers in suits and ties supervised them.

I had noticed on other walks with Craig that there was always a manager involved in anything—one painter painting, one manager supervising, one electrician holding the ladder, one electrician putting in a bulb, one manager supervising. Three plumbers walking in the hall trailed by one manager on a walkie-talkie. The managers were everywhere.

"Craig," I asked, "why are there so many managers?"

He looked at me dumbfounded. "I don't know."

"Is this part of my reexposure therapy?"

"Sure—they call it managed care," Craig said and grinned.

I didn't know what he was grinning about.

I still had a week to go, so Craig took me out to drive around parts of town that might jog my memory.

"This is going to be a long ride in the Oldsmobile." He winked again—dammit.

We set off down Faris Road headed toward the older part of town. The pavement was pitted in places, the roadside thick with old vegetation, azaleas, dogwoods, and huge oaks dominated the city forest there. All kinds of houses planted in between the trees. I could see that it was late fall now. There were still big piles of leaves, and the trees were mostly bare, trunks gray, pewter with age, like silver-backed gorillas or proud old men— white oaks, red oaks, maples, arthritic-looking dogwood trees struggling for the sun and gnarled up wild cherries poking out beside driveways. The fermented smell of leaf smoke from somewhere flavored the afternoon. The golden light made my heart hurt. I remembered everything and nothing. I had been here before, a thousand times, and I had never been here at all.

We drove up and down side streets with big houses and carefully tended lawns, shrubs crowded, and flower beds full of fresh mulch. We drove past other streets that looked shaggy like English gardens then down other streets neat as Versailles—treetops and rooflines visible over brick walls. Little houses set back, big houses, new, next to the curb, and even bigger houses on big lots, with lawns like golf courses.

"Craig," I said, "this place seems familiar." I pointed down a street called Woodvale Avenue.

Craig said, "Well, it should—you used to live there."

"Really."

"Yes, in that gray house. When you and your ex-wife lived there, it was painted yellow. My wife and I live in that brick house four down. We used to have a Christmas party—all of us—for the whole block."

Suddenly, I felt strange, in time and out of time. A switch had been thrown, and only half the lights came on. "Craig, I actually remember that. I brought the ham, right. Well, actually, you brought the ham one time. That was the year you and your wife split up—when your daughters were still young."

He nodded yes.

Still more memories. Red and green ribbons. Christmas smells of orange peels and cinnamon. Clove apples. A bowl of brandied peaches. Trays full of rich desserts rolled in pecans, toasted and glazed. Little finger snacks of rare meats, strawberries from somewhere dipped in chocolate. Smoked oysters. Big platters of ham and turkey and roast beef. I remembered eating all of it one time. I was so skinny from . . . from . . . swimming all the time. That was it. I used to swim all the time, and that year the troubles my wife and I had made me eat my way through Christmas. I got sick from all the cheese and greasy confections that masquerade as Christmas cheer. It took me two weeks worth of milk of magnesia to get well.

This set of memories ran through my mind in a flash, just in time for Craig to stop the car.

"Are you all right?"

The chipper Dr. Olds with the striped bowtie, starched white coat, and creased khaki pants said I had only a week or so to go in the hospital. He intended this time to further orient me to my old neighborhoods, my town, and, if possible, my profession again.

—+—+—⋆—+—+—⋆—

The town was more beautiful than I remembered. Maybe I had taken too much for granted. The area around the hospital for several miles was packed with trees and shrubbery. Olds called the names: camellias, azaleas, roses, rhododendron, wisteria—gnarled up and roped around oak trunks like sailor's knots; oaks—white and red; plum trees, dogwoods—arthritic from chasing shards of sunlight; poplars—tall and proud, straight as Greek columns; maples—still partly in flame gold color from the end of fall.

We usually went out in the afternoons when the sunlight slanted through the trees, over the vivid green lawns, made my heart hurt with nostalgia.

For what? For whom? I couldn't answer. It was only autumn sunshine and the end of summer . . . Other people taking walks or driving with their tops down seemed afflicted with the same feeling too.

Maybe it was the great South Carolina mystery, a compound of weather, old politics, and lost causes put to bed with blood. Why did all that happen anyway? Why did we have the berserk Civil War?

The houses were nestled in groves of trees like afterthoughts. There were no straight lines. Street names did not change at ninety-degree intersections, but they did change in the middle of a block. Whose memorial? Whose right of way? What drama of annexation in obscure county planning meetings.

—+—+—⋆—+—+—⋆—

CHAPTER ELEVEN

Craig and I toured the ring of mill towns that surround Greenville—City View, Berea, Parker, the Bleachery—all named for the huge textile mills that sat in the center. Here, there were no big trees. The houses were smaller and more functional. There was obvious planning with squares and grids and patterns around the mill with small commercial areas for the little towns. I asked why everything was so empty, without any traffic.

Dr. Olds said, "The mills are drying up now. Everything is going to China or India or Asia. The town is changing fast."

I looked out the window, and that made sense. Lots of for-sale signs, barren shops, and grocery stores. We drove through like tourists without cameras. Change comes to everything, even southern mill towns. Maybe especially southern mill towns.

On our last ride from the hospital, we went out into the county and spent all day, from the flatlands in the South to the mountains up to Travelers Rest and Marietta. We took Highway 25 from the southern county line all the way up to North Carolina past White Horse Road, Cedar Lane Road, the large concentration of Mexicans near Lake Saluda in Berea, the vivid colors of late fall still hanging on in the hills and ridges and low mountains going toward Asheville. We swung back across to 276, climbed the winding mountain road to Caesar's Head, got out, and gazed down upon the great plain of Greenville looking like a point of pilgrimage for an ancient culture. We came back down through Travelers Rest, past Furman University and

Paris Mountain, and eventually got back to the hospital. This was our Paris and Rome. Our Berlin and New York. I was now starting to remember it.

"That's it for now, buddy. I'm taking a vacation starting tomorrow, but I'll leave your appointment schedule with Nurse Bolding. After you get settled with Travis, we'll expose you more."

"Thank you, Craig."

"You are welcome."

"Now, Travis is coming tonight and getting you packed up. You will be discharged tomorrow."

—✦—✦—✶—✦—✦—✶—

Travis came at seven in the evening—all business, slacks, and a loose shirt. One suitcase was all I had. Surely I had more stuff somewhere? Where? I took a nap and slept fitfully after she left. Dreams flickered like moths around candles. Who is Travis anyway? She seems so familiar and acts even more familiar than that. I appreciate her looking after me, but I feel like something is missing besides my memory. She is so sure of herself. I am not.

In each dream, I felt hot. In each dream, I was chasing something. In each dream, I felt my skin burn and smelled that peculiar barbecue without hushpuppies and slaw and fried okra.

CHAPTER TWELVE

When I awoke that morning, it was drizzling rain. I looked out my window to say goodbye to the hospital. Out the window, the fall dissolved in the rain.

Late fall in South Carolina is almost the same as winter. The rain knocks the leaves to the ground. One week all the trees are dressed like oriental princes; the next week they're naked as skeletons. Black, hibernating like bears. It seems cold even though the temperature isn't. The atmosphere is full of peril and promise—like a god who can't make up his mind.

The autumn has come and gone in a blaze of color—gold red, soft brown, and piney green. Even the grass is a color that makes you breathless. Lazy afternoons with sunshine lighting the leaves like antique gold. Then that rain starts, and the tree trunks have their golden coats in tatters on the ground. The summer never really dies. It just slips away. You can't put an end to it in your mind. It is as if the trees themselves were in the adjacent room, breathing in gasps on IVs and waiting for more morphine. You can't relax and grieve. There is no end and no clear beginning.

Carolina winters seem so very cold for all that.

Nurse Bolding came to me when I woke from this reverie for good. "Now, Fred, I want you to remember one thing," she said. "Your situation is complicated, way more complicated than you can understand right now. I want to be your friend through all of this, so I am giving you my phone number. I am putting it in your wallet, and whenever you finally need it, give me a call. Dr. Olds is looking after you very well, and I think that woman will try her best too." She whispered all this close to my ear.

"That woman?"

"I believe you call her Travis."

"Oh, well." I looked around to make sure she wasn't there. "You know, Nurse Bolding, I don't really know who she is."

Her eyes opened wide. "Do you want to go home with her?" she said. "Are you afraid?"

"No, no," I replied. "She has been good to me so far, and I like the way she smells even though she overdoes it some. Dr. Olds seems to think she would be good for me as well. I know I need someone. I can't remember which leg of my pants I am supposed to put on first."

"Well," she said and became very nurturing, "don't you worry, honey, you are going to be fine but try to remember this card. I have my name written on it as well as my phone number."

She looked around and then hid it in my wallet and patted my arm softly as she left. I felt her concern, but I could connect it to nothing.

Travis came soon after that . . . I couldn't understand the hospital bureaucracy. Checking out seemed as hard as checking in. I needed Travis's help. Forms to sign, satisfaction this, satisfaction that, agreements to pay, insurance forms, etc., etc., etc. As a lawyer, I should have taken more pains to read everything, but I simply couldn't. I was tired. I wanted to get to some rest—and I wanted to find out who Travis really was.

I wanted a meal—anything except damn hospital forms.

PART II

CHAPTER THIRTEEN

Travis drove me down Faris Road then turned onto Augusta then onto McDaniel Avenue. There at the corner was a huge magnolia tree. Travis pointed it out and said, "We are having a great party there this spring. You should be fully ready to enjoy it with me." This was delivered with no nonsense; why not party in spring? We kept going for another block and turned left onto Crescent Avenue, a street with a high canopy of trees, some privacy walls, and large older homes that exuded wealth and stability. She pulled into the third one on the right, parking her BMW in the circular driveway.

"All right, Fred, this is it. I am sure you will start to remember things once you get in. Mother gave it to me, then Tommy, that SOB, left me alone in this when he finally left town. I fixed it up real nice for you." She pointed with her well-manicured right index finger. Red polish on her fingernail.

This was the first I had heard of Tommy, so I guessed I was going to learn more about Travis in a hurry.

Through doors with leaded glass on each side and a little hall with several flower arrangements, big oriental rugs, rich, heavy pile, and a stairway with Mahogany bannister leading up to the upper floor. There was a living room to the left and dining room to the right—all of it rich and heavy. I felt uncomfortable, although Travis was nice and determined that I should be satisfied and completely at ease.

"What can I get for you now, honey?" she said.

"Well, I have a question that I think I can finally ask."

"Sure, Freddie, shoot."

"Now, please don't take this wrong."

"Well," she said, pulling herself up a little bit, "you can't tell me how to take anything just yet."

"Okay, okay, uh . . . Who exactly are you?" I phrased this the best I could.

Her face was a micro study in modern dance, the play of emotions skipping around to some rhythm I didn't know. After a minute, though, she settled on a wary, questioning look. "What do you mean, darling? I don't really understand the question."

I reached out and took her hand and tried to look at her eyes, although her soft hair had fallen into them, and they seemed to glisten. "You've got to understand, Travis, that I don't really remember anything, anybody, any place. Well, hell, I can't even remember church rituals. I remember nothing about my occupation, and I remember you only from the hospital over this past six weeks."

Then before I could think any further, she stood up and took off her clothes in a kind of languid and self-possessed manner right there in the hall. The black sheath woolen dress fell to the floor. The satin slip followed. Her panties weren't there, and her brassiere was a dainty little French thing that I had to help her take off.

"Well, let's just see if you can't remember anything," she said, pulling me over to the couch and unbuttoning my shirt.

What happened next felt very good. Even though I couldn't kiss her well with my still burned and tender lips, I felt her lips on me, and I did begin to remember something. *Water, cool water, flowing all over strong legs, wet, hot, sliding in and out, fish coupling . . . exhausted . . . I saw her smiling . . . And my eyes opened.*

"You sleep now, baby. I'll tell you who I am later," she whispered. "You remember lots of things."

CHAPTER FOURTEEN

Hours later, after I had rested, she announced that we would walk twice a day, and this was to be our first walk. She started out very simply on this mission to tell me who she was and actually who I was as well. I learned that we live in the city of Greenville in the state of South Carolina. Our street is in "the heart of the heart of Old Greenville." She grinned when she said that. Crescent Avenue is a crescent like the moon that shined through the French provincial windows of the house Travis lived in. Those windows designed by the great architect, Jacques "somebody."

"So this is the house that Jacques built?"

"Ha-ha," she said and pinched me, then bit my ear lightly for it was still tender. Then she whispered, "I am going to bite it off," which was startling and thrilling as we walked in the dusk.

"Where are we going—*quo vadis*?"

It seems we had dated in high school, and then I went off to Washington and Lee University in the great state in Virginia. She partied down at Converse College and then the College of Charleston. We broke up once in college and then again the summer before law school. I worked at the club pool in the YMCA as a lifeguard every summer. She even swam on the team one year with me. She had to tell me this stuff several times before it began to swim around in my mind unaided by flotation devices. She said I had loved the pool more than I loved her.

The dreams I had had of swimming began to make a kind of sense.

"You used to say, 'Water, water everywhere but not a drop to drink. This water is to swim in.' You'd dive in and then start the breaststroke." She giggled, held my hand to her right breast, and I was there in the pool, quick as a swim meet.

The water flowed over my shoulders pure as a mountain stream, blue and clear. The pool, light blue green, like a Caribbean paradise. "Go, Fred, go." Travis was screaming. In the lane next to me, the guy from Spartanburg was a half a length ahead. We pulled to the wall and flipped—when we came out of the turn, I had caught up, and I heard nothing after that except my breath sucking like a steam shovel. I felt nothing except the pool and my arms and the fevered rhythm of my frog kick. I was a bullfrog running from a ten-pound bass.

"Whew! Did I win that race?"

"What are you talking about?"

"You know, the one with old Robert Milliken from Spartanburg back in high school that summer."

"Oh my god! You remembered something." She danced around me like a forest pixie, kissing my cheek and rubbing her legs against me.

We were on a public street. We stopped our walk, and she put my arms around her. She started to cry.

"What's wrong?"

"Oh yes, you won the race that day. You won two things that day." She looked up at me with big tears in her eyes. "Don't you remember?" I remembered something . . . not sure, but I knew to be quiet.

"Well . . . After the race you won me. You had finally noticed me in my Speedo tank suit, and you claimed me for your very own. I remember you said, 'Me Tarzan, you Jane,' just like the movies."

Boy, she was really crying now. She still hadn't told me exactly who she was, but I was getting a very good idea. No wonder I remembered that race.

We made it home as the darkness gathered all around us.

Back in the house, we snuggled some, and although I was tired from the walk, I, as she said, claimed her again.

Tarzan again, right? Tarzan had long hair, and he remembered his way around the jungle, swinging on the vines and swimming in the rivers. I remembered that.

-+--+--+--+--+--+-

CHAPTER FIFTEEN

Travis slipped away to make supper, and I began to sleep.

"Oh, baby, you look so good swimming out there today." "Thank you, Travis . . . You know we shouldn't be doing this here . . . Bubba might catch us."

"Bubba runs the bar . . . We're in the women's locker room . . . In the sauna? The lights are out."

"Is that why it's so hot . . . ? Is that why your face is catching fire and my hands burn . . . ? Yeeeeeoooowwwwww!"

Travis was shaking me. I had been dreaming. I looked closely at her. I touched her face and lips with wonder. She was okay. Her face was not on fire. My hand was rough. It stung. I was crying. She hugged me.

"You'll be all right, darling. Let me fix us a little sweetener."

She fixed us a cup of coffee mixed with rum and heavy cream.

It took the chill off the evening and really woke me up from the dream that clung to me.

Nobody ever burned down Tarzan's jungle.

As the days went by, Travis filled in the details. We had known each other since childhood, and I had grown up in a neighborhood close by. I was two years older, and she had followed me throughout my early life in Greenville.

We both left in high school. She went to Chatham Hall in Charleston, and I went to Virginia Episcopal School. The summers were devoted to swimming, and I became a legend in town for my skill and competitiveness.

"Go, go, go, go, go, go, go, go, go, go, go, go, go, go, go!" the crowd chanted, yelling in unison as the water sloshed up a froth of flailing limbs and rhythmic kicks up and down, up and down—the breaststroke and the freestyle, the backstroke and the butterfly—graceful yet clumsy. My favorite was the breaststroke, frog kicking my way to the state championship, like an amphibian with a Speedo.

At prep school, I learned how to tie my tie right and just what kind of tweeds and khakis you should wear. Your Weejun's had to be polished. They had to be the right color too. After that, I went to Washington and Lee and after that to the University of Virginia Law School, all the while perfecting the persona of a Virginia gentleman.

Once you get into the state of Virginia, you can never get out. From Edgar Allan Poe, the Raven Society to the Secret 7, mysterious benefactors of the university, the whole place is wrapped in idealized southern culture. The equestrian statues of confederate generals surround the capital in Richmond. The ghosts of generals haunt every field, crossroad, and town.

At Washington and Lee, the recumbent statue of Robert E. Lee lies in state in the chapel. You can't graduate unless you take an oath that you have seen him in the early morning riding on Traveler, his beloved horse. Everyone wears a bowtie with their Harris Tweed blazer. We have even had a song in our Latin class commemorating General Lee and his horse. A warrior and a gentleman.

Travis stayed in South Carolina where twin institutions, Converse and the Citadel, educate and inspire. Converse trains women for service. The Citadel trains men. Don't ever question an upper-class South Carolinian about these two colleges. They launch into elaborate misty-eyed memories and talk about their last reunion. It's like Virginia. The Citadel or El Cid owns 51 percent of your class ring to protect the integrity of the corps of

Citadel men. There's even a story of a deathbed confession with voluntary surrender of the ring. "Here, cut my finger off—I've dishonored the corps," the old man said with his last breath.

There was a deputation of Citadel cadets at Saint Peter's gates waiting for the ring.

Converse girls used to marry Citadel boys a lot. Many South Carolina fortunes are wrapped up in the alumni of these two institutions.

Travis's marriage was to a Citadel boy. He lost his ring, and with that, he lost his honor. As our walks continued, I relearned bits and pieces more.

By the time I had become a partner in my old firm, Travis was in the throes of her divorce. I was married then. When she told me this, I had guessed that I probably had been married too, but I remembered nothing. Travis gave no details.

All this information took days and days for me to assemble as we took our daily walks under the trees on Crescent Avenue. Up and down on the sidewalks outside the mansions.

Winter was coming on, so we had to bundle up. Whenever I asked Travis how I was burned, she got quiet and a little misty eyed herself. I had learned enough at this point to know that she didn't want to talk about it. I didn't have the strength to fight over it. She would just reassure me—"When you are ready"—then hug me and kiss me.

CHAPTER SIXTEEN

A woman brushed beside me in the grocery store. Smells of produce mingled with perfume, strawberry and lettuce, musk, and secret sweat. We looked around furtively like fruit flies. She picked up the reddest strawberry, waved it under my nose, and pulled it slowly apart. The inside was pale red and wet, her lips moistened as she licked it. Her lipstick wet too and red as a strawberry. I felt her against me; her breasts warmed up my shoulder. Her thigh against my leg. She brought the strawberry up to my lips and put the tip of her finger in my mouth to open it. Wider. The berry glistened, and she slid it in slowly, letting some juice dribble down my chin. Quickly she licked my chin with her red, red lips and then kissed me as we both struggled not to choke on the pulp of the berry, the juice, and the kiss. Someone was watching. We didn't care. Where was I? Who was this strawberry nymph?

I had grown accustomed to the fragments of memory that would jump to my mind. Each one left another point to connect to what was there.

At least in this one, my hair didn't burn; the strawberry was fresh, not cooked like a pork rind.

"Travis, do you like strawberries?"

"Love 'em. Why, honey? You know we used to go to the Robertson Farm up in Pumpkintown when we were in high school."

"Well, I had a little memory of strawberries, I think. It must have been the stuff at the bottom of the yogurt."

"You want me to get you some strawberries, baby?"

"Yeah, that's a good idea." I scanned her face to see if my request registered. It didn't. The little fragment of memory did not seem to involve Travis. I couldn't really tell if it was truly a memory. Who was the woman?

—+—+—+—+—+—+—

CHAPTER SEVENTEEN

The YMCA on Cleveland Street in Greenville is not an especially imposing building. Like much of Greenville's institutional architecture, it is functional, spare, and moldable. The functional dream of the philanthropic construction community. Shift the front here, move that panel over there, pour some tar on the corner, and voila! An addition or an enlargement appears with just the right level of funding. All right angles, brick and steel. Rectangles, steel-framed windows, and doors. The Y is set in a little grove of trees on the top of a hill beside a wide street that stays busy in the morning. The rest of the day the street is empty, except for the occasional jogger.

Dr. Olds had driven by the Y on our "jaunts down memory lane" as he called them. He knew I had spent a great deal of time at the *Y*, and he felt that he could undo my "*lapsus memoriae*" by exposing me to the familiar. So far, it had not worked especially well, but the Y also formed one border of the trail of my evening walks with Travis; and the more I passed by it, either on foot or in Dr. Olds's car, I began to have a sense of safety or something that might start to pass for memory as my convalescence continued.

Travis had returned to work—she was the chief administrator of our old law firm. She left me to look after myself during the daytime but tried to get home early so we could walk and talk each evening.

Soft evenings of spring were full upon us all around, the promised ritual of azaleas and dogwoods, the buttercups with their buttery yellow strewn upon the ground, and the faint green fuzz covering the oaks and poplars pointing the way toward a heavy, humid summer. We walked two or three miles each evening. Travis had strong legs, and strength was beginning to return to my legs too. Her legs were more beautiful than mine though—her thigh did not have the huge rectangular scar where I had donated skin to myself to cover my face. When I walked, it felt like my face twitched when walking stretched the scar on my leg.

As we drove by the Y one morning, Dr. Olds remarked how good a swimmer I had been and did I harbor any wishes to return to the pool. As ever, he cloaked the question in therapeutic purpose. "You know if you got back into shape, it might help your memory return faster."

"What about my scars? Pools have chlorine, right? That might burn my new skin!"

"We'll ask Bruce."

So ask Bruce we did, and the great plastic surgeon said we could return to the pool next week. So we planned a trip. If I started burning on my face or hands, I was to get out. If I noticed any signs of infection, I was to quit and let them subside. If they persisted, I was to call him immediately.

When I told Travis of the plan, she smiled and disappeared into the attic. She clunked back down the attic steps holding a little swatch of dark cloth in her hand, a cute smile flirting on her lips.

"Here, baby, let's see if you can get into this."

She tossed me an old Speedo racing trunk. It looked like a wide rubber band in two colors.

As I marveled at the tiny waist of whoever had worn this, Travis began to pull my pants down. She had that look in her eye that commanded us to be young again. We were going swimming! Reexposure technique 101.

Thirty minutes after that, I got around to trying on the Speedo, but it didn't fit quite as well as it might have. Travis was giggling and ran up the steps again, this time returning with her own tank suit from years before, which, amazingly enough, she could fit into with some mashing and pushing.

We slept and dreamed and thrashed and swam all night long. Speedos on and Speedos off.

Travis went to work in the morning.

Although she was the chief administrator, she had, as yet, told me nothing about it. I had no curiosity for that just now; primal feelings occupied my mind. Part of the time I didn't know where I was. Part of the time I didn't care. Dr. Olds had instructed us both to take it easy; forcing memories that he said would come in time on their own. I kept waiting. When was I to get in the swim of things again?

"Bye, darling," I said and kissed her. She was a lovely vision in a power suit, fragrant with some new French perfume she had found, eager for me to show more signs of life. I stepped back a moment and just looked at her, my hands at her elbows. Her hair was brushed back in a casual style that had taken thirty minutes to achieve. A saucy gray cowlick hung over her left forehead like the waves about to break on Hawaiian surfer. Her cheeks were blushed as light as the pink on the roses in our garden, and her fine nose softened at the sharpness of her eyes. Thin lips gave her face a sense of purpose and classical beauty.

"Thank you, baby," she said and stroked my chin. I was now fuzzy, showing the hair follicles that had not been damaged totally. My beard was patchy with scars.

"You might need to shave before too long. Now, don't you go and get drowned when you start swimming."

"Not a chance," I said with a bravado borrowed from her power suit.

Really I wasn't sure I could swim at all. Making love to your high school sweetheart in a Speedo bathing suit that doesn't fit any more isn't the same thing as swimming—but maybe it was close. Maybe you just had to practice.

CHAPTER EIGHTEEN

Dr. Olds arrived a few minutes late, and I was waiting for him on the sidewalk under the great oak tree in the front yard. It was a white oak that towered above the house. When the autumn wind had blown through it, the leaves would fall in a cascade, like a Niagara of dancers leaping and turning to the music of the wind. Now that it was spring, a green glow surrounded the tree. In the early morning, it seemed to waken like the sun, as alive as the birds that sang in it. In the evening, it glowed more luminous than the lightning bugs that would start up in the soft May nights.

Craig pulled up in his convertible.

"It's going to be a beautiful day, my man. After we check out the *Y,* we will try and see what you remember."

"So is this the final exam?"

"Not a final exam. Call it a pop quiz."

"Well, then, can I call you Pop?"

"*Nulli secundus,* second to none." He grinned and pulled from the curb after I got in. The Y is less than five minutes away, and we wandered a bit to appreciate the spring and the trees that surrounded our house, driving slowly. Each house is two or three stories tall, well built, old, and solid. All of them have been renovated and passed through several generations of owners. All have different styles, but all of them have large impressive trees.

The trees were the envy of the rest of town, and nothing like them existed anywhere else.

We were in the heart of the heart of old Greenville, and the fortunes that had built it had stayed there for a long time. There was everything from groceries to a country club. You could walk if you wanted. The Y was a short walk down a sidewalk lined with azaleas. Some people never strayed from this enclave of ten to twenty streets. They were born, schooled, married, lived, and died here as if it were a medieval village surrounded by the wilderness, like Rome surrounded by the barbarians or China surrounded by the Great Wall.

When we arrived at the Y, there was a little banner across the front desk. "Welcome back, Fred." Were they talking about me? Such a puzzle, soon cleared by Kathy Cork, the director, who winked at Craig.

"Fred, I am so sorry about what happened to you. But we are very happy you have come back. We have missed you a lot these last six months, and we want to help you as much as we can."

"Thank you. Thank you so very much," I muttered, overcome with this. I tried to hide my still scarred face while I shook a round of hands. "Who arranged all this?" Caroline and Jenny and Shovanda and Charlene and Darlene and Linda and Danni. They all came up and hugged me. Welcome, welcome, welcome.

No memories yet. It was still darkness to me, despite the light of their welcome, even as Charlie gave me the tour.

The men's locker room was to the right, past the nautilus and weigh training facility. Further down the hall, the racquetball courts popped and slapped and grunted in echoes like a dungeon torture chamber. The nautilus athletes were more polite, not making noises. They looked like everything from body builders to anorexics. Slender young women and bulky young men. One of them seemed to stare at me, and when I looked at him, he scowled. I was suddenly afraid.

"Who is that, Craig?"

"I don't know, but he didn't seem to like you very much."

"Yeah, probably pulled a muscle on his bench press." But Craig grew wary too.

I forgot about it as we walked down the long tile corridor to the pool, perched on the end of the building, with long glass sides that could be opened to the sun.

It was a beautiful day, with bright flinty sunlight, striking the new spring as if to summon it to growth—get green now, the sun said, while I gazed at the pool and tried to call up a memory.

At first, nothing came to me. The unfriendly weightlifter had distracted me as well as the joy and welcome of the staff, the hugging, and the happy chatter.

Caroline, who seemed to be the lifeguard, motioned me toward the pool office, a cramped little space all jumbled with kickboards and fins. There on the wall were two pictures of me as a young man. Both of them showed trophies won somewhere.

Craig whispered something to her. "Now, Fred, close your eyes, and I will really show you something," Caroline said—she was a youthful blonde whose eyes twinkled in perpetual flirtation.

I closed my eyes, and she put something cold into my hands. I felt it first before looking at it. Smooth and hard, it was about twelve to fifteen inches long and seemed to have a base of different material, maybe wood. It seemed familiar, although I couldn't remember it.

When I opened my eyes, I found myself crying. "That's your last trophy!" Caroline said, excited as a child.

Suddenly I was surrounded by half-naked people, sleek and fit in Speedos and Tyr Lycra suits that hugged their tight torsos, fit from swimming lap after lap after lap. I was holding the trophy aloft to the cheers of the team. We diiiid *it!* We diiiid *it!* We shouted over and over. We had won the team championship. All around us pouting at our victory and simmering in covetousness, the other teams glowered, defeated in the final race. I was breathless, still wet. It had come down to the final four-hundred-yard individual medley, a killer of a race. A hundred yards each of butterfly, backstroke, breaststroke, and freestyle. When I hit the wall on the final turn, I was two strokes back and had to kick until my crotch popped to make it to the end. I touched out my opponent by a whisker, which none of us had very many of, and we'd shave the ones we did have to make us slick as seals. I touched the wall first on the final pull.

It was the best I ever did, and the YMCA had the trophy still. Three years after I left, the team disbanded and did not revive until I came back to town.

Caroline saw me crying, although I tried to hide it. Men try not to cry. Plus, I was a lawyer. Lawyers never cry.

"What's wrong?"

I shook my head. "Nothing, nothing. I was just remembering the meet and how much fun we all had."

"Yes, yes, and we were all so young then."

"I can't even get into my Speedo now," Caroline said and laughed.

"Surprise," I said as I pulled my old trunks out of my towel.

"I dare you," she said, narrowing her merry little eyes.

Quickly into the locker room, where I pulled on the damn thing. I was careful not to bend over, for it gripped me like shrink wrap on tenderloin. I waddled back to the pool down the long tiled way.

Caroline giggled like a schoolgirl, and before I knew what had happened, she pinched my bottom. Just right there, pinched my Speedo-clad bottom in front of everybody!

"You're turning red." She giggled again.

"I've got to try to swim and just how am I going to explain this bruise on my fanny?"

"Get in the water, boy. Start swimming like you used to."

Everybody was there by the pool chanting, "Fred, Fred, Fred! Swim, swim, swim!" I was transported, and I couldn't remember getting burned at all.

I dived in, and the years dissolved into the water, the magic solvent of all things.

For the welcome I received, the swim had been a success. As for the swimming, well, that was something different. I was too tight to swim the butterfly, and some of my scars prevented me from raising my arms high enough to clear the water. The freestyle was all right because I could roll my body. Same with the backstroke. The stroke I did best was the breaststroke, although my knees were tight and didn't let me whip my legs like I knew I could. I couldn't extend my arms as far as I wanted either. But I got enough air and could do it slowly enough to keep up. The other strokes made me too breathless. Caroline leaned down and kissed me after the first lap. The others applauded, and then they left me and Craig to finish the swim.

When I described all this to Travis at the end of the day, she grinned and pulled off her blouse. "Try this breaststroke." She laughed, and as I fondled and kissed the warmth of her body mingled with the smells of her day, cigarettes, perfume, coffee, and peppermints the rose she had worn, and the lapel of her power suit. I could swim! And smell and taste and see. I drank it all in, greedy as a baby.

It had been a very good day.

CHAPTER NINETEEN

Being burned alive is a powerful experience. It teaches you that you are frail and mortal in a way no other experience does. Every day becomes an escape from fire. Every day is immediate and sweet. You are wrapped in cool blankets and skin grafts. You never get over it.

I began to swim every two or three days and even to venture to the Y by myself. My memory had returned enough to let me remember the route, past azaleas and big fluffy camellias and bright lawns glowing like neon in the morning sunlight. I took a shortcut Travis had shown me, three blocks of streets that were quiet as museums where the hearts of the heart of old Greenville beat slowly. Time stood still here.

Each day I got there in midmorning for a long swim, and my endurance built up gradually. The water aerobics class of geriatric patients filled one side of the pool. They would hobble in with canes and walkers, their swimsuits baggy and tight all at the same time, then they would slip into the pool to dissolve their clumsiness to frolic like fishes.

A pilgrimage to the magic healing waters for all of us.

I watched them with feelings of sympathy and regret. Never will I let myself get in such bad shape, I declared, but just as I declared it, a voice would echo in my mind telling me to quit being so stupid—they wouldn't have gotten that way either if they had had any choice about it. Then I would dive in for another lap or two to wash those thoughts from my mind. Healing waters indeed. To heal, you must jump in.

My old coach used to say, *Cogito ergo Speedo*, and chuckle like a teenager. We had to take Latin at W and L, for it was rumored there that had been the preferred language of the southern planter class—guffaw, guffaw.

The ghost of the classical culture of the agrarian south had aspired to manifest itself in the curriculum of Washington and Lee, Hampton Sidney, UVA, and Randolph Macon. So Latin was it, from toga parties to Latin jokes—all stored up in an atmosphere that you breathed daily. *Cogito ergo Speedo* meant, "I think, therefore I swim in this tight little swimsuit." We all mumbled it like an incantation before and after practice.

Now it was *Speedo ergo sum*—"I swim, therefore I am"—for me.

Each day I remembered some other piece of the past. Every time I'd swim, some new piece of it came to the surface of my own special pool as my endurance strengthened.

CHAPTER TWENTY

I couldn't see her face, but we were alone swimming. The light at the bottom of the pool made it glow blue and inviting. She began to take off her clothes, some kind of uniform, and revealed a perfect body, sleek and muscular and female, as female as an instinct. Her breasts round and pendulous and excited, and her legs shaped perfectly as she dove in, her long hair streaming behind her. She motioned for me to join her, and I felt the cool solvent of the water cooling down my waist and my genitals while my mind heated up with lust. Cogito ergo Speedo. *Speedo ergo amore*—"I swim, therefore I love." *Sum ergo amore*—"I am, therefore I love."

"Are you all right?" she asked.

A cute little lifeguard who sat in the chair crumpled all over herself to hide the beautiful body she had acquired as a swimmer.

"Huh." I shook my head and realized my ventral fin was sticking me. Back to reality. Had it been a dream? "No, I mean, yes, I mean I'm fine. I was just thanking the Lord that I wasn't as broken down as some of those folks."

"Well, Fred, you're not, aside from a few scars. Caroline told me to look out for you, so that's what I'm doing. Swim on and"—looking down in the water, she said, "please try to calm down."

After a minute I did.

What kind of uniform? Who was my mermaid?

———+—+—⋇—⋇—+—⋇———

CHAPTER TWENTY-ONE

That Sunday, we took a drive in the country. Travis had a new BMW convertible. Our law firm had wrangled a deal since they helped set up the move of the company to South Carolina. Travis swore to me that I knew all about it—winking conspiratorially—another damn wink. I could not remember a thing. The car itself was sleek and black and aerodynamic as an arrow. The power surged under the hood and to remind you of the way things seemed to get done in Greenville. The power in the city was like that—you could feel it, but you couldn't see it.

The streets were quiet after nine thirty or so when the church traffic had dimmed down. We passed Westminster Presbyterian Church and the other churches on the Augusta Road, then the downtown churches eased by. We weren't travelling fast. Travis let the top down, and we soaked up the sunlight while the coolness of the spring morning slipped past, all around us. We were headed out to Paris Mountain to view the city from the TV tower at the summit. It was a favored place for lovers as Travis told me, and we had been there often during our "Speedo Summer," as she called it.

We went out Rutherford Road, past Green Valley Country Club, where the nouveau riche hang out, with mansions deliberately more grand than the ones in old Greenville. Houses on steroids, big as clubhouses or gyms.

All along the way, there were churches of every description. The oldest Catholic church, Saint Mary's, the Greek church, whose new cupola gleamed sunlight bright as the Mediterranean Sea. The Greek's ran all the restaurants in town and could tell you at day's end exactly where they stood with every account from hot dogs to onion rings. The Protestant churches were everywhere, Church of God, Church of Pentecost, the Brethren Church, Presbyterian, Reformed Presbyterian, and Methodist. Then came the Baptists—they outnumbered the rest three to one, black, white, Korean, and Spanish. All of them Baptists.

Greenville is a very religious town. Everyone convinced of heaven and everyone working hard to get there.

That Sunday you could feel it in the air, for Easter was close, and every church displayed some sign of it. Several churches had large stark crosses, from weathered wood, large as Calvary's own, with a swath of regal purple cloth draped around the crossbeam. The Sunday sun made the cross and the cloth glow with the sacred melancholy of martyrdom. All awaiting release and rebirth, the stone rolled away from the tomb.

We started out the ride in a jolly mood, packing a picnic. After four or five of these crosses, we had lapsed into silence.

"This can be someplace, honey," she said.

"What do you mean?"

"I mean the Baptists are everywhere."

"Yes, they are," I said.

"But they aren't the only believers, you know." And then she took off on a kind of free and association monologue. This was the kind she had adopted to reorient me to Greenville and to myself.

It was partly a history lesson, partly a catalogue of current events, told partly to herself. It would start with pies and ended up with grocery stores and the time the Community Cash had a milk riot. Or it might start with dresses and end up with the gay community in town and how they own some of the nicest shops. I could never tell exactly where these talks would go. Today, it started with Baptists.

"We believe at Christ Episcopal Church too. You know that's the big one we passed on Church Street."

I remembered a weathered brick building, majestic as a piece of England, mature and full of authority. There was a cross there too. The steeple climbed up, clad in old copper, and dominated the corner next to downtown, with a discreet and exclusive cemetery surrounding it.

"I think we were here first actually. The planters founded it to escape the low country heat and malaria. The Foothills were good, for the Scotch-Irish had driven the Indians out. We hired them, you know. Christ Church is the biggest Episcopal congregation in the whole country, but we don't run the town like we used to."

She began to list the fortunes of everyone she knew in town. The Rughs's family daddy was a sharecropper; now they "own shopping centers" and even have a place at Pawley's Island, the ultimate status symbol.

"You remember Pawley's. That's the beach where we all played in high school. Keeler had a place, and Judy Earlham had one and the Judsons and the Thompsons. Judy was the one who thought up the slogan 'Arrogantly Shabby' at lunch one day in the eleventh grade at Ashley Hall. Anyway, you wouldn't recognize the place now, all packed with new stuff, houses line the beach like lemmings or rats, waiting for the next hurricane. Everybody used to come to Christ for Easter and then head to Pawley's for the Easter break. Now, the Baptists and Presbyterians and that Bob Jones crowd seem to run things—it's just not the same. They're everywhere."

We were out in the country now with low hills, big Gregorian style houses with white columns, back from the road. Big lawns. Then there was a patch of poverty, broken-down cars, trash in the yard, just to remind you this was still Appalachia. We began to climb up Paris Mountain, and the road resembled a serpent sunning itself, a big black asphalt snake.

"Just look around you here." Travis paused at a lay-by and gestured with her hands and eyes. "All these folks have come since the fifties."

We were on a kind of plateau most of the way up the mountain. Houses had been perched on the mountainside going up but hidden by trees and rhododendron patches with honeysuckle and dogwood. The homes we saw now were an order of grandeur above the others, lower on the mountain. Some were close enough to the edge to put decks out like cliffs. You could see downtown below; the valley stretched out in the spring sun, the spires of the biggest churches still visible.

"I remember when they built these houses," she said, "and we all wondered who would come here."

We drove by one gate that looked almost menacing with a big pad lock, but there were signs of disuse, rusty hinges, weeds, and brush in the flower beds.

"Then, of course, you have Butch Canal and all his stuff." She turned at me in an accusatory way like I knew Butch Canal.

She suddenly turned on me. "You do remember, don't you?"

"No, I don't remember anything. I feel something, but I can't tell you it's a memory."

I didn't like her accusing me of anything, especially something to do with memory.

"Well let me tell you all about it. You and Butch Canal," she said this somewhat tenderly, although there was a knife hidden in her words.

It was as if she would help me remember so I could feel guilty about it.

Then she said, "I was ashamed of what you did." And she looked at me earnestly, eyes full of reproach.

"Can we wait until we get to the tower?" I said. Now I didn't want to remember anything. Maybe she would forget it too.

"We're almost there," she said and stared off the mountainside.

We pulled off the road just as it began to descend from the top plateau, took a cut back to the left on a steep, ill-paved road that mounted back and over the cliff to the mountainside. She accelerated a little around the curve and kicked some pavement loose, but we made it, and then we could see the high-tech tower about our heads. A relay for all the gossip and text and digital reality of cell phones all around us. I wanted to drape it with a huge regal purple cloth, but it was too technical and too hard for that.

In the valley, we were Easter; on the mountain, we were an electromagnetic Easter Island, mysterious with the energy of artifice. The valley was the Holy Land. The mountain was the spaceship for a ride to heaven.

We stopped at the base of the tower in a small parking lot then clambered over some rocks to see the valley laid out before us.

"You and Butch Canal." She started her story. She had not forgotten as I wanted. As I had become more oriented and less dependent, as my open wounds had healed, as I had gained strength from swimming, she had become less patient. Her teaching was more to moralize at me about my past. She liked to inform me what I had done and then judge me for it. It wasn't all positive. Now, I was about to meet Butch Canal again, whoever that was.

I still remembered nothing.

"Yes, you knew Butch Canal well. He started life as a Joneser, a fine product of the Bob Jones School of Evangelical Christianity, and he was one of the best. I heard him preach once, and he was good, made you feel like you were going to hell if you didn't give money to his ministry, as he called it. He and some friends bought a little radio station and called it World Broadcasting for Jesus, even bought a big globe to put on top. The mill owner, Old Mr. Stoner, gave him the land to buy a place in heaven. He was afraid of going to hell for the way he used to treat his employees.

Anyway, Butch went to work. None of us knew him then. We were all busy at prep school and college. He amassed a fortune in little properties given to his ministry. "Give your land to God," he'd cry out on the radio. "He needs the promised land for Jesus."

She stood up and spread her arms, quivering her head a little to imitate an emphatic radio voice.

"He had been going for about ten years by the time we got back into town, and his real estate ventures had attracted so much attention he had to donate 'his ministry' back to Bob Jones—except it had no assets. He hid them somewhere else. I wish I had been at that meeting. He really got rolling then, and that is when he began to need the services at our firm, specifically—you." She pointed at my chest.

As Travis talked, veiled foggy memories came to me. Silvered hair swept back like a motorcycle helmet, heavy cologne, sweet as the muck on a greenhouse floor, pudgy little soft hands in a baritone voice that invoked "gawd" and the "ahwmiitey" every other sentence.

"Tax shelters, complicated land swap deals, money here, there, and everywhere. He had to screw his old buddies first and break the ties to his old churches. No problems until his wealth had grown. By then, his sister had married the chief of police. But you, Fred, didn't have to visit up here at 'the castle of the lawd' until he got into trouble with his mistress. Then things became a bit sticky."

So here was Greenville at Easter, full of true faith with a history of something else woven all around and through it. The crosses and their purple clothes called us to redemption.

We all needed it.

Travis said, "I had just come to the law firm, so I knew nothing—I know a lot more now." Travis arched her eyebrows. "Let's just say I was naïve—I never knew my daddy would do such things."

Her daddy used to be the managing partner of the firm. He had passed Butch Canal on to me.

"I was married then, and you were occupied with your first marriage, so we were just friendly. Anyway, there were some other dealings cooking up, like a gourmet chef at a slime-cooking contest. Nobody liked him, for he was always quarreling about his bill. 'What do yawl mean, closing costs? Where did all these fees come from? How much extra are you guys getting?' He raised so much hell one time my daddy kicked him out of the office. You were the only one who could tolerate him because, somehow, he didn't fight with you as much. You didn't mind cutting your fees a little bit for him, and he loved it. Eventually, you were his only lawyer, and he brought everything to you including that damn phone call."

The sunlight was bright on top of Paris Mountain and warm in the little pocket of rocks where we had taken our rest.

The morning fog was gone, and with it, my memory had become sharper. I thought I could see the purple of the crucifixion robes scattered in the valley. Travis continued to talk for the next half hour with little interruption, and I just made myself listen to a sordid tale of dope and corruption. It seems that ol' Butch had let his real estate empire go to his head.

In the process of acquiring their land, he had acquired three different mistresses who had started to blackmail him once they discovered each other. One of them had owned the land on Paris Mountain, and Butch had built her a nice little hideaway love nest, which we had passed on the road coming up here—the one with weeds. She was found dead of an overdose, and Butch was the only witness. He called me, and I sped up there in the middle of the night. The police came after that, and it looked, at first, as if Butch and I had conspired to kill her. It took two months to straighten all this out to the satisfaction of the detectives or rather, to get me out of it. In the process, Butch had left town for a while. The gossip about our law firm died down eventually but not before we lost some clients.

Before I could ask where Butch was now, Travis said, "I would say we don't consider him our client any longer." She said this with exaggerated finality, like she was hiding something. She offered nothing more.

The image she had conjured up nagged at my mind. The encounter with the police stuck out. Something about the police or uniforms or something. I remember Butch standing there trying to preach his way out of it while the detectives stared at him like he was totally crazy. I remember a detective who seemed like a lady's man. And I remember something else as well, a young woman who was an EMS technician. When her image floated into my mind, I jumped.

"What's wrong, honey, am I boring you?" Travis said, suddenly sweet as pie but sarcastic.

"No, baby, go on. I can't believe this stuff, but I know you are telling me the truth." I dipped my reply in honey as well, although all this had felt like torture.

I couldn't tell her about the memory of this young woman, whoever she was. And as I focused on the memory, it began to leave.

I looked out into the valley for redemption, but all I could feel was burning on my face and hands.

CHAPTER TWENTY-TWO

My memory now worked in spurts. Sometimes whole pieces of it would return. Sometimes just shards and splinters. I could never tell what would stick and remain with me into the next day. I tried to find themes; none would appear. An EMS ride. I wasn't hurt. Sensations in my groin. Dark hair flowing over my cheeks like a waterfall, something illicit but sweet Latin phrases. My partners were looking at me and shaking their heads. Old Butch really taught you a thing or two. Heh, heh. The judge calling me back into his chambers for a discussion. Plea bargains, admonishments. Fear. Respondeat superior. The buck stopped at the top.

It was fragments of a bad dream.

＊－＊－＊－＊－＊

Nights and days were interrupted with scraps of near memory. It began to disturb Travis.

"What's wrong, honey?" Travis asked, awakening from sleep.

"Baby, it's the same old garbage."

"Well, I thought you were doing better."

"Ever since you told me about Butch, I have been remembering little things. Little things every day, and I don't feel good about it. It was almost better when I couldn't remember anything. I'm scared I have done something really bad."

"Well, Fred, my dear. You have," she said and broke into a smile. "Everybody has." She put her finger on my lips and began to caress me where I wore my Speedo.

"No, honey." I pulled away from her for the first time since the hospital. "I'm getting really down about this."

She was hurt and said quickly, "Well, I am going to get depressed too if you don't pay attention to me."

So I had to become a zombie with an erection again.

I tried to moan in pleasure while my mind flickered between memory, shame, fear, and dream.

CHAPTER TWENTY-THREE

After Travis's revelations, I began to think Butch had basically changed me. The more I had helped him with one legal entanglement or another, the more I had been drawn into his moral swamp. The morality of expedience and the rules of the first church of money. He was like a parody of Greenville or an embodiment of the worst traits of the whole place. Charming, conniving, and cunning—he existed just to make money for himself, and while he preached Christian altruism, he didn't practice it at all.

I had been the upright and righteous gentleman in all my legal dealings. I had learned at Washington and Lee the example of the great General Lee himself, and I did not want to besmirch my own personal honor by any actions unworthy of the great Virginia gentleman, shepherd of his people during war.

Butch was a siren from a different class. As I saw him through his problems, I became the same immoral cad that he was. This was the picture that Travis had painted for me on Easter morning at Paris Mountain.

She had piled me up with details of Butch's misadventures, of late emergency meetings with police and zoning boards, of favors delivered through intermediaries, of condos at the beach, one trip to the Caribbean. She had seemed so unforgiving, even as she massaged me and kissed me on the mountaintop, as if she enjoyed the catalogue of my sins, and it somehow absolved her of whatever her part of it all might have been. She was in the firm, just like me.

As she talked, my memory stirred up and awakened. After so much of it, I had to stop her and continue the tale myself, even though it was fragmentary, *non nova sed nove*—not new things but in a new way.

Mendacem memorem esse oportet. It is fitting that a liar should be a man of good memory, Quintilian wrote. *I had learned that I had become a liar, and with that knowledge, my memory was returning.* Great.

In my mind I could see General Lee riding away from me on his great horse, Traveler, shaking his mournful head. What had become of the South?

⸙⸙⸙⸙⸙⸙

I could share some of this with Travis, of course, but I wanted to share it with no one, and dwelling on it just impeded my recovery, so I put it in the back of my mind—the little private damaged file. There. Like a manila folder scorched in an office fire.

There were other things I had to do now besides mourning something I had done in the past.

Tempus edax rerum. Time the devourer of all things. The past, after all, is past, and I can't undo whatever harm I had done back then.

So I bent myself anew to the task of rehabilitating myself more completely. I reached for the phone to call my good friend and rehabilitation doctor, Dr. Craig Olds. He would keep pushing me, dragging me around town, quoting Latin, and he had never mentioned Butch Canal.

I couldn't have been as bad as Travis made out. Was she exaggerating? Was there more to the story?

I stayed befuddled when I slipped into questions like that. A lawyer learns to not ask a question unless he knows the answer. I didn't know the answers to anything now. My memory is still slipping gears like a bicycle with a loose chain.

⸙⸙⸙⸙⸙⸙

CHAPTER TWENTY-FOUR

"How's it going?" asked the chipper Dr. Olds, bowtie in place, a nice blue blazer that matched the tan—along with the slightly peppery mustache.

"Very good question," responded the evasive brain-damaged lawyer who was me, without a tan.

"Look, Fred, don't be so down in the mouth. Travis has done a very good job with you. You are well oriented now. You know who you are. You have some good ideas about who you used to be, and you are determined to get back the rest of your brain function. '*Ab ovo usque ad mala,*' as you used to say to me when I was on the witness stand. The first time you told me that, you said it meant from start to finish, right!"

"Dr. Olds . . ."

"Call me Craig. Again I have to keep reminding you."

"Okay, Craig, then, I really don't know what you are saying. Some Latin comes to me but not very much. Occasionally, a phrase will slip in, but then it doesn't bring any meaning with it. A fine phrase like you just told me is beyond me right now, still."

"Well, you used to use Latin all the time. I thought at the time just to impress people, but then as I got to know you, I realized you really cared about those things. The Greek myth—you were fond of saying this or that judge was Narcissistic, like Narcissus. People all over town thought you were a snob—a 'pointy-headed intellectual' some folks said. I knew different, but so it goes. Most people are very suspicious of higher education or any display of it, but you never were."

"Well, that's the idea I was getting from Travis on our walks. She tells me little stories about this or that piece of gossip—God, there seems to be a lot of it. Nobody seems to enjoy anything much except making money or showing up at church."

"Yes, that's the way it is, and you used to help some of the best of 'em." He said this poking me with his finger.

I stared at him blankly and tried to focus on this last set of thoughts. Lawyer, intellectual, Latin snob, defender of greedy capitalists. I couldn't put this together with my memories of swimming and my dreams of making love.

"You will pardon me, Dr. Olds—I mean Craig—if I don't remember this exactly in every detail right now, fully."

"You are not well enough yet, but it is time we start the reexposure therapy intensely and see what you can tolerate. Your burns are well on their way to healing up completely, and Bruce tells me you will have minimal scarring. There is a chance that you weren't as badly hurt as we thought, and the skin grafts look pretty good. Maybe we will have to go hiking."

"What!"

"It's getting to be spring, and you used to like to spend time in the mountains. It might jog your memory some."

I felt vaguely upset just after he said this, like I couldn't hike, or maybe the mountains held some secret I wasn't supposed to remember. The memories of Butch Canal still haunted me.

The mountains sit up there at the north end of the county, dark, dark purple in the evening with a soft fog in the morning. That part of the county is called "The Dark Corner." I know all sorts of things hide up there, not just liquor stills.

Maybe I really don't want to remember everything.

CHAPTER TWENTY-FIVE

Spring comes to the Carolinas like a shy horse. At first, it gallops through the meadow dragging a thunderstorm. The rains drench the ground, flood the parking lots, and summon the flowers. Their green fuses lit; the daffodils explode everywhere, lawns and forests, meadows and woodlands, all over Cleveland Park. The trees begin to bud. The flowering Judas trees come out robed in the regal color of Christ's blood, promising warm days but delivering a few more weeks of cold rain, maybe snow. People become furtive and restless, appearing for walks in the evenings and runs in the mornings, hiking up their skirts behind their cars in the park to get the first sun on their legs.

Finally, the dogwoods bloom, and we are home free. Next, the azaleas—coral and red and purple and white—then there follow a riot of blossoms and bees. Everyone is doing "yard work," and the landscape companies charge around dispensing mulch, fertilizer, and pesticides. The sun takes forever to set. Every plant and tree and blade of grass—anything green—is luminous in that last light of the evening.

Travis and I sat on her deck partly hidden by the stonework that "Jacques" built, looking into the vacant lot next door.

"I am glad Tommy hasn't sold that thing yet," she said with a gesture next door, indicating the partial woods in the gathering darkness. "You remember Tommy, don't you?"

She went on to tell me all about Tommy, and the evening turned to tears. She was in an unusually talkative mood, which for her meant very, very, very talkative. Usually, it was just idle gossip and idle commentary about her surroundings; but this time, she was revealing herself, really.

Tommy had been her first husband. He was the scion of the Von Lapper family and plugged into Greenville with all three prongs. That got to him later, for he blew it all on real estate deals and tax problems, trying to maintain the frantic growth of his fortune in the booming Greenville economy.

That's when he lost his Citadel ring.

"I was there that night," Travis said, "three old men and one young guy in a Citadel uniform appeared at the door. They looked sad and stern. I hated them the minute I saw 'em. Poor Tommy was drunk as a coot—he'd always say that and wink at me because neither one of us had ever seen a coot, much less a drunk coot. I don't even know what a coot is. This time, he wasn't winking at anybody. I let them in, and they brushed past me. 'Thank you, ma'am,' so damn polite. One of them had even been Tommy's roommate at the Citadel! Then they read a little speech. 'It is with grave intention that we have embarked on this mission to recapture and preserve the honor of the Citadel Corp of Cadets.' I still remember that part because Tommy burst into tears and sat there sobbing. The ex-jock, swaggering real estate whiskey-soaked bastard, was bawling like a baby!"

She still couldn't believe it. She couldn't believe Tommy, and she couldn't believe the Citadel, and she couldn't believe "the whole damn night."

"After the little speech about honor and duty and service and all that other Citadel stuff, one of the guys who is a lawyer in our firm, just like you"—she glared at me—"read a short note about the contract that involves the ring, and then they reached over and took it from him. He held out his hand, and I thought they were going to have to cut it off his pudgy little finger, but they got the ring off after I put some Ivory soap on it. 'May I have a towel to dry my hand off, please,' the leader asked in a whiny little voice, and I threw a roll of paper towels at him. They left after that. Tommy stayed drunk for a week, and then I left my own house until the bastard left. I couldn't stand any of it anymore."

Travis trembled, and her eyes were moist. When I tried to comfort her, she pushed me away.

As she sat there, remote and full of grief, a memory surged into me, like a tidal wave in a swimming pool.

I felt wet, as though I had been swimming, and I felt cold. She was still beside me but younger. It was the time I left her to return to college. Speedo Summer we called it, named after the swimsuits we liked to pull at when we were making out. We would close the pool and lock the gates and disappear into the locker room until the darkness made us go home.

The pool closed on Labor Day. That summer had been cooler than most, and one evening she started crying. I don't remember any words, anything that would have hurt her. Maybe the prospect of my leaving was enough.

That fall, with no warning, she wrote me a breakup letter. I didn't hear from her the rest of the year. The next summer, I came home, and she was with Tommy.

She stayed with him through his drinking and infidelities, through his bad land deals, and through all the "horrid" gossip.

When he lost his Citadel ring, she could delude herself no longer. The romantic dream was gone. The shining armor of the Citadel knight had been taken from the Converse queen. She was still so bitter she couldn't comfort herself even now, even by nursing back her old "burnt to a crisp" boyfriend so he could be a lawyer again.

—♦—♦—♦—♦—♦—♦—

That's why they call someone an "old flame." Travis had her own third-degree burns.

CHAPTER TWENTY-SIX

After this memory, Travis reached for a bottle of whiskey. She began to drink. Almost knocked me aside with her arm reaching for the big decanter of bourbon she kept in the dining room. Her wretched face contorted by the crystal reflected all her disappointment, sorrow, and fury. I knew I couldn't stop her, and I knew, too, that she would refuse to be comforted, so I just sat there with her until she was so drunk she had to lie down. Then she snored—god, how she snored. I just watched—curious about all these permutations of love, bright feelings, and hopes turning to despair—all over those silly things that southerners understand, and only South Carolinians understand in their peculiar institutions, their schools for dreams.

I had almost lost my life in a car wreck. The burns still hurt and ached, and I was curious about my life, but Travis, in her attempts to love me, had to clear away her own bad memories. She wanted to get back to our days of swimming, naked in the sunshine, little tiny bathing suits, and hot kisses that are clumsy, wet as rain.

I stayed up as long as I could, and then I, too, drifted to sleep on the big couch with Travis's liquor-soaked breath and big snores bumping at me all night.

The next morning, she had a horrible hangover, so she didn't go on the walk with me. "You go on, you go on," she said, holding her head, "but please get me some aspirin and fruit juice, okay." I complied now that I knew my way around the house. Then I slipped out the door into the glories of springtime. Every day seemed fresh and new, yet to be discovered.

As I walked, I thought I saw something unusual. Down about two blocks away, there was an EMS van with its lights off. It was barely daylight. The engine was running.

I kept walking, but I felt myself grow a little wary. A shiver of recognition or a memory or a flashback or something came over me. When I got closer, the driver of the van turned around, and the engine turned off. I kept walking, but I wanted to go to the other side of the street. Just as I started, the door of the van opened, and a young pregnant woman stepped out and looked directly at me. I stopped walking.

I knew I recognized her, and suddenly I felt in that kind of knowledge I had begun to call dreamtime—a mix of yearning, dreaming, and memory. I couldn't take another step as she approached me.

She looked over both shoulders, furtively. She was beautiful. Her breasts swollen with pregnancy. Her abdomen stuck out and firm. She seemed strong. Her face high-cheeked, hair long and dark in a ponytail for work.

"Are you all right?" she said, hesitating. Then she reached out and kissed me first on the cheek, then next full on the lips.

I just stood there, dumb as a stone or one of the great trees that witnessed all of this. She looked at me again and felt my face, her fingertips shrinking yet touching me, still tentative, not to hurt me, almost clinical. She gave me no name.

"I can't forget you," she said and then turned and walked quickly back to the van, started it up, and left. Still no lights.

I looked around the street aware only that something important had happened. I wasn't sure exactly what. Some of it had been familiar. I wanted to know more, but I was paralyzed. Still in dreamtime.

CHAPTER TWENTY-SEVEN

I knew I better not tell Travis of course—somehow she might not like the fact that a beautiful pregnant woman had stopped me on the street and kissed me. I didn't think that was part of Travis's plans.

As I continued my walk, I kept looking for this mystery EMS woman, but she was nowhere to be seen. Of course. I began to mistrust my memory, but no, this was real. Something had really happened just now. But what?

How had I got to all this anyhow? I was deep in a mystery.

There were things to sort out. What was the story? How had I been involved? I didn't know, and now I wanted to remember just so things would make sense.

Were there any other clues I'd missed?

Who was this woman?

The cool spring air helped me calm down and try to plot how I might get Travis to help me more or maybe Dr. Olds, or maybe there could be somebody else. Maybe an old friend. I couldn't think of anyone.

By the time I got home, I was ready to suggest to Travis that we should get someone else to help me. She needed someone to take some of the burden of caretaking off her so she could get back to work at the law firm—and let me get to my former self.

When I got home, I heard the blender going and saw Travis mixing up what she called her "old favorite hangover remedy"—part raw egg, part orange juice and B vitamins, part coffee, and a half a teaspoon of bourbon, of course.

She was haggard from the excess of bad memories and alcohol last night. No mood for my kiss.

It's a funny thing—alcohol mixes nicely with memory until the memory turns toxic, and then the alcohol turns toxic too, creating tears you can light with a match.

Travis brought such intensity to everything—it fatigued me—and confused me. Were we supposed to help me get my memory back—or something else? Whatever happened to Butch Canal? Who am I now besides her lawyer animal-rescue project? Who was that girl? She'll never tell me all this.

—+—+—+—+—+—+—

She settled down on the sofa and patted the seat next to her. "How was your walk, honey?" she said, sipping the concoction she warmed in the microwave. "Oh," I said, "it was fine. The birds are chirping, the light was just right, and my legs feel stronger every day."

We rambled on talking about various things, never mentioning last night except once she said, "Thank you for listening to me" and touched my cheek and head.

Eventually, I saw an opening and said, "Travis, you have been looking after me so well, and I love you for it, but I keep wondering if I had an old friend or two that I have forgotten about, somebody who could take me on walks and drives and talk to me about court—maybe another lawyer."

She said, "Funny thing that you say that. I just got a call from Wiley yesterday evening, and I wanted to see him soon and to talk about just what you are describing."

"Wiley? Wiley who?"

"Wiley Kayne," she said. "He was on the swim team with us. He was your chief rival then but later became your best friend until you were hurt. I've kind of kept him away from you for a while." She almost blushed and looked away when she admitted that. "Now I think it's time to bring him in on things."

She said this looking into the air, almost as if she was confirming a detail of a plot she had made a long time ago.

I certainly knew of no plan or plot. She had never mentioned Wiley before, and I couldn't remember him at all. But Wiley might fit the bill, plot or no plot. I was at her mercy.

It turns out that I had known Wiley rather well.

He was on the country club swimming team and a bitter opponent of mine throughout adolescence. I'd win one race; he'd win the next. He was very good at the butterfly, but I always beat him in the backstroke and breast. It was a tossup in the freestyle. He went to the University of Virginia for college, and because of his swimming prowess, he lived on the Lawn—that magic part of the campus where the stalwart young heroes of Virginia grew up under Thomas Jefferson's watchful eye and listen to Edgar Alan Poe's Raven every night.

Unfortunately, he was accused of cheating; and like Travis's ex-husband, he was kicked out of the great ol' UVA fraternity. The University of Virginia had an honor code, and if you were seen cheating or suspected of cheating, you were hauled before an honor court and expected to answer the charges. It was a shame and disgrace, like losing your Citadel ring.

Wiley couldn't answer the charges, and it was a dark blot on his life ever after. A dirty secret—as most secrets are.

Fortunately, he was smart. He transferred to finish school elsewhere and worked hard to rehabilitate his reputation. After that, he went to the University of South Carolina to law school; he ended up practicing in the same law firm as I did. We used to swim together at times, but then he decided to get wet at a different time of day. It was my pool in the morning, his pool in the evening. We still had meets together.

The outcomes remained the same.

Once you start racing, you can never quit. Travis told me this entire story, and I simply had to believe her.

CHAPTER TWENTY-EIGHT

Wiley was a big boy—at least two inches taller than I am and twenty pounds of muscle heavier. He looked like a marlin, actually, with the kind of long sharp nose, big shoulders and chest, tapering down to feet that could paddle a boat. He had that curious trait of backslapping bonhomie that could turn in a flash if he were thwarted. The bully in him would rise up, and all that extra testosterone would flood into his face. He was grinning and laughing one moment and then mean and cunning as a snake the next. Apparently, he did very well at our law firm. Clients liked him. His nickname was "Bulldog."

I thought they should have called him "Bulldog Fish," but I don't think bulldogs can swim very well. Maybe there is a kind of shark like that. Lawyers are sharks, right?

The first time Wiley came to see me he was his happy, good ole backslapping self. "Fred, Fred, Fred—we gotta get you back. Travis tells me you can take visitors now."

"Yeah, I think I can. I am sort of getting a little restless here, and I feel like I'm burdening Travis too much." I said nothing about the EMS girl.

"Naw, naw, I am sure you are not burdening her, but I have just stayed away from you until she let me know when I could be helpful."

"Well, I need to get around and start exposing myself to some other things. I remember nothing about law practice, and I don't know what my old partners think of me. My skin grafts are still red as peppermint, and I need a guide. I can't remember where anything is in Greenville. The only street I know is Crescent Avenue."

Wiley rolled up his eyes, and something about him made me want to remember more and more. I felt safe enough with him, but questions began to make me itch—like there was something I really should know before I gave him too much trust. Was there a plot? When would we get started? Travis had hidden as much as she had revealed.

CHAPTER TWENTY-NINE

I was a regular at the Y now. I would go into the pool in midmorning, when no one else was there. My Speedo snug about my hips with my little gentle bulge firmly in place. A warm-up swim of two hundred yards, easy, then a variety of strokes for a thousand yards, a rest, then a slow five hundred. It was good that I could do that, although I wasn't fast anymore. My scars still held me back.

I loved the way my Speedo felt around me and the way the water flowed over my head and my shoulders, swirling around my legs.

I tried to go every morning or every other morning at least.

After a week or so, I noticed the same EMS van was there in the parking lot when I came out. Nobody seemed to be in it, but I didn't really know. It made me nervous. It was *Ipso Facto*, unusual. Was it an omen?

I tried to remember any fragment. Something came to me while I was swimming—the smell of floral perfume, so different from the chlorine smell of the pool. It was dark; the only lights were those in the pool. We had come there by an EMS van—was this a dream? She had to close the pool for the day. Who was she? When she took off her clothes, she had the most beautiful body I had ever seen—athletic, slender, muscular with the long graceful muscles of a swimmer—firm breasts, her hair, long and dark, down to her shoulders, her skin olive, with a natural tan. Her eyes furtive and playful, almost shy, inviting me to her.

I had to stop swimming a moment and collect myself. I had grown a ventral fin again. This time, I knew it wasn't Travis I remembered.

"FRED! FRED TOOTHUM!" a voice exploded my reverie. Again, loudly, "WILEY, HERE." I looked at him, a big thug in a Speedo three sizes bigger than me with a little paunch overhanging the Lycra stripes in his suit.

"Well, yes, Wiley, are you going to make me race like you used to?"

"We've spent many an hour in here, my man. When we weren't beat'n' 'em up in court, we were beat'n' 'em up in here. Heh, heh."

Images click through my mind like a slide projector in overdrive. Wiley as lawyer, Wiley as prosecutor, Wiley as swimmer, Wiley as bully, Wiley as nemesis.

He had been my chief opponent throughout high school and then college. From Gower and the club to prep school and college, in one terrific meet, I swam against him three times. He touched me out the final lap in the four-hundred-meter relay, but I beat him the other two times, and he never forgot it. It was in the Gower versus Country Club meet, and that was the only swim meet that ever mattered to anybody who ever swam in Greenville.

"*Quo Vadis*, my man?" I couldn't fully feel anything toward him, but now I had another source for my past besides Travis. Maybe Wiley could help me reconstruct my mind and my personality. Whither goest me?

He suddenly turned tender in the way big gruff men do—half conspiratorial, half ashamed. "Whatever happened to you? Travis wouldn't tell me everything."

"Let's finish our workout and get a cup of coffee, deal? I'll tell you everything I can remember."

"Hell, boy, I'll take you to lunch at the club like the old days."

One grin and a few laps together, and I was back in the swim of things. *Gandeamus igitur.* Let us now rejoice.

One grin and a few laps together, and I was back in the swim of things.

"Wiley, can we go for a little drive?"

"Sure, big fella, let me check out my office for a moment."

As he muttered something into his cell phone, I climbed into his big BMW, all leather and power. He usually parked on the metropolitan side of the YMCA, a kind of elite health club for the downtowners, zip code 29605.

"But I think it's all right. Sure, sure, don't worry about anything. No, I wouldn't do that. Talk to you later." He hung up. Just then an EMS vehicle left the parking lot.

"Not to worry. I had to call my secretary down, if you know what I mean." I did not know what he meant, but it seemed that he had been talking to someone about me somehow. Who?

I let it pass with a dull nod.

CHAPTER THIRTY

Over the next several weeks, since I had begun to swim regularly in the grip of my old Speedo, my alertness had improved. I didn't feel so dull and lifeless. With this, improvement had come a kind of paranoia and lawyerly suspicion again.

The lawyer, after all, tends to explain everything with a few simple rules expanded ad infinitum, making them apply everywhere. Reality is evidence, and evidence is reality. Everything happens with due process, and in the end, something is right, or something is wrong. That's it. There's nothing else.

But you'd better write it down, or it disappears.

Was everything I had observed related? Had I even observed it? Wiley might know, but I wasn't about to ask him yet. Furthermore, I wanted him uncontaminated by Travis.

I felt I was in a crowd of conspiratorial plotting. With the fog in my brain from the concussion, nothing seemed pure.

"Oh, Wiley, don't be talking to Travis, okay."

"Yeah, I heard you been shacked up with that little piece of honeysuckle, eh?" He leered.

"No problem."

As he said this, I felt a surge of recognition—the big bad bravado of the good ole boy that he pretended to be. Wiley was no good ole boy. He was a cunning big city lawyer in a small town that was growing faster than cancer, and he was always on the make for something or somebody. I had been, apparently, the same in some way, even as I impress people with Latin phrases and references to mythology. A narcissist in a bass pond.

Now, Wiley was going to help me find myself; plus I needed him for swimming practice.

As far as Travis and honeysuckle goes, there is an inn in Charleston, the Meeting Street Inn, that is upholstered in honeysuckle. The balconies are festooned in the sweet stuff. On a spring night when you head to your room, you are drunk on its perfume by the time you get there. It follows you down the balcony, a nocturnal companion, like a girl on your arm. Sort of the way Travis slips around in her sheath dresses and ballerina legs. She wasn't just a little piece of honeysuckle; she was a big piece of that southern vine, full of blossoms.

Something else was going on though, for as we drove around, Wiley kept stopping to answer his cell phone or to place a call himself. *Beep, beep-beep, beep-beep-beep*—the new rhythm of the times in which we live. All these sounds had made me an alarmist. There are alarms everywhere now.

Just yet, I took no part in them, for I had left alarms back at the burn unit, back with the slimy packages of skin graft stock. Now my world was my Speedo, my girlfriend, and my increasing store of mysterious memories, with Wiley as a new guide. Travis had hesitated for some reason to bring me back into the game, the swim of the law, for some reason unknown to me. She thought I wasn't ready, but maybe there was more to it.

Wiley had already made my mind work better. Something about past athletic rivalry sharpened the senses better than the silky soft pleasure and comfort Travis had given me day after day.

After all, I did swim fast in my little swimsuit.

Putting my Speedo on was not just a prelude to pulling it off for Travis or anybody else.

—⸕—⸕—⸕—⸕—⸕—⸕—

"Let's go for a tour of the town first, Bubba," Wiley invited me.

"Where is that exactly?"

"Well, all you have seen so far, if Travis had much to do with it, has been the gold coast of old Greenville, the Olympus of the old town, you used to say."

"My doctor tried to show me some more," I said, and I didn't tell him all about what Travis had shown me. Something made me hesitate about Butch Canal and that whole story.

"Was Dr. Olds a Yankee?"

"Midwest."

"That's worse. They have about as much imagination as a row of corn. Plus, they count their money. Did you know they bought up Media Plus?"

"What's that?"

"Old Man War started it. Robert War. He is kin to Travis somehow. Ask her. Anyway, I am going to show you this Greenville you have forgotten about, where old Butch Canal made his fortune. After that, we will go to Zorba's."

Off we roared in the BMW, growling with power and making a noisy show. "Heh, heh."

"Greenville is laid out like the dream of a free market economist in the nineteenth century. An urban core with parks and mansions, surrounded by unincorporated mill villages where the mill and the housing for its workers existed. The company store was there. The small Baptist church at one end and the Methodist church at the other looked after their souls. The cheap loan shops took care of personal hard times.

The urban center has the owners, while the perimeter has the workers.

"When the mills from Lowell, Massachusetts, relocated down here, they moved into Poe Mill, City View, the Bleachery, Judson, and Mills Mill, lured by the cheap labor of the post reconstruction south and the proximity to cotton, still king and ever king of textile finery.

"Ask yourself why the South went to war in 1860. Ask yourself why the mills moved to the South. Then ask yourself this—how does it feel to slip into your jeans, all washed and soft as baby skin? What are your favorite bedtime sheets made of? Ask yourself what is softer, your wife's cheek or your cotton sheets? What are your shirts and underwear and pajamas—all cotton, every one.

"That's what the mill villages were all about. Every village was named for the mill at the center, and every village developed an independent character based on the owner, the management, and the workers of the mill. City View, for example, incorporated eventually and for a long time had a police force of two or three deputies. Was this to be sure to break strikes more efficiently? Or to gather to the owner the powers of a municipal government? Who knows now?

"Over here is Poe Mill, which just closed down in the depression and left all its housing in place. Still the most dangerous part of the city after dark.

"Once it was dangerous because of the poverty of the mill where everyone worked. Now it is dangerous because of the crack houses."

Wiley lectured as we drove along, telling stories of people he had either prosecuted or defended. The knifings, the orgies, the sex crimes, the domestic violence—all in the name of some kind of family honor that made no sense to outsiders but defined the lives of the people around us, including ourselves.

"Don't you be talking bad about nobody's mama," Wiley said with a grin as we passed the slumbering giant of an obese man sitting on a porch in Poe Mill. "That's Ronnie J. He is about thirty years old now, but five years ago, he killed three guys in a fight about his mother. One of them stabbed him, and he pulled the knife out of his blubber and slit the guy's throat. I thought it was self-defense. Heh, heh. They still talk about it around here. Nobody bothers Ronnie. We didn't even prosecute him."

⸙ ⸙ ⸙ ⸙ ⸙ ⸙

"What's that patch of ground?"

"Oh, that used to be the Green Avenue Grocery Park. Ole man Hyman would get discontinued groceries off the shelf at Winn-Dixie, buy them up at salvage prices, and sell them back at a four-hundred-percent mark up. That worked pretty well until the Cash 'N' Carry opened, and everybody got cars. He moved over to City View then and left the building empty. The city repossessed it and tore it down after thirty years of negotiating with the bastard."

So we moved around, roughly taking White Horse Road in a kind of perimeter through the manufacturing district of Greenville. I now saw the town as a big egg. The yolk—sweet, yellow, and rich—was around old Greenville. The Poinsett Club, the park, Crescent Avenue, the green, green grass of the country club. The egg white, colorless and made to sustain the yolk as it grew, was the belt of mill villages, and the white shell was the Eastside where the new industries had sprung up to service the old ones, where the New South had its prosperous Greenville version—tires, transmissions, and fancy cars.

We drove through the "other side" as Wiley called it with the new Harris Teeters sporting gourmet coffee and emu meat—no salvage groceries here. At Earth Fare, things were no different. The miles of tasteful treeless and expansive subdivisions, Miller Lake, Stonehenge, Woodruff Pond, Willow Creek, Rocky Falls, Throneglade with million dollar houses, Chanticleer with older million dollar houses, and Silar Creek which gave way to Silar Ridge, and on and on. Greenville was three cities—the yolk, the white, and the glistening shell; and as Wiley said, "Only the lawyers keep the damn thing together. On Saturday night it might as well be Beirut."

CHAPTER THIRTY-ONE

It was one o'clock when we got to Zorba's. It was at a wild corner close to the zoo, close enough to hear the howling of the samarangs when the traffic was slow. *Hoot, hoot, hoot, hoot.* "Give me a Greek salad," they said, "some feta and some lettuce."

Across the street sat a country-looking building, relic of World War II with a curved roof like a Quonset hut. Greenville Feed and Seed, the sign proclaimed, like the battle flag of a lost regiment of confederate farmers that had been surrounded by the union infantry of urbanism but vowed to fight on. You could get anything you wanted their sort of big livestock. Chicks, baby rabbits and dog food, grass seed and chicken feed, tomato cages, hunting knives, and wire fencing.

Zorba's was one of the only Greek restaurants in town that wasn't named Pete's or The Clock, and according to Wiley, they had the best Greek salad in town. He also said that I used to come here a lot, and the crowd of Zorba's was a floating banquet of scandal and rumor and gossip.

Outside, only a sign of a fake gaslight distinguished Zorba's from the dry cleaner right next door and a rap record shop further down the strip mall. On the corner, a convenience store with gasoline got robbed twice a year. The ownership changed every three years, swapped among Indians and Pakistanis and Syrians and Lebanese and Palestinians as they climbed up the ladder. The Mexicans owned Berea, on the west side of town.

Enter the door of Zorba's, and it all went away. No light, just soft pornography, plastic, video poker, and alcohol but great Greek food. Criminals, would-be criminals, almost criminals, and all their lawyers came here to feel a little sleazy while they ate the food which came out hot, served by a buxom waitress who had a special smile for everybody. "Hi, hon." She knew your name after you had come twice, and her memory was legendary. If she liked you, you got your burger hot. If she didn't, well, it might not be so hot.

"Fred, honey, I was so worried about you, babe. It's good to have you back." She planted a voluptuous wet kiss on my cheek and rubbed her big bosoms on my shoulder before my eyes had adjusted to the darkness.

"You don't kiss me that way, Toni," Wiley said, pouting.

"And you don't deserve it either," said Toni.

We sat by the jukebox. Everything was near the jukebox. Across from the plaster statue of a nude with little pearls for breasts perched on a lighted beer sign that looked like a fountain.

"Is it the usual, men?" Wink-wink went Toni—usual meaning some illicit delicacy, in this case Greek salad.

"Yeah, with sweet tea this time."

"No bubble stuff, Bubba?"

"We gotta work."

"Oh," said Toni, pouting.

Wiley reached his arm out to comfort her, and she slid just out of his arm's reach while turning to get the silverware. He did it half-heartedly—a game they had played over and over again.

I had been quiet the whole time, letting my eyes adjust to the dark, taking in the late lunchtime crowd.

Toni went to the kitchen, and Greek-American-English spewed out a menu over the half door.

Wiley leaned over to me. "Poor thing. I helped her with her divorce last year, and she hasn't quite got it together yet, but she is as sweet as apple pie."

"Did I used to come here?"

"All the time, all the time, my man," Wiley said dreamily with a ghost of a voluptuous grin on his lips. Soon our lunch arrived, and we directed our attention to our full plates.

My eyes were used to the darkness now, and I could see couples at the other tables. Secretaries smoking, plumbers and HVAC men, and guys in the blue pin-striped uniform of lawyers and bankers. Through this small crowd were sprinkled a few pretty young women who pressed close to the men beside them, pulling at their arms until the food came. Wiley identified one of the men.

"Gene Borgias came here with Michelin ten years ago. They kicked him out over a scandal there, something to do with the vice-president's wife who was actually a Michelin herself—Quelle Scandale! He went into business himself, running the tire stores that got into malls, and now he is another wealthy Greenvillian. I think that's Mandy with him, although I have heard he has got somebody new now."

Monsieur Borgias was a slender little man, who looked like an old greyhound, half rodent, intelligent like a fox. He was laughing with Mandy, but I sensed a predator, *Lupus est homo homini,* a real wolf.

Wiley knew several others in the room, and occasionally he would nod to Toni. She would nod back in some secret code that seemed to be the whole reason you came to Zorba's. Rumors to go with the Greek salad. Underneath the plaster statues of nudes and the tacky outmoded beer signs, a whole narrative of a part of Greenville played itself out. It was like the Rosetta stone with the first language being American English in a southern idiom, the next language Greek. The last language carved in was just oohs and aahs, raised eyebrows and shoulder shrugs.

The jukebox came on to pure country.

"You don't love me anymore 'cause you just walked out the door of our bedroom, where so many times before, the smoke and fire would drive you wild"—or something like that. Toni sang along, and I noticed she looked down, away from Wiley, while all the girls seemed buried in reverie, their lips whispering smoke and fire while the singer raised the pitch and mourned her lost lover.

The door opened, and a burly man rolled in, moving like a weightlifter. He looked familiar, and I nudged Wiley. "You know him?"

"Maybe," Wiley said and grew a little tense. He nodded his head at Toni as the song ended.

Our lunch had been delicious, mounds of feta cheese on sweet lettuce, chopped tomatoes and peppers, all glistening with the sheen of olive oil and vinegar and Greek spices, *nulli secundus,* second to none.

The big guy looked over at us, and I suddenly remembered him from the first day at the *Y.*

I smiled.

He glared.

Toni went to him and placed her hand on his arm, resting on the vinyl-padded bar. She whispered to him and squeezed his arm lightly.

"Let's get out of here," Wiley said tersely.

The guy was muttering something to Toni as we slid by him, and he extended his foot backward in a clumsy effort to make us stumble.

Wiley caught my arm before I tripped, and we both got by without even touching him. Toni seemed to be pressing his arm and talking to him more urgently. While that seemed to keep him at the bar, we wasted no time in cranking up the Bimmer and speeding up Washington Avenue back toward town. Safe in Lawyerville.

Wiley said nothing. He was big, and there were two of us, but we were lawyers, and the other guy seemed to be serious about something.

"What was that guy's problem?" I asked, trying to sound calm.

"No clue," Wiley said, meaning he wasn't going to talk about it.

No "heh, hehs" this time.

"Wiley, if I've done something to that guy, I'd like to know what it is. What if I see him again? *In cauda venenum.* There is more to this than some muscle head wanting a brawl."

"We're safe now. We'll talk about this later."

With that, the long day now closed, Wiley put on his character armor and zipped his mouth firmly shut.

I did the same but had a secret sweet marvel at the fact that I had remembered a little Latin today. In fact, the last thing I said was *in cauda venenum—this guy was the tale of a scorpion of intrigue that was hidden from me,* I thought as Wiley stopped the car. Scorpion's can sting you pretty bad.

"Now don't you go anywhere, hero. I'll get you again tomorrow, and we'll eat somewhere else. Now, git!"

I smiled and thanked him as I clambered out. He pulled up his cell phone to report something to somebody, and I felt a tug of mystery swirl around me like the undertow at Edisto Island.

This would all reveal itself in good time. *In tempore opportune,* I muttered to myself, savoring Latin like the garlic from the Greek salad at lunch.

CHAPTER THIRTY-TWO

The house was empty, the kind of early summer afternoon when the deep shade of the big oaks kept the house cool. The fragrance balms that Travis had littered about the house made an intoxicating atmosphere with the rays of the sun slipping in through the windows. The play of shadow and light, perfume mingled through it all, made for involuntary reverie. Where was I in all this? I felt like a confederate Proust, reconstructing a South lost after some battle I couldn't remember, waking up on a scorched battlefield with no memories of cannon fire.

Let's see. So I woke up in a hospital bed, burned and beaten. From the moment I could think a bit, this beautiful permanent debutant is by my side, loving on me. At first, this was wonderful, and she led me into a thicket of dependence I needed at the time. Gradually, as I got better, I became her love slave clad in Lycra, her Speedo king, there with passion.

Meanwhile, she had begun to impede my return to active life for reasons I couldn't fathom. Suddenly my old rival Wiley appears and gives me a whirlwind tour of Greenville, the Greenville that still exists despite the modernizers, and we run into a belligerent bodybuilder, snarling at us as we escape an old haunt that I can't remember. Wiley seems to be reporting to someone. This whole time, an EMS vehicle appears at odd moments, as if it were on an errand of observation, and part of the whole thing sounds more and more like a strange conspiracy as I describe it to myself.

Is paranoia one of the stages of healing from a head injury?

Suddenly I wanted to go swimming. I needed to go swimming. I hated to leave the cool, calm sun-striped interior of the house, but I had to go swimming.

Did the house really belong to Travis? Is this just a scene in a movie directed by someone off stage?

I wanted to slide on my Speedo and do some comfortable mind-numbing laps. This reverie had cost me my peace of mind, and I needed to baptize my soul in the cool water of the swimming pool. I needed redemption.

—+—+—*—+—+—*—

I walked to the pool the long way, back up to Crescent Avenue half a block and down by the crook in the street that led into a cove lined with mansions. Now a ghetto for the high bourgeoisie of Greenville. An arboretum with azaleas and rhododendron and dogwood and cedar. I tried not to think anymore as I walked through this wonderland.

Samarangs from the zoo filled the shade with wild whoops and howls, reminders of the jungle surrounding us.

I gave up when I saw the EMS vehicle at the end of the street, going slowly, pointed in my direction. It seemed to pick up speed as it moved toward me. This was the same van from my dreamtime encounter? It was happening again. I was trapped on the narrow street, but I started to sprint for the nearest driveway.

The ambulance slowed, and the window on my side cracked open. A contralto voice whispered my name, husky as a lover's moan. Last time she had just kissed me.

"Fred, Fred, calm down. It's me, Eva."

I pulled myself down from the front steps of Polly McGillicuddy, the rich Yankee girl who had come to town to seek refuge from a series of marriages to Latin playboys. I hoped she wasn't seeing this.

I walked warily to the ambulance, and Eva lowered the window further the closer I got.

When I got within five feet, I could see her.

She was the girl. The girl I had been dreaming about. The girl who'd been haunting me. Now I had her name.

My memory flooded back, and the whole thing began to make sense, although it was still foggy and full of smoke.

Her beauty and energy shown through her uniform and the unlikely vehicle. What was she rescuing me from?

I could see the soft swell of her breasts and the full lips that were perfectly formed.

Her hands were long and elegant, strong and muscular, an athlete. I had to know just one thing.

"Do you swim?"

"Ever, Fred," she whispered. "Of course I do, darling. Don't you remember?"

⊹ ⊹ ⊹ ⊹ ⊹ ⊹

Oh my god, did I remember. Her wetness in the pool, the slithering breaststroke with my ventral fin attached, erect like the mast on a sailboat. The Speedo pulled back like the sheath of a fish scattering milt, injecting it, seeking the great mating. We wriggled through the water attached together like amphibians in the spring. Her lovely legs wrapped round me while I moved my arms, her back supported on a kickboard.

Honk-honk.

A BMW passed us. "Who was it?" I jumped back.

"I don't know," Eva said in another whisper. "Watch out now, Fred."

"Watch out for what?" I said, my chest aching for her.

But she jumped into the ambulance and sped away.

Somehow, I was afraid. My reverie blasted. I felt the energy of something from my former life overtake me. Exhilarating fear. I climbed the hill, fondling my Speedo and imagining Eva, Eva, Eva.

─✢─✢─✦─✢─✢─✦─

How could I trust her? She had emerged from my mind like the shadows in Plato's cave. Professor Labban had always taught that the shadows never came off the walls of the cave. They always danced in the dim light of the fire. This girl was real though, and she had come off the wall of my fire-scorched mind into my dreams and now into my actual memory. She was real. I wanted to touch her. *Quis fallere posit amantem?* Virgil reminded us, who can deceive a lover?

But then lovers can deceive themselves readily enough. Especially ones with head injuries—or did I forget something? Like how I was going to explain this to Travis.

CHAPTER THIRTY-THREE

It was just late June, and the heat was building up like the morning birdsong and eerie cricket cries at night. I felt my Speedo again and knew this time I really needed redemption more than ever. I needed a swim.

I came to the Y with no fanfare anymore. The girls at the desk, Caroline and Susan and Darlene and Sharonda, just nodded and smiled. Something told me to tell them I was swimming today, although usually I didn't bother. I just waved and smiled. But today, I asked Susan to check on me.

Sweet little Speedo, cloth of my loins, wrapped me in Lycra wonder like the codpiece of a knight, my armor, the muscles tight around my shoulders and legs.

I dived in after stretching and began a slow warm-up, pulling myself through the water and feeling the water glide through my mind. It dissolved my fears of Wiley and Travis and washed clean my memories of Eva. Eva with strawberries, Eva with breaststroke, Eva pulling her Speedo down and off. Eva, Eva, Eva.

Cogito ergo Speedo, I muttered to myself, as the memories began to come unbidden and to slow me in the water. The lifeguard had left soon after my warm-up, and I was alone in the pool at the shallow end.

That's when the bodybuilder grabbed at me.

The guy at Zorba's, big and hairy, like a Goth, grabbing a Roman in the baths of the capital. Couldn't he see that he didn't belong! The Barbarian!

Not in my realm, my Speedo province, not in my reveries of Eva!

Ira furor brevis est. Anger is brief madness.

Before he could growl out whatever he wanted to say, his face contorted in surprise.

"Whaaa," he shouted as I knocked his hand off my shoulder and drug him into the pool.

He hit his head on the side and was dazed; plus his big lean muscles sank like stones. He was stiff and heavy as a piece of iron. I couldn't have handled him on the ground, but in the water, I dragged him out deeper and held him under.

I would have drowned the wild boar had Susan not shouted at me.

"Fred, Fred, what are you doing? Let him up!"

I let him go, and he began to sink.

"He attacked me."

"So what, you idiot, that's Eva's boyfriend."

"What?"

"Don't let him drown."

As I dived down and pulled muscle boy out of the water, I was genuinely puzzled. Susan and maybe the whole Y knew something I didn't. I pulled him onto the pool deck and pushed on his chest. He vomited some water then started breathing on his own and roused himself to try to struggle with me again. He had learned nothing.

I backed into the pool after knocking his hands away.

"Susan, you look after this jerk right now, and he better not hit me. I just saved his life."

I swam into the middle of the pool and began to tread water, while Susan ministered to muscle head.

"Incidis in scyllan cupiens vitare charybdim." Out of the frying pan, into the fire.

What else was this day going to bring.

At least my Latin was with me.

"Eva thinks I tried to kill you," the big muscle said, "in the fire."

"Did you?" I asked, like a lawyer.

"No, hell, no!"

We were still on the side of the pool.

Muscle boy turned out to be named Jason. Susan had calmed him down and told us to get ourselves together. She would not tolerate any "crap" like this at her *Y*. If she hadn't known us and "the whole story," she would have kicked us out, and she still might, so we had to get along or be banished.

We moved to the lobby so Susan could watch us.

So we talked and talked and talked and talked some more. Jason was one of these guys you can't quite pin down to anything. It was a flaw in his language skills because he was pretty bright, at least as bright as a head-injured, Latin-loving lawyer type. He thought "approximate" and "unusual" sounded sophisticated, so he used them all the time.

I preferred Latin.

CHAPTER THIRTY-FOUR

Jason had been in the army once. Now he was a part-time student, part-time security guard, part-time truck driver, and part-time philosophy.

"I just get along, mister." He said he liked philosophy, and I thought about throwing a little Latin at him, but his muscles were too big to be very philosophical. Maybe he was a gladiator. I did not want to damage his inflated opinion of his own intellect while we had to get some business done.

"Now, did you try to kill me?"

"No, Fred. I did not really try to kill you."

"What do you mean, really?"

"I have wanted to bust your face in for what you did to Eva, but killing is against my moral code."

"So busting my face in, as you so delicately put it, wouldn't kill me?"

"Not where I come from."

I was glad we sat in one corner of the lobby under Susan's watchful eye.

"Okay, okay, let's start right there. Did I do something to Eva?" I thought of the urgency she breathed onto me through the ambulance window. What had I done to her?

"You impregnated her."

"Please say that again."

"You got her pregnant, man. Can't you understand good English?"

"All right. I don't know if you will believe this, but I can't remember any of that. When am I supposed to have made her pregnant?"

"Fred, there is something the matter with this. It would be highly unusual if you don't know how somebody gets pregnant."

"Jason, let me tell you this straight up. I know how somebody gets pregnant. What I don't know is how that's supposed to happen when I have been in a burn unit with a concussion."

"You just don't make any sense," he said irritably and got up to leave.

"Please stay," I said, and I waved at Susan who began to move toward us.

"Fine, you got her pregnant last year."

"When did she have the baby?"

"In February," he said tersely. "I was with her, February the 28th."

"Now we're getting somewhere."

"Now you tell me what exactly you're talking about. I have not heard of a burn unit or a concussion."

"I was in the hospital for about six weeks in December, January, and February. I was found somewhere in northern Greenville County all burnt over my left side, beaten, unconscious. I have no memory of anything leading up to it, and I have no clue why it happened."

"Well, I didn't do it, honest." He crossed his heart. "I have known Eva for a couple of years, but we just got close this last four or five months. You know, you were really a bastard, but I can't get Eva to talk about it."

This certainly did not fit anything I could remember, nor with Eva's continued expression of affection for me, but I couldn't tell that to Jason. I wanted time to sort this out.

I looked up at the clock. It was about time for Travis to get home. I did not want to alarm her.

"All right, Jason, let's make a little deal. We meet at Zorba's tomorrow at lunch."

"Are you kidding? That's where you and Eva used to eat."

"Well, I don't remember it. That's how bad I was hurt."

"Okay, fine, tomorrow at twelve fifteen."

We both smiled and shook hands and then waved at Susan who smiled back.

Jason went back to lifting, and I walked fast to the showers, still looking over my shoulder. My head was spinning with this new information that was old news to everyone else.

Why hadn't Susan told me?

CHAPTER THIRTY-FIVE

It was dusky when I walked home, my head still spinning from a full afternoon. First, the urgency of Eva rescuing me away from something, then Jason making me remember her, and the threat in the pool, then Susan who mysteriously knew everything while she volunteered nothing. The coolness of the evening was a balm to my bruised mind.

The sunset filtered through the trees like red gold, gilding everything it touched.

Our house was in a grove of giant oaks that made the sun fall sooner. All around lay odd pieces and rays of the dying sun of the day, but the oak towers kept them out. The house stayed cool and shady. Dusk grew up from the tree trunks and bushes, gathering in silence.

Wiley's BMW was parked in front. As I walked up, a big dog padded down the street and stopped on our little sidewalk. He lifted up his leg, marking his territory with urine.

Was this like me? Maybe I hadn't urinated enough to recognize my own territory. When you have a head injury, all sorts of things come into your mind. Maybe they catheterized me too much.

I did not want any more surprises—what was Wiley's car doing here? Did he see Eva?

"Hey there, big buddy." Wiley grabbed me with his paw and half pulled me into the gloomy house.

"Good to see you again."

"We were getting worried."

"Who are we?"

"Now, I say, don't be a smart aleck, college boy. Travis and me of course. Haven't we been worried, honey?"

I wanted to tell Wiley not to call me honey until I saw Travis. She popped up from the couch and strode over with the tiniest miniskirt I had seen yet and an angora blouse that made her look as fluffy as a dandelion, black on the top and beige leather on the bottom. Her legs stretched out like a dancer, and I almost asked her if she was wearing her Speedo, but I could have seen it if I had looked for it. She had beautiful bare feet. Toenails red as hybrid roses.

"Now don't get any funny ideas." She said this with the same tone she always used in greeting. She meant for you to shut up and not ask questions, but she had a look in her eye that beckoned you into her web.

"We are taking you out."

Wiley was gently steering me toward my room. "Wait a minute, guys. Can you tell me what's going on?"

"You want to get back in the firm? Then do what we say." Travis looked drawn and tense, more anxious than usual, unlike her. She smelled of cigarettes and coffee, not musk and flowers.

"Just please tell me exactly what this is. I need some more information."

Wiley broke in. "Travis, let me explain this."

"Okay." She seemed relieved but didn't drop her guard.

"Fred, Travis, and I have been thinking how to get you back into the swing of things for a long time. Frankly, your reputation isn't as good as an egg-sucking dog after your head got banged up. You weren't capable of anything except makin' trouble. But now your Latin is starting to come back. You are oriented. You know how to dress. You are *redivivus,* so to speak." He winked at me. "But to get you back in the firm, we got to trot you out around town a little bit to see the reaction. Now there is a big party each year at this time, and we have all been invited. We are going to do this first, then troll you through the firm to see if any of the fish are biting."

Travis sprayed a little mint vapor in her mouth, refreshed her lipstick, and put on Chanel Coco perfume. This put us in Zorba's sure enough again. It was effortless for her. She was nodding her head the whole time. The essence of honeysuckle.

I debated what to do. I was tired. Who wouldn't be? I had gone to the Y for swimming practice, had a brawl, met a new player in this big mystery, and learned I may have fathered a child. Wasn't that enough for one day?

However, the sight of Travis, beautiful and smelling good, and Wiley, good old boy, energized me. This plan they had laid out sounded good.

But a party? *Plures crapula quam gladius,* the Roman's had said. More people die partying than fighting wars.

I had been threatened with death two times now—once in the wreck and earlier today by Jason. What had I done to deserve this? *Quid nunc?* What now?

"I'll go," I said.

Might as well, I thought to myself. At least I will have them with me, and after seeing Eva today, I am not sure what I'd say to Travis, especially with her dressed like that. It's hard to choose between two beautiful women.

"What clothes am I supposed to wear?"

"Hey, man, did you forget where you are? This is South Carolina. You wear khakis and a blue blazer with a polo shirt, of course," Wiley said, pointing at his own clothes. "Weejuns and no socks. All this is a given, if you remember." Travis nodded, arching her eyebrows, already made up.

"Fine."

What a full day this had been. Maybe I was *redivivus*, brought back to life, indeed.

My skin grafts were throbbing.

He led me back to the bedroom, and there, laid out on the bed, was a blue blazer, an ivory polo shirt, and a pair of khakis starched and pressed with a razor crease. My Weejuns were polished and sitting on the floor, red as a cabernet or a rib eye done rare.

"C'mon, get dressed."

I did.

CHAPTER THIRTY-SIX

This party was called Sprummer, part spring, part summer. Ten years ago, ten couples had a party; the next year they had a party again. It grew and grew and finally a quasi—formal organization had developed, with "rules and informal bylaws." Each of the ten original couples continued their participation—through divorce and remarriage even—and now they each invited ten others.

Over the course of the evening, all the "old Greenville crowd" wandered through the party. It was held at the home of "Big Camelia"—an older woman that was somewhat related to Travis. She was Big Camelia because her daughter was Little Camelia and part of the Sprummer crowd. The house was three blocks away from us, and Travis wanted to walk in her new semi-spike high heels, even though they hurt her feet. The walk up to the house afforded a kind of runway entrance. She wanted to observe everybody's reaction to our arrival from the moment they laid eyes on us.

Who were they trolling really?

The house was balanced and symmetric, modern with big windows and a geometric presence. The lawn stretched off into the night. Beside the house stood the largest magnolia tree in the state. The leaves of it made a circle a hundred fifty feet in circumference. It had about thirty trunks sprouting from a common root.

I thought the whole place was a symbol for Greenville, rooted in a common southern past, thick with spring blossoms. The huge blooms floating like moons in a green night secreted incense like a temple for the great lost cause, the South—of myth and legend.

The tree was only decoration though, for the ultra modern house was where everyone slept and ate. Greenville is the New South. After all, you can't eat magnolias, nor moonlight. Something else must sustain us—parties!

Mimbbee, ruh, ruh boom chicky, hey, hey, hey, hum-ra-buzz—hum-ra-buz, hum-ra-buz,

Mimbbee, ruh, ruh boom chicky, hey, hey, hey, hum-ra-buzz—hum-ra-buz, hum-ra-buz

Mimbbee, ruh, ruh boom chicky, hey, hey, hey, hum-ra-buzz—hum-ra-buz, hum-ra-buz

The closer we got to the party, you could hear a kind of low hum, like a beehive in honey time, beach music, laughter, greeting cries, voices began to distinguish themselves. The Weejuns hurt my feet, and Travis had managed to stumble against both me and Wiley, righting herself with a sideways thrust of her hip clad in leather. She couldn't walk in her shoes either. As we got closer, a kind of party glow enveloped us, and I could see Travis wet her lipstick, already luscious, with her tongue, wet as the inside of a spring flower.

Wiley winked at me—wink-wink—I tried to wink back, but I still couldn't do it. My right skin graft was too tight.

The first person we heard was "Bertha," a beautiful little dark-haired woman with black hair, flashing eyes, scarlet red lipstick, and red, red nail polish. Every word she said was a delighted shriek or a cute little scream! "TRAVIS, HOW GOOD TO SEE YOU!" Arms open wide, hugging our little mini-skirt, honeysuckle close, and knocking us over with noise, perfume, beautiful grooming, and fine clothes.

I couldn't tell you who looked more provocative—her or Travis. Her clothes looked more expensive, and she had a head start on what Travis coveted.

Bertha was part of the textile people that always seemed to have money and property, but you never knew exactly how they got it. When Bertha saw me, she flinched, and that registered with Travis, but she grabbed me anyway and hugged me close and whispered, "You watch out now, baby." And then she held me at arm's length to smile a cautionary smile.

Watch out for what? I thought this was supposed to be a party.

Bertha smiled a radiant smile at Wiley, gave him a squeal and a hug, and then drifted off through the gathering crowd, hugging and shrieking as if she hadn't seen her friends in years, instead of the tennis lesson that morning.

I had become as vigilant as the emperor's watchdog—thanks to her.

Was something hiding in the magnolia tree? Maybe a Yankee sniper.

⸻ ⸙ ⸻ ⸙ ⸻ ⸙ ⸻ ⸙ ⸻ ⸙ ⸻

Travis was in her element now. She grabbed Big Camelia, and they started whispering. After we rambled over to the drinks, everybody seemed to look at us then look away quickly, too quickly.

Yes, it's true they are together now. He looks good after all that, but she looks better—imagine that dress. Who invited them anyway? Party mumbles.

One partially bald fellow seemed excessively friendly even in that friendly atmosphere. He was tall and looked like a rat, sharp features and hair slicked back. He stood beside a tiny beautiful woman with big hair and a big mouth, even louder than Bertha, trained at the same school of opera party talk.

"And I said to Randy not to sell that Rolls Royce, people around here are just not ready for such vehicles. Waste of money and time." A small crowd of people, well dressed and tan, surrounded her and her tall husband like courtiers around a king and queen.

"Who's that?" I asked Wiley. Travis was now mingled into the throng but glanced back at us periodically checking for something, anything.

"That, my good man, is one of the Schnaffer's. Old man Schnaffer used to sell Packard's, and now his sons sell the finest cars made from Europe and Japan. Got into it when the Ford Motor Company turned them down for a dealership. He gave me a good deal on my Beemers. We will have to check with him when we get your car for you. He's a great guy."

Apparently, he had given a good deal to lots of folks because half the cars there were Beemers, little ones and big ones, convertibles, coupes, and sedans.

His wife was Melinda. When she saw us, nothing registered until Wiley reached out and gave her a hug. "Melinda, I'd like you to meet Fred Tutem." She looked breathless for a moment "The Fred Tutem! I thought he was supposed—"

Wiley cut her off.

"To be well and getting better, right?" Wiley finished her sentence for her.

"Travis and I brought him with us tonight. By the way, you're right about the Rolls." He winked and pulled me away, while Melinda gasped, quiet for the first time in the last ten minutes.

Another quiet man with another beautiful wife, this one sweet and pretty and silent as a sphinx, stood on the edge of the crowd, not really mixing but acknowledging everyone.

"That's James Milkuns, our most esteemed head of the democratically controlled legislature. Good guy."

He gave me a politician's handshake then moved on to another opportunity to press the flesh.

Here was South Carolina politics happening right before my very eyes, in the presence of a big magnolia tree, a modern house, moonlight, and whiskey.

I wished I knew what was going on and what Bertha was talking about. I was still worried.

I stood there wishing Wiley would leave me alone. I wanted to leave yet talk to someone at the same time. I felt threatened by the crowd and Bertha's ominous whisper. The buzz and hub-bub and music just confused me and added to the threat. Who were we trolling for? What were we trolling anyway? Was I the bait?

My Weejuns hurt. Everybody was drinking, but I was afraid it would make me collapse.

I wanted one anyway.

—⊬—⊬—⊬—⊬—⊬—⊬—

"Hey, I'm Amy, remember me?" An attractive girl appeared out of the crowd and stuck out her hand.

"No, I don't remember you, but I would like to."

"Well, I've got a message for you."

"Please let it be nice." I winced and braced myself for another warning.

She touched my arm. "Look, Fred, it's none of my business. Jinny just told me that she hoped you'd be careful of Travis." She said this conspiratorially close to my ear, watching Wiley's back. He was ogling somebody's wife.

"Who's Jinny?"

She looked disappointed. "Well, she's your ex-wife, and she is a good friend of mine."

"I was married?" I asked. It startled me that I remembered nothing.

"Up until three years ago, you creep," she said with a fake smile. She began to turn on her heel and walk away, but I reached out and stopped her.

"Please, we need to talk," I begged. I pulled her aside so we could talk. Wiley turned and looked at Amy.

"Wiley." I tapped him on the shoulder. "Amy and I are going to get some drinks. Do you need anything?"

"Let me come with you, buddy."

"I'd rather let Amy chaperone me, big guy." I punched him on the shoulder. "You wander over to Melinda and get me a deal on a Beemer."

With that, I pushed through the crowd a little away from him. The crowd closed in around Amy and me. The perfume and cologne mingled with the cigarettes and whiskey and magnolia.

All I could hear now was party buzz. Amy was coming along with me.

Wiley just shouted at us to come back with the drinks, and then he gave his lustful attention to some other bare-shouldered beauty.

"Please, Amy, I was hurt badly, and I don't remember huge chunks of my life, almost nothing before the wreck, including my marriage."

"Well, Fred, I always liked you, so I'll tell you whatever you'd like." She had softened.

The drinks were behind the magnolia. I suggested we just go into the middle of the tree to talk. We could drink later. Big Camelia wasn't looking.

It was very dark and quieter there; the big dark green glossy leaves hid us while she told me my story . . .

⸎⸎⸎⸎⸎⸎

CHAPTER THIRTY-SEVEN

How strange it is to contemplate your own life through the eyes of a friend. Amy was kind as she recounted my marriage to Jinny. She had been a Randolph Macon girl, bright and sweet. I was the super swimming Speedo man from W and L. After the failure of our first pregnancy, she got depressed. The longer she stayed depressed, the more my behavior changed. Then I got entangled with Butch, and I started to run around.

"I ran around?"

"Well, yes, you used to swim half naked with that damn little Speedo. Why not take it all off?"

"With Travis?"

"At first we thought so, but then it seems there was someone else. We couldn't really track it down, and Butch was involved somehow—that was as far as we could get."

She continued the story, and it was clear that I had not acted like a Virginia gentleman.

"Finally, Jinny left town, nursing a broken heart," Amy said, "but she had spent so much time with the Junior League there was no time left over for you. No wonder you had the affair."

"I wish I could remember this," I said.

"No, you don't," Amy said quickly and leaned over to kiss me on the forehead then turned to leave the magnolia thicket.

"Amy, one more question."

"What's that?"

"What do I have to be so afraid of now? People keep telling me to watch out."

In the dark, I could see her eyes widen.

Someone had crept into the other side of the tree right then.

"Fred, I'll tell you later. Let's get out of here," she said with some urgency.

I followed her out quickly, while behind us, somebody or bodies struggled to get through the tree.

I turned to see who it was, but just then, the lights went out for a minute, and the crowd surged forward, cutting off my view, which had not been that clear anyway.

Was this why Travis wanted Wiley to protect me?

I needed a drink.

—ψ—ψ—ψ—ψ—ψ—ψ—

The lights came back on.

Amy and I wormed our way over to the bar as quickly as we could, looking over our shoulders the whole time.

Two black men in tuxedos poured the drinks and tried to be pleasant, while everyone jostled each other to get a glass of the available intoxicants. Just to the side, a precariously perched display of liquors caught my eye. Each bottle had a silver tag around the neck. Scotch, bourbon, gin—but the one that caught my eye the most hung around the red wine. *In vino veritas* inscribed in a Latin script.

I needed some *veritas*, truth, and I wanted some red wine.

"Red wine, please. Make it a double," I said to the bartender. He broke into a grin.

"Okay, wait, wait just a minute. Shawn, get a load of this—Fred Toothum!" The bartender, a handsome black man named Rufus, recognized me. He seemed happy to see me.

"I thought you was supposed to be daid."

Shawn, the other bartender, paused and looked me up and down just shaking his head. "Mmm, mmm, mmm, Mistah Fred. Why you are quite a sight!"

"How do you guys know me?" I said, clutching my double red wine with one hand and Rufus's hand with the other.

"The Poinsett Club. Don't you remember? You used to eat there all the time. The cornbread sticks? C'mon, man, I don't believe you can't remember as many as you 'et. Those guys couldna beat you up that bad."

Then he pulled me close as he could over to the bar, grabbing my biceps with his right hand and saying in a low voice, "You better get your Speedo butt outta here for your own sake. They're comin' after you."

Shawn pushed at Rufus. "Rufus, that ain't none of your business."

"Hush, Shawn, Fred needs to be warned."

Then just as quickly, both of them resumed their party faces.

I thought I had clutched my wine tightly, but it was gone. Did I drink it?

Rufus poured me another one.

I looked at Rufus and then looked around the party. I recognized no one, and when I looked back at Rufus, he was hiding behind his eyes. They were as glazed over as they were at the Poinsett Club. Seeing nothing, hearing nothing as gossip swirled around the cornbread sticks.

In vino veritas. I drank it down fast and decided to follow all this advice I was getting. I was going to get out of there.

I began to make my way back through the crowd, but I couldn't see Wiley or Travis or Amy. Suddenly I felt something hard sticking in my back. It did not feel like a wine glass.

"Don't turn around. Just keep walking to the street." *In vino veritas.*

I didn't know who it was, just a gruff voice. About my size.

I had faced damn Jason in the pool though, and swimming in this pool of partygoers wasn't that different. If he was pressing me with a gun, then too bad.

I screamed "*IN VINO VERITAS!*" I screamed it again. The crowd suddenly got a little quiet, and the hard thing against my back vanished. I kept screaming about wine and truth and began to run toward the street. I would tell Travis I went crazy. I shouldn't have had the wine, heh, heh.

In fact I felt *Dionysian*, crazy with the great mystery surrounding me. Spring was the right time.

Who were these people? How did they know so many things? Who am I?

And who was trying to kill me?

Everyone was staring, and I didn't care.

Travis and Wiley began to push and pull their way toward me, but I ran in the opposite direction.

As I reached the street, an EMS vehicle rounded the corner at McDaniel Avenue and Augusta Road. I ran toward it instinctively. It was Eva. The second time today.

As I reached her door, she motioned for me to get in, and I did, pretending not to hear Travis and Wiley shouting back in the crowd at the party.

―✦―✦―✶―✦―✦―✶―

CHAPTER THIRTY-EIGHT

"What are you doing here?"

"Somebody called us twenty minutes ago."

"Who could that have been?"

"I don't know who, but it doesn't matter now, does it? I got word from the dispatcher, and somehow I knew it had to be about you."

In the rear window, a little of the party crowd had spilled onto the street; and Wiley, at least I thought it was Wiley, was running toward us. I caught a glimpse of Travis and her two long legs as well.

"Where are we going?"

"Why don't you take me home? It's just around the corner."

"I've got a better idea. Let's go to the hospital and call Craig Olds, tell him something happened to you, and you need to be seen."

We made it around the corner out of sight of the crowd, and she began to reach for her radio.

"Wait a minute," I said. "What's the hurry?" *In vino veritas.* Eva looked good in her uniform.

I put my hand on her leg. "The park is down there, let's, uh, talk a little bit."
Dionysius, I whispered to myself.

Without a word, she took the next turn and drove into the darkness.

-+--+--*--+--+--*-

We didn't know what was coming next, and we simply didn't care. I don't
know what the ambulance looked like from the outside, but I know we
made love fiercely on that tiny stretcher bed in the back. She had to keep on
some of her uniform in case the police stopped by, but at least she took her
metal name plate off, for it was scratching my chest and cheek. She unbound
her long dark hair, and it flowed over my shoulders like water.

The Samarangs were howling, and the darkness was everywhere. Lots of
places to hide. I wanted to drag her into the grass and go back up to the
forest along the park's perimeter.

Her breath hot in my ear, she whispered, "I'd like that—but it would mess
up my uniform."

I agreed, "Of course it will mess up your uniform—that's the point."

"Why would you want to mess up my uniform?"

"It just stands for everything that the crash and burn took away from me,"
I said and suddenly began crying.

What the hell . . . I choked it out, but the feelings stayed and grew as I cried
more grief spilled out—my profession, my memories, my position in town,
my ability to think, even my Latin. It all gone—but it's got to be there
somewhere. I know it is there . . .

She murmured softly as she patted my shoulder and dried my eyes with
her shirt. "Sweetheart. Remember, we are in an ambulance. I am a rescue
worker."

"Well, rescue me then."

She kissed the top of my head. I felt like a little baby.

All this made me cry a little more, but I clutched to her tightly and suddenly began to twitch and convulse with something that went into darkness as soon as I began to feel it. I knew it wasn't familiar. I don't remember anything more in the ambulance in the park—just a big space with darkness . . .

—+—+—*—+—+—*—

I woke up in the emergency room, Eva by my side with her professional demeanor on, her name tag in place, her uniform almost pressed, only a few tear spots at the bottom of her shirt next to the beltline. She presented my case as I tried to listen, but all I wanted to do was sleep.

"Patient is a forty-three-year-old white male with a previous history of head injury approximately six months ago. Emergency vehicle was called to 103 McDaniel Avenue at approximately ten o'clock due to presumed signs of intoxication. The patient was picked up and decision made to escort him home. He seemed disoriented, and then an attempt was made to restrain him—he had a grand mal seizure, and a decision was made to transport him to the emergency room. Under direction of emergency room physician, an IV with Valium was started. He has received about half the ten-milligram dose. The vital signs are stable—pulse 75 and regular, temperature 98.2, respirations 20, blood pressure 130/80."

Again, the scene of doctors buzzing around me like bees on a honey pot played itself out.

Examples are great devices for learning anything, but I was tired of being the example for medical problems.

As the Valium began to take hold, I simply slid into sleep. I remember looking into Eva's eyes to see an exotic blend of pity, empathy, love, and fear. Where did this woman come from?

How many truths our faces convey without words—what is it falling from the light in your eyes, a tiny muscle next to your eyebrow, the shape of your nostril? Whatever it was, I knew surely how Eva felt.

CHAPTER THIRTY-NINE

I was disoriented in the emergency room and for days thereafter. Eva drifted away that night and returned to her duties somewhere else.

Travis came back strong. Wiley was nowhere to be seen.

I learned much later that Eva thought the whole thing was some trick of intense lovemaking. She had tried to quiet me, but when I butted my head against her mouth, she suddenly became professional and recognized a seizure—that's what she told me later. It was almost funny then.

With all the commotion and my most recent set back, I missed the appointment for lunch with Jason. He never called back. It didn't seem important.

⊬ ⊬ ⊬ ⊬ ⊬ ⊬

Travis was up to her old beautiful tricks for a while. The dresses with the slit sides, the soft texture of her skin, the rich oriental musk of her perfumes. Wiley waited on the sidelines.

Had all this changed their plot? Did they even have a plot? Was their *truth* in wine? Did I have to fear anything?

After a couple of weeks or so, Travis took me to the neurologist to check my new medications.

"Seizures aren't unusual after head trauma," said Dr. Foxshire who appeared slightly disheveled and distracted with multiple cards in his shirt pocket and one half bleached ink splotch on his white coat. He mumbled things about my medication, how it demanded liver tests and blood counts but that it had proven extremely safe, and it shouldn't make me drowsy, "though it might." It also shouldn't hurt my stomach, "though it might," and he warned me not to drink with it. He explained how my EEG had been somewhat unusual, but he expected this to go away with the medication, and then he was gone. The whole explanation took maybe three minutes, then he disappeared. We had waited an hour and a half.

Travis was there, taking notes. Then Wiley arrived. This was the first time I had seen him since the party, and I had only a dim memory of that. He looked serious, and this was unusual.

"Hey, ole buddy, I heard all about this from Travis, and I've got to tell you I think we . . . we . . . we . . . we need"—and he glanced at Travis—"we need to change plans." With that cursory introduction, he took Travis into the hall. I heard voices raised, heavy whispers, and a sharp bark—like a fox. High heels clattered away down the hall. *Clack-clack-clack.* When he came back in the room, it was without Travis. He walked to my side and said, "I am in charge now."

"What are you talking about?"

"You are coming to my house when you get out, and we are going to get you back up to your office." He gave my arm a squeeze and left with a sense of mission. He turned at the door and said, "By the way, you're not going to be able to drive for six months because of that seizure. We will see what we can do, but the doctors have to stop you. We will talk about it some more later."

I had known something was up—something big, and it had felt good. Especially after the seizure. Not driving would be a complication, but I trusted Wiley now despite the way I had felt at the party. The seizure had cleared the air for now.

A goal at last: "We are going to get you back to the office." I would be a lawyer again—a swimming lawyer with seizures who found truth in wine. Who was burned and beaten and paranoid at parties and who had two girlfriends. That sounds just about like all lawyers.

I still couldn't quote Latin easily. My memory was undependable, and I knew nothing for certain. I missed Eva, but she was a mystery.

Travis was waiting for us in the lobby when I got discharged. We waited together, while Wiley got the car.

I remember being in the hospital the first time. I could remember the scent of my burned flesh—like steak on a grill. I could also remember the first time Travis came to see me wrapped in that tight black sweater dress with the slit up the side, smelling like a pheromone. There is nothing like a big dose of Je Reviens or Shalimar or Poison or Coco—to drive away the nightmare smell of your own skin burning.

She gave me something to touch besides my own scabbed and skin grafted body, something more than the soft hands of the nurses and the oily ointments they taught me to apply to the last places that had not healed.

She shook my desire awake as surely as she had shaken me out of my nightmares.

She fed me, clothed me, bathed me, and sheltered me.

And now . . . it was time to go.

So when I kissed her goodbye, I meant it, although even all this could not make me trust her again. I meant my gratitude, and I held her as close as I could, breathing in deeply one last cascade of the perfume she always wore.

Her eyes were moist as she whispered, "Well, I'll have to wait again. I won't let Wiley hurt you this time."

Won't let Wiley hurt me this time?

I thought he was rescuing me from her. She had said this as if we were coconspirators. Was I a blind man, and she was leading me through a labyrinth that would have rivaled the one King Minos built on Crete? Was Wiley the Minotaur? Was Travis Ariadne?

I held her strong shoulders at arm's length, took one more gulp of perfume, and said, "Please watch my back."

Her face dropped, and she handed me my bottle of anticonvulsant medicine. She pointed at it. "Make him help you take your pills right."

"Yes, ma'am," I said.

"Thank you." And then she patted me as I turned around and headed toward Wiley who was waiting at the door.

"Come on, buddy, it's time to try something different. I don't smell as good as Travis," he said and snickered, "heh, heh."

——+——+——+——+——+——+——

PART III

CHAPTER FORTY

The next couple of days were a blur of independence. When I first got away from the hospital, Travis had eased me back into life. Now, Wiley threw me into the pool of living to see if I still knew how to swim.

As we drove off, he said, "Well, the first thing you are going to need, boy, is a driver's license. I think I have arranged for that, plus we gotta finish up that insurance crap and get you a new car. They have just opened up a new office of the DMV, but you remember your ole buddy, John Erwin?"

He didn't give me time to reply, but it didn't matter because I didn't remember "Ole Buddy John Erwin."

"He is one of the DMV commissioners now, and he helped us a little bit, heh, heh. We are going to the new office."

So we buzzed happily along with a CD of blues and greatest hits of the seventies. When we pulled into the parking lot, there was already a line. Wiley just pulled over to the side, and we knocked on the back door. The security man opened the door and said, "You, idiot, get in line like everybody else. Is this the one?"

"Yes, he's the man."

"Well, go check in, and then we will see what we can do." Then he slammed the door like an exclamation point. Back at the front door, we nodded at another guard who eyed us suspiciously—everyone in line looked at us. Wiley's jaunty air made us different enough to create suspicion.

"Hello, Suzanne," he said. She had on a nametag that said "Suzanne." This didn't fit with the paramilitary uniform she wore but no matter—Wiley said in a whisper to me, "Our new governor has made the DMV 'customer friendly.'" Heh, heh. "So I'm being friendly." Big grin.

We waited in line—oohh—fifteen minutes or so, like everybody else. Wiley assured me this was the least he had ever waited for anything from the DMV. When we got to the front of the line, he saw "Linda" and whispered, "I believe that Commissioner Erwin has left something for me, Linda."

"I don't know what you are talking about," Linda said, smiling officially. Wiley was flummoxed at first and searched his mind for a different strategy.

During this pause, Linda said, "Your name please?"

I said, "Fred Tutem. This is Wiley Kayne."

Linda smiled. At last these unruly citizens were acting properly. "Oh," she said, "you're Mr. Tutem."

"That's correct."

"Could you show me some identification?"

"Well, the only identification he has is his scars at this point. All of his personal documents were burned in the fire," Wiley intruded.

"Oh," she said, "so you're the one . . ." She turned around and conferred with someone who appeared to be a supervisor who then got on the telephone to finally start the circle of patronage and nepotism that Wiley had hinted about. Linda said, "Ya'll need to come over here and go see Jane." She seemed to inspect my scars.

It was a wonder it had not taken longer.

After a few moments in a rather sterile government office with Jane, she took some documents out of her desk and made me get a new driver's license photograph.

She then said, "Now, it's time to take your driver's test." Wiley was surprised again. Jane turned to him with a kind of revenge and said, "Look, he has to take a road test," exasperated. "You don't want him to have another damn wreck, Wiley Kayne. So calm the hell down." Wiley gaped at her.

So off we went, leaving Wiley there in Jane's office. It seemed he had to repair some patronage. I passed the road test, and when she came back, I had my new driver's license #306751SC 2007, expires 2017.

Wiley and I left, happy. The day had just begun. "Okay, well, buddy, that went pretty well. Let's go to the car lot."

"Car lot? I don't have any money."

"What do you think Travis and I have been doing for you?" he said, with mock surprise.

"Well, I didn't know. All I was doing was going to the hospital and trying to remember things. Then I had a seizure."

"Well, we settled your insurance claims. Freddy, my friend, I know that you believe someone was following you and caused your wreck. It appears from our expert's investigation, however, that your Porsche had a defective steering column. The manufacturer was recalling all those models to conduct an investigation. I wrote just one demand letter to the manufacturer, and we settled your case for a handsome sum. It was a 'no-brainer.' You are well fixed, and we will talk more about the settlement.

"First, we gotta swing by Tommy's office and sign the papers. They're fighting the last two hundred thousand dollars, but they have given up a big enough chunk to get you a car without fighting too hard. We made sure that was only a partial settlement."

I thought, *Wow! Maybe I can trust them after all*. But why don't they trust each other? So we duly went by, collected the insurance check, deposited it at Duke Furman's Bank, and went to the BMW place.

"Wiley, these are expensive cars," I said and looked around the interior of his car—all leather, tanned, soft as Italian gloves, wood grain, and just enough chrome.

"You're one of us," Wiley said. "This is the only kind of car we drive here in Greenville." Then he leaned forward. "Besides, we are going to get a used one any way."

So there it was—the BMW lot, packed with cars poised to speed run like race horses—German engineering meets Greenville money, the full circle of Protestant work ethic landing like a drunk German playboy among the Scotch-Irish in the Piedmont of South Carolina.

We picked out a gray one. Wiley assured me this was the color Greenville lawyers drive. A few minutes in the manager's office, Mr. Harris brought in the keys himself. "You've done good work for us, son," he said, although I couldn't remember anything I had ever done for him, and Wiley handed me the keys and my new license and said, "Follow me home—oops, I forgot—we have to let somebody drive you."

Whereupon he produced a nice twenty-year-old boy, Austin, who was clerking for our firm. His job was to be my driver until enough time had passed for me to drive myself. A car and a chauffeur . . .

—*—*--*--*--*--*—

We drove slowly. Wiley's concern and worry had been hidden till now—his fake, jovial manner, like boys nudging each other in a fraternity party—concern and worry that came out as I watched him drive carefully on the way home, always checking his rearview mirror to be sure I was close.

Traffic seemed confusing at first, and then it gradually came clear—even though Austin was clearly in charge, I was learning my limits almost as if I had been driving myself. This wasn't so bad. Each day and every adventure brought me closer.

CHAPTER FORTY-ONE

They told me the seizure medicine would make me dizzy at first, but I had felt nothing except exhilaration that I was going back to swim in the pool of lawyers, all the strokes and race tactics that are all part of the big swim meet. My mind would slip in and out of the mystery of how all this happened and what any of it meant.

Who exactly was Eva? My girlfriend, but then how did Travis fit in, and this relationship with Wiley seemed to spring from nowhere? All three of them seemed motivated by things that I didn't understand—yet. Thinking about it made me dizzier than the medicine.

We got to Wiley's house and pulled into the double driveway. "This, my friend, is your new castle. We'll look around later."

We were in and out and on to the last errand of the day. I rode with Wiley. Austin took my new car and left me his cell phone number. I had to wait six months to get to drive, but Wiley was making sure that I could get around—the firm was also making sure they had a spy on me whenever I was in the car, although Austin didn't look like the spying type. I knew, as well, the swimming pool was my haven and rest. Austin didn't swim, and he wasn't built right to wear a Speedo.

* * *

"Next, we gotta get you some clothes for the office. That bad burn made you so skinny. Your seersucker suit hangs on you like a scarecrow. What you need is two dark blue suits in tropical wool. You need one light gray with a pin stripe and a seersucker for the summer, two or three bowties, a few regimental stripes, a couple of paisleys, and two or three khakis we can press like razors. And your blue blazer has to always look fresh, so you will need two of 'em. That ought to about do it. Now you can dress like a lawyer in Greenville. You never wore anything except that anyway. I see Travis has your loafers picked out—a black, a red, and now you are going to need a tan pair too."

We accomplished this clothing run, as Wiley called it, during the rest of the afternoon . . . and then we were back at his house making my bed and establishing the plans for the next day. I was exhausted, but I could remember almost everything we had done. That was encouraging.

The next morning was Saturday, and Wiley was up before me and already had a pot of coffee going with some fruit laid out.

Wiley was fairly sly, I knew, but I didn't know how much his public image was carefully crafted to hide his vulnerabilities. To the public, he was a jovial, back-slapping, aggressive bully. But here, alone in his house, sipping coffee with his old friend, he was a thoughtful introspective man—although I didn't fully trust him. Can anyone trust anybody?

"Well, you're in Gower now. We like to say on this side of town that Gower is a dreamland, and the country club is a nightmare. Ha, ha." He then made a sweep with his hand all around him. "You see, my house is fairly plain—outside a beautiful lawn, nice camellias, gardenias, spruce trees, all the trappings. I am surrounded by houses like this, and we have so much here. On one side is Quail Hill with million-dollar houses. We are in the middle. And at the other end are starter homes, where everybody begins the mortgage rat race, the starters. If you take Parkins Mill from one end to the other, you will see just about every kind of house and every kind of neighborhood that exists on the planet except for really poor ones." He bent over the table and clutched his coffee. "My friend, we don't have any ghettos."

He rolled the word ghetto out with his mouth wide open as if he personally had had something to do with that—maybe he did.

"The thing we have here, Fred, in case you don't remember, that makes us different from every other part of town and maybe different from the whole rest of the world is . . . is . . . Gower Power!" Here, he raised his cup of coffee above his head and brought it down as if to slam it on the table. Then he started laughing.

"Wiley, I am not completely with this. Two days ago, I said goodbye to Travis and left her sweet arms of security. Yesterday, you threw me in the pool of reality like a baby fish, so forgive me if I don't understand."

He was laughing more.

"You helped established Gower Power, my friend. You and I did, in the early days of Sail Swimming league. The swimming league that has graduated many a Greenvillian into the ranks of college stardom. From May through August. We swam twice a day, went to swimming camps during the winter, and whipped ourselves like racehorses all year long. There were only two options. You either tried harder or you tried even harder. That was it for the Gower guy and Gower girl."

"Wiley, please refresh my memory."

"All right, all right." Wiley got a little serious and waxed less fun. The lawyer in him came out, and he told me the story of the swimming league that dominated the summer time activities of every neighborhood pool in the county. Almost every one of them boasted a nice big pool suitable for racing—twenty-five yards long, four lanes, and a big deck for spectators. The two oldest pools were Gower and the Country Club, and they were "kings of the hill." On the Country Club side, you had all the wealth—the

Jaguars, the Cadillacs, the tennis courts, the poker games and betting on golf, the full decadent spectacle of wealth in motion and on display.

On the Gower side, you had the striving, upwardly mobile-driven managers and entrepreneurs that had only begun to make it. The Country Club was old Greenville. The Gower side was new Greenville, and both of them were locked in a death grip of swimming competition involving their children.

As he described all this and reminded me of my role and his role in the swimming meets, I began to remember details that I had forgotten even in my rediscovery of swimming months ago—the chanting crowds, the stunning teenage girls striving, the lifeguards, the tanning oil, the days spent in grueling race after grueling race after grueling race all summer long. Travis had made me remember the events of our Lycra swimsuits. Now, I began to remember the rest of it and gazed at him as he compiled detail.

"In fact, today is the Country Club meet, my friend, and if you don't remember this after we go see the pep rally, then I will know your brain has been permanently squashed. Eat your grits and come on."

I finished my breakfast, brushed my teeth, and followed him out the door into the fresh morning with the early summer heat rising up with the mist from his lawn. Three steps out the door, and I could hear in the background a low chanting. *M-m-mm—m-m-mm—m-m-mm*. This continued and grew thunderous. I rolled my window down to keep listening as the sounds sorted themselves into words.—*Gower Power Now! Gower Power Now!*

Wiley winked. We drove about two blocks through the urban forest that held the lovely homes, beautiful lawns, and long driveways and came down a hill where the sounds reverberated like an echo chamber, GOWER POWER NOW! GOWER POWER NOW! GOWER POWER NOW! GOWER POWER NOW! GOWER POWER NOW!

Louder and louder and louder. We parked on the road with hundreds of other cars and joined the spectators that thronged the parking lot. Young swimmers were shaving their bodies and daubing themselves with war paint.

The parents had already daubed on their own paint. Some were half naked. All of them striped like Apaches. There was a big drum that pounded, and somebody had a bugle. Here was "Custer's Last Stand" right in front of us. I was glad I didn't have long blond hair like General Custer—or else these Indians would scalp me clean I was sure.

GOWER POWER NOW! GOWER POWER NOW! GOWER POWER NOW! Cars festooned with ribbons and banners that said, "Gower Power" and "Beat the Club."

All got quiet for a moment as the swimming coach addressed the crowd with a handheld electric megaphone, "I am here to tell you today is a historic day. Last week, we crushed Stone Lake. Before that, we outswam Devenger three to one. Tommy here"—and he gestured toward a handsome, strong young man built for swimming with broad shoulders, skinny waist, legs like whips from a willow tree—"Tommy just broke the state record for the breaststroke. Let's hear it for him."

Yah-yah-yah-yah! Gower Power Now! Gower Power Now! Gower Power Now! Yah-yah-yah-yah! Drown the Club! Gower Power Now! Gower Power Now! Yah-yah-yah!

Everyone was screaming—the parents as loud as the children, and the children were screaming as loud as they could—fourth graders, fifth graders, even little guppy swimmers three feet tall.

Wiley leaned over and said, "That's Tommy Leatherwood. He's my neighbor. He is going to swim against Billy Mann today." And then he paused. I could barely hear him. "Billy held the record until the last meet when Tommy set a new record by half a second. Today is going to be a great match. The country club doesn't stand a chance."

The coach gestured for everyone to be quiet. "Now it's time for our premeet prayer. Bow your heads everyone."

As he said this, I had a flashback that almost knocked me down. I had been Tommy—I had been Billy—I had been all of them, every last lean swimmer, rolled up into one—that was my summer of love when first stardom grabbed me tighter than a kudzu vine. A vision of splendor in a Speedo. I suddenly remembered it all, and I felt like the coach was praying for me directly to God.

"Dear God, give us guidance today that we may exert all our strength in the service to the greater glory of your kingdom. Amen. Now," he shouted again into the megaphone, "let's go!" All the SUVs and vans in the parking lot revved up at the same time. All of them sprayed with shaving foam. GOWER POWER, DROWN THE CLUB. The swimmers marched into their preordained vans—their parents frothing to get this thing going. They rolled around the parking lot in one ritual convoy and then out the exit they went—all the spectators cheering too. The whole thing had taken an hour.

"Wiley, how long did it take for them to organize this?"

"Oh, we have a special committee that does that, but we try to add something each year. Today, we added the coach. Last year, he just waved from the side, but this year, we made him rehearse the prayer so he would get it right. Heh, heh."

He looked at me. "Now, are you remembering?"

He had a leer of pleasure, for he had been there too—a swimmer just like me.

As we walked home, all I could think of was swimming.

Earlier in the day, I had asked Wiley about his wife—it was a very short conversation. He said while looking sad, "Well, Fred, buddy, she left, just like your wife. From a very small statistical sampling of lawyers I know with a sample size of four in our firm, I'd say practicing law and practicing marriage don't go along so well together. Come to think of it, they were swimmers too and maybe that was important." Then he turned to me with a kind of grin that said, "Let's don't talk about it anymore." And we never did.

So there, that was that. The modern attitude revealed in two sentences. How can you build lifelong love when you are always swimming, swimming, swimming in those tight little Lycra suits and those big pinstriped coats, with regimental ties. Gower Power indeed.

PART IV

CHAPTER FORTY-TWO

The next day, we went to the office of the firm, "the big pool" as Wiley called it. It occupied a downtown corner as tall and stately as a modern skyscraper can be. Red brick and those modern windows, double sealed against the air, and the weather and stained against the light. The law is a hermetic world, closed off from reality but undergirding it like the steel skeleton of the skyscraper itself—big parking lot, big enough for platoons of lawyers, men and women, to troop through the pneumatic doors past the huge library in the lobby; clients sitting in plush modern chairs on the colorful rug with swooping designs of circles and squares under the watchful eye of justice, pure as a Greek ideal.

Wiley made me greet everyone all along the way—any old client he saw, all the partners and the young lawyers, some people I hadn't met, all the secretaries. He wanted them to know I was back. And he told me in a low voice, "Don't act ashamed—you don't look like a zombie in those new clothes, even if your scars are still red."

I could remember no one, but like the vagueness of dawn before the sun comes up real good, something was stirring in my head.

Occasionally, Wiley would lean over and say in a conspiratorial half whisper, "Hang in there, Fred buddy, this is the warm-up. We have got awhile before the main event gets started." And he would give me a slap on the back between my shoulder blades right where I had a skin graft.

"Wiley, I've got a skin graft there. That stings when you slap me."

"Oh, ole buddy, I'm sorry. I won't do it again."

And then ten minutes later, of course, he would do it again. Maybe that's part of being a lawyer. You've got to hit 'em where it hurts—but I didn't remember all that yet.

The firm's receptionists hugged me, enveloping me in a soft cloud of Chanel perfume that had been tastefully daubed just behind her mandible, as if she and Travis shared a common parent, or she was the older cousin. Both of them members of that now lost female tribe of Southern women who spring nice smells on everything. Nobody did it better. All the women were gardenias.

We dropped by Travis's office. As the office manager, she was supposed to be there every day, but she wasn't there when we came.

Wiley muttered, "Well, she did what I told her to for once." And a brief scowl clouded his face. We worked our way up, floor by floor, past cubicles, filing rooms, little rooms with elite secretaries—though windowless and almost airless—other mini libraries, and conference rooms with large rectangular tables and leather chairs.

All of it bespoke reasoning cold as the arctic *this is the truth, the whole truth, and nothing but the truth, so help me God!* "And, by the way, we have got an army of secretaries and lawyers to produce documents upon documents upon documents to prove it. Anything we need to have for you, our beloved client."

As we swam through the floors in this big pool as Wiley had called it and made our way up floors, things got a little quieter. There were fewer people around. The offices got larger and more plush.

By the time we got to the uppermost floor, something had clicked. I thought I saw my office on the last floor.

I pulled at Wiley's sleeve, which was in keeping with everybody else—a nice dark blue suit with a regimental stripe tie and a button-down collar on his white shirt. "I think I saw my office."

Wiley stopped in midstride. "Well, sho nuff," he said. "I was waiting for this." His grin reached halfway up his face. "Lisa will be ecstatic."

We turned around immediately and almost ran to the stairs, hopped down them, and walked back to the door that I had seen. There was only a number on the outside, but inside there was another door with my name on it, and in the anteroom, a friendly face looked up, startled.

"Oh my god, Fred, it's you." And her eyes were wet.

"This must be my end of the pool," I said to myself, and just as suddenly as I said that, everything began to come back in bits and pieces. I had to sit down.

Wiley watched me like a hawk, and I noticed that he was watching her too. I had that sense again—the sense that I had had all along—that something was up, and I really didn't know or understand exactly what it was.

Wiley walked me around the rest of the building. I visited the old chief partners—Mr. Featheroak, Mr. T. Hambone Fleschner, Garrett Bosman, and Terry Wellner. Each of them had their own personalities, and each exuded an air of confident victory or power, not ready to fight but just ready to win and accept their due—good lawyer psychology. I knew I would see them again for, in addition to their gray suits and baldness, they seemed extra wary around me.

Were they part of a plot too?

I couldn't shake my conviction that it was right to be paranoid—maybe that's what a good lawyer does anyway. Never trust anybody, they say in law school.

Back downstairs, Wiley took the elevator—one story—just in case we might meet somebody else, which we did, held the elevator door open, a few quick hello's . . . I was getting tired and confused . . . Greetings here, greetings there . . . It became a blur like just about everything else, dissolved in the smear of the day on my mind.

All I wanted to do was get back to my office, sit at my desk, and try to clarify what I was feeling. Could Lisa help? It seemed that I could trust her. She didn't look at me with the same startled eyes after the initial greeting. It was as if she was trying to talk to me without saying anything, trying to reassure me and not trick me. There was a frank, candid quality about her whole being.

I was plugged in, like an old appliance you find in the attic, but I wasn't on yet. Yes, I was in the big swim again, but I had to recharge in my own little office. Wiley suddenly became expansive, looked at his watch, and pronounced, "It's lunchtime! Come on, and then I will leave you in your office the rest of the afternoon."

Lisa would have to wait.

"You gotta get some of Gene's iced tea—which will give you a case of diabetes. Heh, heh."

CHAPTER FORTY-THREE

Gene's was stuck on a rather bleak corner of two major streets. One street, West Street, led through an historic preservation district. The other was Academy Street, now one-way after the latest rounds of downtown zoning. The old Greenvillians never got over it, but that's the nature of things, and now everybody else took it for granted. Gene's had stayed the same. It was a watering hole for the legal power of the town.

He was the only guy in town who still made a living at a restaurant using canned food. That was one of the first jokes told when we got there. Everybody seemed generally happy I had returned, but a few people turned away and muttered things under their breath that I couldn't hear, but maybe that was my concussion again. Scattered among the tables were lawyers, judges, police officers—some eating together, some apart—and Gene presiding over it all like the major domo of a gourmet palace.

Wiley led me straight to an attractive but familiar-looking woman who was politely diverted from eating her salad by Wiley. He showed a peculiar deference to her, so I figured she must be a judge by her manner. She had a rather dowdy female assistant seated across from her, and both of them were dressed conservatively. Wiley approached. "Your Honor, I wanted to let you know Fred was back."

When she looked up, her face beamed. "Mr. Tutem, we have all been so worried about you, so I am extremely happy to see you back at work."

"Um," I said, "Your Honor." And I could feel Wiley holding his breath. In fact, he nudged me a little in the side, and then he said, "Yes, Your Honor, thank you so much for putting a hold on things for the extra time Fred has needed to get rehabilitated and to get back to work. I know the parties are all pounding the table to get on with the case, but Fred still needs a bit more time to finish his research."

"Well, I can give you a bit more time, but as you know, I have a duty to move the case along, as swiftly as possible given the demands of probate court administration. I have postponed the matter three times." Here, her eyebrows arched. "Because of your unexpected misfortune, Mr. Tutem, but I knew you could do a thorough job, and I wanted to continue with your good legal services because of your reputation for scholarship." And then she leaned over. "And in spite of your reputation for other matters." Judge Poe's eyes twinkled with mirth. I gulped under her stare, even though I didn't follow what she was talking about.

"Uh, uh—well—thank you, Your Honor. Thank you for still having faith in me. I'm thinking a whole lot better now, and I shall get back to work on this as soon as I—" Here she interrupted me.

"You have thirty days." And then she smiled a radiant smile revealing beautiful white teeth and lips worthy of a playboy bunny. Those thoughts jumped in my head in spite of her august presence. In fact, as I turned, I noticed her legs underneath the table, and they weren't bad either.

I caught Wiley looking too. As we were leaving the restaurant, he said, "Well, she usually hides that short skirt under black robes, so you can't blame us, ole buddy."

We got in his car and headed back to the office.

When we got back to the office, sure enough within the hour, an official order from the judge came over by courier—from the Honorable Alexandra

Poe, Greenville County Judge of Probate—directed to Fred Tutem, Personal Representative of the Estate of Louise Putnam. There was also a Notice of Final Hearing on the case which had been scheduled at the Greenville County Probate Court for August 17, 2007. The pleadings further directed: "You will submit your final report on the results of your determination of the heirs of this estate pursuant to your investigation and findings. Please serve Notice of this Order and Notice of the Hearing on the other attorneys and all unrepresented interested parties."

Wiley abandoned me with Lisa for a while, saying he had a few errands to do.

I felt overwhelmed and scared. I did not know exactly what all this was about, but by now, I had some inklings.

This hearing with Judge Poe had to be part of all the intrigue surrounding my accident and the careful reentry to my office that Wiley and Travis had engineered.

Lisa would have to guide me. Could she?

When I looked over at her, she stared at me and said with a heavy sigh, "I can't wait for all this to be over."

CHAPTER FORTY-FOUR

The next two or three days at the office were spent "dusting the cobwebs" as Lisa said. Everything was neatly arranged, and at first, it just looked ready for my return. Then I began to notice things that were foreign to any of my old habits—at least the ones I could remember. The pencils were lined up straight. Papers in various stacks had no dust, and every corner fit perfectly. There were a couple of drawers in my desk that were totally empty, and the bookshelves seemed sparse to me.

All of it seemed prearranged and pawed through, discarded . . . or stolen. It was too neat.

I began to wonder if anything was truly missing or if; in fact, my compulsively neat secretary, Lisa, had just straightened up for me preparing for my return. I voiced no suspicions because I couldn't be sure until I looked in the back of the big drawer on the left of my desk. It had a false back. I could tell because of the depth of the drawer in relation to the desk. There were eight inches to spare, and when I knocked, it was hollow.

I knocked again, and suddenly a memory came to me—the way you remember the combination on a lock after you haven't used it for months or years. I just knew with no explanation. I reached to the right and pushed the button there and then held down the button on the left to a count of three. The lid popped open, and the drawer slid out so I could open it. My face got warm, and I felt my breath catch at what I saw. I got up and closed the door to my office. As much as I trusted Lisa, I didn't want anyone to see these documents yet.

There were four files, and I hoped they would hold the keys to my destiny, and the new life I would have to assemble in the wake of my personal fire. I spread out the files on my desk. Number one, a divorce agreement and final order. Number two, a deed to a mountain house. Number three, a journal and sketches for a novel with poems. Number four, a rough draft of a letter to the judge. There were no notes on the outside of the folders—big clunky legal things with clasps and reinforced binding on the back, with long thick red rubber bands. I wanted to study them one by one, and I began to return them to the hidden drawer.

Before I could get them put back fully, there was a knock, tentative. I thought to say come in but then stopped. "Wait a moment."

Lisa's voice said, "Okay, but just a moment."

I stuffed the files back in the drawer and closed the lid with a soft click. "Come in."

The door opened, and there stood Lisa with a scowl and moving her head and darting her eyes over her shoulder as if to warn me. Behind her stood Wiley, and behind him stood Travis. There was another figure that turned and left. Wiley said, over hearty, "Have we left you alone long enough?"

Nihil agendo homins male agere discunt, I thought. "The devil finds mischief for idle hands," I said.

I could smell Travis's perfume. It smelled good. Too good.

Later, I tried to remember this first dive back into the swimming pool of my profession, and the thing that stuck out was Travis's perfume.

"See, I told you he wasn't ready," she said to Wiley and almost slapped him.

Underneath her breath, Lisa looked at me and said, "Puh-lease." Wiley looked abashed.

I came to my own rescue, sort of. "What do you mean, I am not ready Travis?"

"You are just not ready for it."

"It—what are you talking about?" I began to assume a legal authority, and I took pains to get around my desk to put on my blazer—all without seeming too obvious—a trick even for someone who didn't have brain damage. I wanted to divert Travis, with her eagle eyes, away from my desk and signal everyone in the room that it was time for lunch.

"It's time for lunch!" I said.

I thought that might be subtle enough. Everyone looked at each other.

"Fred, you may be hungry, but it's only ten forty-five. We don't eat lunch around here until noon. That's the custom established by Mr. Weatheroak and another one of the unwritten rules—something else you are going to have to remember." This was all from Travis.

Then with the edge jumping back into her voice, she said, "I want to talk to you alone, mister."

"Well," I said, "let's go to your office." Wink—I did it at last! "I'd like to be alone with you too." I didn't know how to rescue this except to rely on the familiar pattern of seduction. That perfume will do it every time.

I wanted to protect my office at almost any cost. The indication that Lisa was displeased with all this made me even more convinced that something was afoot. These folders must hold the keys to the mystery. I wanted no one to know exactly what I knew, what my questions were, or what my actions might be once I had planned them.

Practicing law is like that. You have to find out what the other guy is thinking before you know what you are going to think-and both lawyers go round and round and round circling each other in a dance of advocacy, both serving points for truth, tracking it move by countermove, slow-motion tennis, or chess. Lawyer's instincts.

Travis announced, "Come to my office then."

When we got to the big door leading down the hallway, I noticed Wiley was talking to Lisa and eyeing my door.

"Travis, stay right here a moment—you have to lead me to your office. I don't remember exactly how to get there." I went back in, grabbed Wiley's elbow, and pulled him away from Lisa gently. I whispered to him, "Wiley, I am going to need you—you better get to your office quick." And I pushed him ahead of me. Then I whispered to Lisa, "Lock my door and don't let anyone in. I'll be back as soon as I can." Lisa nodded at me with a blank face, indicating with her eyes that she understood.

I announced jauntily as we made our way down the hall, "Well, this is an interesting day back."

Travis glanced up. "What do you mean interesting?"

I wasn't exactly sure, so I said, "I'm not exactly sure. You are going to have to explain to me why I am not ready 'cause I feel ready thanks to Wiley . . . and you, darling." I winked again!

Wiley puffed up a little bit. Travis clenched her teeth and shot back, "Well, I don't think you're ready."

"Please explain," I said. "As soon as I get you behind closed doors." I then shook my head and followed them down the hall, pushing them away from my office.

Our little platoon left Wiley at his office, and we continued around the corner to the one that Travis occupied. Her office was fragrant with her perfume. On the back of her door was a crisp new blazer with a transparent bag from Coplon's emblazoned in gold just as neat as a pin. Except I knew from living with her, there was probably some clutter behind the doors of the drawers—it didn't matter. Sometimes the appearance of efficiency and control is as good as the real thing. This is another truth lived daily by someone with a brain injury. "Fake it till you make it," Dr. Olds had told me.

When the door was closed, Travis changed tactics. She gave me a big kiss and tried sweet talk—the same way she had done when I was in the hospital.

"Now, Fred, honey, you have just to understand things can't go this fast for you. You know you can't remember enough to take on any new cases or even get through your old cases very well."

I said, "How do *you* know that? Travis, how could anybody possibly know that, when I have only been back a couple of days?"

"All right then, who did you see at Gene's two days ago?"

"Well, first of all, how do you know I went to Gene's?"

"Wiley told me."

"Second of all, what difference could it possibly make?"

"Uh, well, making contacts and remembering things is one of the most important tasks a lawyer has to build and keep his or her reputation. Gene's is where you go to make deals with people and keep up appearances for the firm. If you don't know who you met, then you need to think twice about coming back full-time, just yet."

"I saw a lot of people, but the one I remember the most is Judge Poe. She was happy to see me back at work. I saw Travis go suddenly pale, and her expression changed.

"So just exactly what did Judge Poe say?"

Suddenly, we were in the deep end, and the pool was bigger than I thought. What was up? "Now, you got me." A thought passed. "I don't remember exactly what she said. Whatever it waswas—was unimportant."

Travis then said, "Well, there you go again. Anytime a judge speaks, it's important. Just ask them."

"Now, Travis, you are not showing enough respect. Going to Gene's was a social call just to show to the legal gang that Fred was back in town, swimming along with the rest of them."

I couldn't tell whether she was relieved at this announcement or, not but I had pretty much had it. Why ever she chose to grill me would have to come out. "Travis, what is your problem? I am trying to get back at work. I am trying to find the parts of myself that got burned up in the fire. You were so good to me at first, and now you seem to have turned against me."

"No, honey, I have not turned against you. It's just that I am worried about you, and I am scared you are not going to be able to deliver for the firm."

"Well, Travis, that hasn't come up yet at all. I have only been here for a couple of days. Quit being so afraid." I took her in my arms. "Now, look, I appreciate so much what you have done for me, and now Wiley is going to have to be the one to get me through this—with your help. So keep watching my back, please." She dropped her stunning eyes, and a strand or two of her hair came loose, drifted over her cheek. Oh, I felt an old tug at my Speedo and took a smell of her perfume.

"Then I will call you tonight," she whispered. "I miss you."

"I'll look forward to it," I replied.

I left down the hallway and walked back to my office and promptly got lost.

Heather Laurel, a young attorney, saw me and squealed happily, "Fred, Fred, you're back. I heard you were back."

"Oh, thank you so much, Heather . . . right?"

"We were working on that Putnam case together."

"Oh, oh, that case," I said. "Well, I'll have to talk to you about that."

"Fine, fine, I'll be here tomorrow and the next day, and then I am off on vacation."

"Have you heard from the judge?"

I looked around to be sure no one was in the hall, and we were, in fact, alone. "Let's talk about that tomorrow, okay?"

"Sure, Fred."

"Now, Heather, is my office back down this way?"

She looked at me quizzically. "Oh no, go over to the other side and turn left—it's three doors after that. Tell Lisa hello for me."

Whew! I think something important just happened. I am going to have to sit down and review this lest I be so lost I will never find my way out. I was suddenly back in the thick of things, *in medias res*, and I'd better start swimming. I would see Wiley later.

CHAPTER FORTY-FIVE

Back in my office I sat down with a legal pad to write down all I knew or thought I knew. Lisa had brought me a cup of coffee, looked at me, and said sternly, "Now, this is the last time for coffee." And then she turned and added, "And don't trust those two. Got it?"

"Yes, ma'am," I said, and she closed the door. I believed at this point I should write a memo to myself—from the beginning. So I pulled out a long legal pad, asked Lisa not to disturb me in any way, and then locked the door. I could see one narrow section of Greenville, busy with commerce and construction out my window.

From the beginning:

ITEM 1: My car was wrecked.

ITEM 2: I was burned and knocked unconscious.

ITEM 3: Spent time in the hospital—amnesia and mystery.

ITEM 4: Travis rehabilitated me and rekindled old romance.

ITEM 5: Memories of Eva, mysterious, came back to me in pieces.

ITEM 6: I began to mistrust Travis.

ITEM 7: I became reoriented to Greenville—azaleas, churches, commerce, engineers, and intrigue. Ghosts of mill hands, restaurants, and swim teams.

ITEM 8: I began to swim—again.

ITEM 9: Eva dropped into my life, an erotic angel.

ITEM 10: Latin phrases began to pop into my head, unbidden.

ITEM 11: There was a party. Something happened. I felt threatened. *In vino veritas.*

ITEM 12: Later that night, I had a seizure in the back of Eva's ambulance.

ITEM 13: Wiley took me from Travis's house.

ITEM 14: He dragged me to work, back into the swim of things, in the shark's pool.

ITEM 15: Here, in my old desk, I have discovered four sets of documents that I had hidden in a secret drawer. I don't know what these documents say yet.

ITEM 16: Throughout all this, I have had problems with my memory, my orientation. I have had problems trusting myself and others.

ITEM 17: The only thing I can really count on is swimming—free and clear and focused in the comforting water. The neat outlines of the pool and the lane markers on the bottom, the ropes floating in between lanes, keeping me, like a floating Sisyphus, to the task at hand.

All this took me twenty minutes and some head scratching. It left me with more questions—such as the fundamental one—what was I doing here in the first place? A question every man asks, and no man ever really answers. Each life has a big question mark in it.

Although I could remember, fairly reliably, day to day events, I still did not know myself or the weeks, months, and years just prior to the wreck. I only had the portrait of selective details painted by Travis and Wiley—what they wanted me to know. The brief, intense, and passionate interlude with Eva left me wanting more from her. My senses were intact there. I remembered how to kiss—at least Eva said so—where was she now anyway? Who was she really? Travis told me I kissed well too.

Now, after the memo, I pulled out the documents. Somehow I knew these papers must hold the key to the questions I had. I leaned back in my chair to see the sliver of Greenville that was mine, but all I saw was the documents—just like a lawyer again.

You see, when you are a lawyer, there are only two things in the world. The first is a fact, and the second is a law or vice versa. Sometimes the law fits the facts, and sometimes it doesn't. That's when the fun begins.

Here in the early part of the twenty-first century, with my head injury, I had reencountered an age old fundamental about facts. They are basically what you say they are or what the judge says they can be. Six pairs of eyes can look at the same events and come up with six different statements—"it was red. No, it was blue. No, I saw the green all the way. There was no crash. I was overwhelmed by a crashing sound."

So here with my untrustworthy memory, I had made a list of facts that I thought I knew. The elusive nature of facts themselves magnified by short circuits in my brain. What is a fact anyway? I had no one else to judge it in this case, for these facts had to be only what I remembered. They could be nothing different.

A lawyer again.

As I pondered these things briefly, the telephone rang with a Beethoven melody—*tata ta ta, tata tata*—a symphony, I believe. Lisa was calling.

Another memory peeped through with the music. It dragged me back to the old role of busy legal warrior with trusted sidekick, secretary. The lone ranger and Tonto. Me Kemosabe.

"There is someone to see you, sir," Lisa said through the intercom with a note of warning. I looked around quickly. So I put the memo in my drawer on the left and scattered some pencils and paperclips and rubber bands on top. I closed the drawer with the presumably secret documents and then slid over to the door with my back to the wall.

Why, I can't say now, but it seemed the thing to do. Who wanted to see me? There was a reason I had a secret drawer.

The analysis of the facts I had conjured from my broken memory and the rush of events would have to wait. It didn't make sense to me completely twenty minutes ago, but I had moved closer to finding the truth—the Holy Grail for a lawyer. Even if I could not remember it all.

I opened the door a crack and saw Lisa speaking to someone in a uniform.

When I opened the door fully, there she was—glorious in an EMS suit, clutching an envelope with my name on it. There's nothing better than a woman in uniform.

The door to the hallway was closed. Lisa turned to me and said, "Quick, ya'll get this over with." She turned away. Eva stepped forward a little too quickly, pushing me off-balance, back through my door, into my office. I stumbled backward, and she closed the door. All I wanted to do just at that moment was unbind her hair. I had not seen her since the emergency room and the seizure.

She breathed her words with a swimmer's breath—a quick pant as you raise one arm from the water in between strokes. "I can tell you are doing fine.

Here, take this letter. You better hide it." Then she gave me a big wet kiss on the lips. "It's a love letter."

I hid it as she wiped my lips off with the sleeve of her blue shirt.

I said, "I hope there is no blood on that."

She laughed. "No, I am a professional, silly." Then she did it again. "I have got to get out of here," she said and turned around just as the moment began to surge through me, pulling me off the ledge of lawyering I had managed to climb up to today. She turned and walked half-backward, eyes twinkling and misty, to the door. She opened it carefully. Lisa hissed at her, "Get out now! Take the stairs."

After this encounter, Lisa said nothing, but her eyes said "Watch out, you don't need this to start up again." I felt an ancient mystery drag at me despite my memo of "facts."

What is the love of a woman anyway? Is it a fact? Or the love of a man? Is that more of a fact? The devotion of a friend? What kind of fact is that? A loyal secretary? Is that a fact?

Feelings change like mercury. Does that make them nonfacts or facts forever? Are facts just smoke signals or shadows on the wall as Plato warned? Do the facts speak for themselves? *Res ipsa loquitur?* Why do we need lawyers and lovers?

All this while I touched my lips with my fingertips savoring the urgent wet kiss from a beautiful woman in a uniform, trying to conjure it up again. That was definitely a fact.

All Eva's letter said was, "I love you." Nothing else. I crumbled it.

It was the end of the afternoon. Wiley and Travis had left me alone to reorient myself and, I presume, to find whatever they wanted me to find. I could not shake the feeling that they watched me every moment.

I didn't think Lisa reported to them in any way. She expressed her distaste for them so openly I had to believe she would not cooperate with anybody if it deviated from the work she knew and thought we should be doing. Was she as loyal as I thought?

That left me with mystery as I reached the end of the day.

CHAPTER FORTY-SIX

Wiley came by just as I sat there in my reverie. He always gave the impression of barging in some place—never subtle—I knew I couldn't trust him.

If you want to make a man paranoid, just knock him out good. When he wakes up, he can't believe anything. "Come this way," he ordered.

He began his questions before we got out of the building. I had leaned over to Lisa to say goodbye. Her head was turned away, so I had said in a loud whisper, "I'll see you tomorrow. We'll talk more." I caught a glimpse of her tight-lipped smile, and that reassured me.

Wiley witnessed this. His first question was "what did you say to Lisa?"

I said, "It was nice getting back to the office, and I would depend on her."

"Well," Wiley said, "watch out—playing—you know how she is. Heh, heh."

Well, I didn't know how she was. I didn't remember anything about that yet. I could only trust my dawning awareness so far, and thus far, nothing past my imperfect awareness made me mistrust her the same way I mistrusted Wiley and Travis and even Eva. So I said, "Well, I am sure you will tell me everything I need to be careful of, right?"

"You bet," he said as he thought of more questions as he barged along, the old prosecutor. We hadn't even left the parking lot. "What did you do today?" This was in Wiley's manner, a soft introduction—it looked like a knuckleball to me.

"Not much. I looked around for any old work memos or letters you know, that kind of thing, whatever Judge Poe wanted."

His ears perked up. "Well, I am sure there were a few things."

"Yeah, I found a few things."

"What were they?" He turned to me face on. I was at my car, and he was at his right beside it.

"Well," I lied, "I don't remember exactly."

"Surely you remember something." He began to walk closer toward me.

Suddenly, I felt very strange. My head filled up with fluff, and my stomach turned over. I started to try to formulate some kind of answer but came up only with garbled sounds.

Meanwhile, in my mind, all this felt as if I had been here before. Then it became a cartoon that I couldn't remember—the same way a dream rushes from you just at . . . the . . . point . . . you . . . wake . . . up. A shiver ran down my right side, and I couldn't get my breath. Wiley—"I said, what did you find?"

"Mengtishabahtenblehtyebob . . ." He shook me. I couldn't tell from fear or concern or frustration.

"Fred, Fred, what's wrong?"

"Ggihtenablehtelkhhbleaghbhahg."

"Here, sit down—no, let's go back in the building. No, oh yes. Oh hell!" He made me lean against his shoulder, although I didn't want to. I wasn't sure what was happening. We made it back in the lobby of the building, and he called somebody. Meanwhile, I went to sleep. Sleep came upon me so suddenly I couldn't resist in the big leather chairs in our spacious lobby filled with a beautiful collection of law books. They had never seemed so inviting before. I fell into a chair, and sleep rolled over me before I had another thought.

I woke up totally refreshed in about twenty minutes. Wiley, Travis, and Lisa by my side. "We have called the ER," they said in unison—or it seemed like in unison. I still wasn't hearing properly. I just nodded assent and waited yet again, for the ambulance.

Maybe Eva would rescue me again.

She didn't rescue me, but I got to the ER all the same. The ER doctor said I'd had another seizure and called a neurologist.

CHAPTER FORTY-SEVEN

So a new wrinkle. Just what I needed. I was just starting to sort out what I needed to do to find myself, so my brain delivered me a reward. "So you're starting to think you're something—well you depend on me, and if I, your brain, am not working right then, you will be more confused than ever." Good ole brain.

You can count on your brain to do what it needs to do, and whether that's what you want or not is irrelevant. It's kind of like your liver or your stomach or your foot. If you like to drink, your liver goes haywire. If you like to eat, your stomach gets fat. If you step on your foot the wrong way, it sprains itself, and you might be able to walk. Try to think if your brain doesn't want you to.

The neurologist, a friend of Dr. Olds, was Dr. Latika, a handsome oriental man. "Vell, Meester Toodum, you have partial complex seizures. These are a common problem following severe brain injury such as you had last year."

"Doctor, did you say partial complex seizures?"

"Yes, yours originate in the temporal lobe on the left."

"Well, doctor, you know I am a lawyer."

"Yes."

"Could you tell me what partial complex seizures mean?"

Dr. Latika launched into "Neurology Speak"—the same kind of multisyllabic obscurity spoken by Dr. Olds. He explained how the "earatabilittyy" of the neuronal impulses in one section of the brain cause the neurons to fire out of sequence, "generrating" aberrant messages to affected parts of your body. Your arm lifts up when it shouldn't. Your stomach growls when you are not hungry. You imagine the room is spinning. You think you've done this before. You might see cartoons.

"So basically you're telling me, Dr. Latika, that this is a seizure that is incomplete. It is a partial seizure and, further, that it is complicated, potentially involves many different neuronal pathways, and is therefore not fully predictable."

"Well, yes, that's right."

"Can I really tell what I am thinking is what I'm thinking?"

Dr. Latika grinned. "If you vant to be that feelosofeekal . . . we don't know why people theenk anywhaythey don't really have to." And then he looked out the window. "Of course, they act like they don't theenk very well much anyway."

He looked back at me. "Don't vorry so much, Mr. Toodum, you're going to be fine. Thees medicine I have given you will make you sleepy for a few days, then you vill be able to resume your normal activity."

"Will I be able to swim? Right now that's the only thing I care about."

"Of course you can svim. The nice theeng about vhatever you are doing— just goes off inside your head and not your whole body. Call me at the end of the veek, let me know how you are doing, and set up an appointment for two veeks for blood levels."

At the end, Austin, my driver, had waited for me dutifully and took me back to the office.

I couldn't digest all this at once. The careful notes I had made in my memo—where was it exactly—seemed to dissolve as I tried to remember them. Car wreck, fire, coma, rehab with Travis, then Eva rediscovered—as if I had been put to sleep to extract my rib, and she was it—then Wiley takes over. Now this, dreams, and déjà vu cartoons while I mumble.

Each event made for more questions, and each question led to another mystery. Now this. I couldn't even be sure that what I thought was what I had been thinking. It wasn't enough that my memory was faulty. Now, when I finally ascertained a series of facts, I couldn't be sure I understood their implications or even knew the facts.

These thoughts floored me for a while until I realized that's the way it is any way all the time. We don't know what we're doing even while we do it. Life is illusion. That's why we depend on documents.

Now that thought was comforting, and although it didn't change the realities I had to deal with, it made me humble enough to keep burrowing at the puzzles surrounding me—specifically Wiley, Travis, Eva, and why in the hell somebody wanted to knock me in the head in the first place. That wasn't an illusion, despite Wiley's assertion that my steering column was faulty.

CHAPTER FORTY-EIGHT

Days went by in a sleepy blur for about a week. The new medication did that. I would watch television at Wiley's place, sleep, and swim. No calls from the office.

Swimming was my glory and salvation. I like to paddle in the deep end in between laps.

I had worked up to a four-hundred-individual medley—butterfly, backstroke, breaststroke, free—butterfly, backstroke, breaststroke, free. I could chant the order of the strokes like a mantra that defended me from my brain injury, partial complex seizures, mysterious motives of old friends, and the perils of newly rediscovered loves. I went to the Y every day during this time. It is the only clear memory I have.

Then, I started to come out of it. I was adjusting to the new medicine. So . . . little by little, the fuzzy sleepiness in my head began to recede. I was awake again—awake and feeling the urgency of my quest. I returned to the office to renew the search for answers, no matter what. Wiley and Travis seemed to leave me alone.

They didn't know exactly how to take me. First, I was the cripple they had to pet and protect. Next, I had been the out-of-shape swimmer who had to get in the pool and swim again. Now I was an epileptic fool they couldn't predict. Was their scheme possible at all? They didn't know, and I didn't know either. In fact, I didn't even know what their scheme was, although I knew it was there. One morning at the office, I just sat there thinking through all this. I had found my memo, so I pulled it out and wrote on the side—"Is there any way all this might be related?"

I still didn't fully trust anyone, but Lisa called me just then. I decided, impulsively, to trust her more.

"Mr. Tutem?"

"Yes, Lisa."

"May I come in?"

"Certainly, Lisa."

We both said "I've been meaning . . ." at the same time.

"You first," I said.

"Mr. Tutem, things have happened very fast, and I am not sure you have been told exactly what has happened in a way for you to understand. I would like to try to do that if you would let me."

I pondered this for a very small moment.

"Yes, I would like that—but before you start, I don't need a catalog of my injury and the various medical things that I have had to endure—I know those pretty well. What I don't know is what I used to do and what was going on here at the office just before I got hurt."

"That is what I want to tell you."

"All right."

"You know I have worked for you for fifteen years." There was a pause; I didn't know what was coming next. "And early last year, you were open about everything you did." She blushed and looked down. "Really I knew more than I should have, but I remained professional and just observed things. You were involved in some type of big matter that involved Butch again. He disappeared—"

I interrupted her, "Now, exactly who is Butch?"

"You mean you don't remember Butch?"

"Not really."

"He is the biggest developer in Greenville County and the Upstate and a scoundrel and SOB, if you want my honest opinion. You were the only one who would represent him in whatever matter this was. You had represented him once before when he was in legal problems, and he kind of disappeared from the firm. But then he came back—in his manicured and scented vanity one day to the office, and you had a long meeting with him. You told me that you had refused to represent him because you had a conflict. He left here in a huff after you told him that. Thereafter, you were perplexed and distracted.

"You told me that you had a lot to do on a probate case that you were appointed as personal representative. You didn't work on anything else, and you didn't tell me what it was exactly you were working on. You would go away for afternoons and days on end. I never knew exactly where you went, although you always left your cell phone number which, by the way, we need to get for you again. There was some issue concerning a probate question, and I prepared several form letters inquiring about addresses for different people. Then, you were hurt." She looked to see that no one was listening, and in fact, she got up and locked the door.

"After you were in the hospital, Travis and Wiley came by and rummaged through your desk—you know how prissy Travis is, so she said she was just 'cleaning up the mess,' but I am sure they were looking for something. I took the files that I knew had your private information and hid them in your desk. There were two files in your brief case, and you had left your briefcase. So I also took the files out and put the empty briefcase back in there for them to find. I saw them shuffle through it and then put it back on your shelf. So I don't think they found much.

"When they asked me if I knew of any other documents you might have, I said no. So now here we are. I want to show you these files now and see if you can use them to understand what is going on because I really don't."

I acknowledged her truthfulness and thanked her for her candor and loyalty.

She showed me the hidden drawer in my desk, popped it open for me—I pretended I couldn't do it, and the files were all there just as she had prepared them.

"Well, they're here. And what's this?" She looked in the main desk drawer and saw the memo.

I reached for it and said, "That's just some notes I have been making for myself. I can get serious about it now that you have shown me the files."

She looked at me with a kind of question and then shrugged.

"Well, at least I have done my duty here by you and the firm. Now please tell me what to do."

"Lisa," I said, "you have helped me through some very difficult times, and maybe they have all been in preparation for what we are about to go through next. Something is up as you know, and I don't know what it is yet, even though I am at the center of it. Maybe this Butch is a bad man, but I have been sworn as an officer of the court to do the right thing on my cases, even though I'm not sure what that may be in this case. Now I need you more than ever to help me think through these matters and see what needs to be done next." I then grinned. "You see, now I am brain-damaged and epileptic. If you're lucky, you will get to see me have a seizure." I laughed.

She seemed horrified. "No, no," she said.

"Just kidding! I need you more than ever, so please stay and help me through this and protect me from Wiley and Travis—and Eva, too, for that matter. We will have to talk about all this at length, but I very much appreciate everything you have done."

I assumed my best Washington & Lee manner, bowed curtly, and escorted her back to her desk.

"I would like to check in with you every morning, once during the day, and every evening, and I am going to stay in my office most of the time. Please alert me if Wiley or Travis show up or if you see them snooping around, and please get me a cell phone." She smiled, and I smiled. A mission established. Unspoken—I now had an auxiliary brain for the tasks ahead. I needed it.

"Oh, by the way," she said, "Judge Poe's clerk called and reminded you not to forget about the information the court needs."

"Yes, we talked about this when I saw her at Gene's—she's good-looking too." Lisa looked at me distastefully. "Now, could you tell me what this is about?" Lisa looked startled.

"By the way," she said, "Heather called while you were gone. You can trust her."

With all this old/new information, I had crossed back over the River Styx without fully knowing it. Lisa was the boatman, Charon, taking me in her paralegal rowboat back to the land of the living, the undead, the breathing, and the swimming.

This was a new swimming pool and a new race—perhaps the race I had been swimming all along. The race I had been swimming when somebody tried to drown me. It was the deep end of my pool.

Lisa went on to explain the Putnam case file was one of the files in my brief case and thus, probably, untouched in the "organizing" that Travis and Wiley had done to my office while I was in the hospital. Lisa had rescued these files the first day they had come searching for whatever it was they had wanted.

I had to have some lunch, so I asked Lisa to check if the coast was clear. It was, and I was about to step out when the phone rang.

It was Heather—apparently she had worked on the Putnam file before I was hurt.

I decided not to bring the file since I had not looked at it yet. Maybe just lunch with Heather would be a good start. Lisa said I could trust her.

CHAPTER FORTY-NINE

As Heather and I made our way out of the labyrinth of the building, I had a brief déjà vu—something I knew was part of my new partial complex seizures—it felt like a memory, and as I looked at Heather, her face changed. She reminded me of my mother or of pictures I had seen of Greek mother goddesses, statuesque and determined in the way only female lawyers can be.

I felt a sinking in my stomach when she said, "Are you all right, Fred?"

Her touch was electric, and the feeling and the déjà vu passed from me as suddenly as they had come. Only a little cloudiness remained.

Heather was now Heather and not the determined goddess of the labyrinth. She was just Heather.

"I'm fine," I said. Clear as a ritual gong in a Greek temple, echoing down the halls.

Just as we got into the parking lot, Wiley hollered from the door.

Before Heather could invite him to come along, I said, "Heather and I have so . . . uh . . . work . . . uh . . . We have to . . . uh . . . do, you know, that case."

"I'll get up with you later this afternoon." I put my hand on Heather's arm. "We are going in Heather's car." Fortunately, we were right there. We slid into her messy Buick SUV littered with papers and baby toys, cameras, legal books, food wrappers, and paper.

"Why did you say that, Fred?"

"I didn't want Wiley to come along."

"Well, why, he has been very interested in this case."

"I'll tell you later. Please don't ask any more questions just yet."

"Now, Fred, telling a lawyer that is like waving a red cape in front of a bull. I'll go along this one time just 'cause I know what you have been through but not anymore after this. Wiley is a partner of this firm, after all, and I am only an associate."

"Well, I appreciate that very much, Heather. I have always thought of you as an excellent lawyer."

I thought to myself that maybe it was time to expand the circle of trust—but I didn't really know Heather very well. Young, captivating, determined, distracted by her children, accustomed to lots of money, and no leisure time to spend it. Makeup perfect, clothes perfect, legal documents perfectly prepared.

Could I trust her fully? Was she part of the plot? Am I going crazy?

We settled in a booth at the Bohemian, not too crowded. This was a popular local restaurant on the edge of downtown.

At the Bohemian, Heather came right out with it.

"I am very puzzled, Fred. There is almost no information about this case. You worked on it for exactly six weeks and three days before you got hurt. You didn't share what you had, and even though you knew I was to be your associate, you didn't give me any of the work. So before we get started again, I want it clear that I want to be trusted to work on this case and be an integral part of it. Otherwise, please don't waste my time."

She looked at me firmly in the eye awaiting my reply.

I closed my eyes for a moment. "Oh my god," she said. "You're not having another seizure, are you?" A crack in her assertive will. I kept my eyes closed and moaned a little bit, just for fun.

"Fred, Fred." She touched my arm. I reached out with my other hand and grabbed it, opened my eyes, and shook my head gently.

"I'm fine, Heather. You just reminded me of why I always liked you." Gotcha, I thought. I'll remember this trick.

"And just why was that?" she said in a manner that made me realize her assertiveness was only as deep and lasting as the documents in front of her. All she wanted was a little respect.

"Yes, Heather. You always get to the point. That is why I like you. And yes, in fact, we are in this thing together. I apologize I didn't include you earlier, and I don't know why I didn't tell you more before the wreck. Do you have any ideas?" I was fishing because I truly did not know anything. Just in the brief time I had spent with Heather, some of the memories of her competence and personality had come back to me. She had always been easy to work with, as long as you did things properly. So maybe she could tell me something about it—whatever it was.

"Well I don't really know, Fred. I have heard that your brain was pretty . . . uh . . . uh . . . smashed around, let's say, to use a technical term." She smiled.

"Yes, it was. I don't know the full extent of it, but my memory keeps returning, and sometimes a fragment of it will open up a whole landscape in a way I hadn't fully anticipated. Regular swimming again has helped me a lot."

"Well in this case, the only thing I can think of pertinent beyond the actual facts of the case is your relationship with Butch, the mad dog developer who has used and abused our law firm for many years. He has something to do with all of this in some way—although his exact involvement has never been clear to me."

"Butch, you say."

"Yes, but let's put that aside for the moment. That fact is a separate fact from other facts we might know. As you may remember, Louise and Robert Putnam were an eccentric couple who lived outside Marietta, which is located in northern Greenville County. Robert owned and operated a local grocery store there. Louise taught business courses at the local technical college. Robert, unbeknownst to most folks, owned vast tracts of land in Pickens County, including land adjacent to two highway interchanges on Highway 123 between Easley and Clemson. They also owned a thousand-acre farm near Marietta where they raised cows, pigs, and chickens. Robert was a 'dirt' multimillionaire with all of his huge land holdings. You would never guess it because he and Louise lived like paupers, but they were happy.

"They did not have any children, but they loved animals. Louise gave a home to any stray animal that wandered onto their property. Don't you remember all the school buses? Robert had collected farm equipment and old school buses to house all the strays, including about thirty cats and dogs. He would just park the school buses beside the barn, open the door to each bus, and, voila, an instant pet motel! I can't believe you don't remember all the problems we had with the cleanup and finding homes for all those poor animals!

"Louise and Robert had joint Wills prepared by our law firm many years ago, leaving everything to each other and then to their parents if they were living. Louise was predeceased by Robert when he had a fatal heart attack at the grocery store. His will left everything to Louise, including all the land holdings in different counties located in the upstate.

"Unfortunately, Louise never updated her will after Robert died. Her adoptive parents died about twenty years before Robert. I say adoptive parents because when Louise was about five years old, she was adopted by an older couple, the Smiths, who were neighbors of Ruby Gentry, her biological mother, who lived in a mill village here in Greenville. They had no children of their own, and Louise's mother was a poor single parent who believed that the Smiths could give Louise a better home. Louise also had a younger sister who was raised by their maternal grandmother. Of course, as you know, when Louse was adopted away, all legal ties to her biological family were severed by the adoption, including inheritance rights from her mother's side. Louise thrived with the Smiths whom she considered her real parents. She even graduated from Clemson University where she, incidentally, met and then later married Robert Putnam.

"When Robert died, Louise was devastated. She seemed to fall apart. I guess part of it was that she had no children to lean upon and no family left. She got so depressed that she had multiple hospitalizations at Marshall Pickens Hospital before she died. Apparently, the only person that visited her in the mental hospital was Tammy, her younger biological sister, who kept in touch with Louise over the years. It was also rumored that Louise became an alcoholic and hosted multiple male friends at parties on the farm. Don't you remember how she died? She was found naked and frozen to death under a bush in front of her farm house!

"So you ask, where are we as far as the heirs to this estate, and what still needs to be done? I think it's probably pretty straight forward. Louise's will is of absolutely no use because all the potential heirs are deceased, including Robert, her husband, and both of her parents. The only benefit of the will was that it appointed you as her personal representative. How this happened I'm not quite sure, except that Butch and Robert Putnam were close friends for many years. Butch must have recommended you as the substitute personal representative for both wills in the event something happened to Robert which is exactly what has happened. Butch probably knew that Judge Poe would never, in a million years, appoint him as personal representative because of his sketchy personal history and record.

Bingo, you got the designation in the wills. Also, it seems that Louise had some sort of romantic relationship with Butch before she died. One of our now-deceased law firm partners prepared the wills, so we, as the law firm, found out you were the personal representative when Butch dropped by the office with the original of Louise's will. The bottom line is that Louise's estate will have to pass by the laws of intestacy in South Carolina, meaning it will pass to unnamed statutory heirs as if there was no will.

"If Louise had children, which she didn't, they, of course, would have been the legal heirs. Therefore, we must, by law, climb the family tree to determine the legal heirs. Since Louise's parents had brothers and sisters, which would be Louise's aunts and uncles, that is the first level of heirs to consider. Since all of Louise's aunts and uncles are deceased, the estate will go by law to Louise's living cousins, the children of the aunts and uncles in their proportional shares. I believe you had located most of them after her death and before the accident, but I'm not sure about that. I know that you saw them at Louise's funeral, which was delayed due to the autopsy.

"You told me that you met Louise's sister, Tammy, there. You also commented that you were appalled by the behavior of two of the cousins, who had told Tammy to leave because she, according to them, had no business attending the funeral. Dumb as dirt they called her for thinking she was to be treated like family! You told them that you were in charge of the arrangements, and she had a right to be there if she wanted to be. I think you had concluded that even though the cousins have a right to the estate, they don't need to act like a bunch of greedy rednecks.

"That's as much as I know," she concluded. "I have no clue how Butch might be involved. I can speculate that it has something to do with the land. It always does with Butch—always." She said this with a bit of bitterness.

I could remember only bits and pieces of all this, but once she stated the law so clearly, the situation had shape and color that it did not have before her words. So I was the personal representative for the estate. I was hunting down and determining the rightful heirs. The will was no good. Had I finished my work? Where was I in the process? Where was my lost memory? Thank god for Heather.

This might be easy, or it might be hard.

We finished our lunch. A blend of arugula, romaine, bleu cheese, and pear halves misted with vinaigrette and a hint of lime. Heather, who was trim as an athlete despite two babies, insisted she had begun to eat "Ayurvedic" because Kristi, her yoga teacher, had encouraged her to do so.

"I feel so much lighter now. Up-dog and down-dog no longer hurt my back."

I got up before I could imagine what that meant. We both agreed lunch was on the firm.

In the big old city cemetery, there is a memorial to Robert E. Lee erected in 1956. Robert E. Lee looks to the west, resolute in his purpose—just like me again. I wanted to touch the statue as we drove past, but Heather was from Pennsylvania, and she would have none of it. "We won, remember?" she said.

"So what," I said, puffing out my chest.

I needed to be alone and to think. I told Heather to drop me off at the Y for some swimming therapy. We agreed to meet back at the law firm in two hours.

I needed to swim in clear water.

CHAPTER FIFTY

Now as I stroked through the pool, reviewing my thoughts, I felt some confidence. Heather had given me the right framework, and I was hoping the rest would be in my notes. They might jog my memory to full awakening. Lisa had ferried me back across the River Styx, but I wasn't fully alive yet. Heather's crisp presentation of the facts she knew left room for more questions—just like everything since my car wreck—and like life itself.

Right arm in, breathe, left arm, right arm in, breathe—I settled into an easy rhythm for my freestyle.

Why had I not told Heather everything that I might know? Why had I behaved in a furtive and secret fashion? Why was Wiley so interested? What would Butch have to do with this exactly? Is Travis involved? And what did any of this have to do with my wreck and the frying of my brain? Will I ever find out who burned me?

When I got burned and beaten, the connections between my neurons had been severed. Growing them back meant growing new memories as well. An oxymoron—how can a memory be new? All memories are old. But when they disappear completely and you rediscover them, what do you name them then? Old, new, made up? A "made-up" memory doesn't sound exactly right.

I had had enough partial complex déjà vu feelings to believe that terms like old and new mean nothing when applied to memories. All things are always mysterious. Old and new are convenient illusions, especially when it comes to memories.

As I approached the office after clearing my head, I thought Wiley might be lurking somewhere to accost me with a set of questions worthy of his solicitor past, a cross examination on Louise, et. al. Cool water. Cool head. I got lucky. No Wiley.

I found Heather in her office, and I shut her door. "Heather, let's agree to do this. Do you agree that Wiley should have no direct responsibility in this case yet?"

"Well, now that you say so, no, he has none."

"All right, then. Tell him that I really didn't remember anything, and then tell him exactly what you told me but leave Butch out."

"Okay, but what are you going to tell him?"

"I'll tell him that I remembered nothing, and I didn't see how I could write an accurate report to the judge. Tell him I was perplexed. Both of those statements are true and cover our lunch pretty well."

"What if Wiley isn't interested?"

"Oh, I think he is interested. I think he will see you this afternoon—I have no doubts."

"Okay, I'll agree to do all that, but you must agree to keep me informed about anything you might learn. I understand you took several trips over to Pickens County and even explored county records in Anderson County—is that right?"

"Well, Heather, now that you mention it, I can remember vaguely afternoons and summer heat driving around in that area of the world, but I don't remember exactly what I did. I am being totally honest. If I find out exactly what I was doing, I will tell you immediately."

"That's fair enough."

"Also, please tell me if Wiley gets in touch with you, and I will tell you the same."

"Agreed."

Now, a counter conspiracy has been hatched. Heather and me and Lisa (*Omne trnum est perfectum*. Everything in threes is perfect.)

The Minotaur of our legal labyrinth had a new monster to contend with.

Memory, don't fail me now, illusion or not.

CHAPTER FIFTY-ONE

Wiley was true to form. He was hanging around the lobby as Heather and I meandered together toward the canteen for an afternoon snack.

He pointed at her and nodded with an indication that he would talk with her later. She headed to the canteen without me.

I stood there waiting. "Now, Fred, heh, heh, I see you enjoy spending a lot of your time with Heather, our best-looking associate. She is almost as good-looking as the probate judge."

"Well, for once, we weren't talking about anybody's looks." He was beginning to irk me.

"Oh, really, well then, what were you talking about?"

"Well—we were discussing how to rehabilitate my blasted memory, to pull together my probate case, and how she can be of greatest help to me in doing that. I need lots of help. The judge is obviously eager for certain information that she wants and needs from me to end this case."

Wiley got a little excited. "Yeah, I understand she is expecting something important from you. Do you have any clue what it might be?"

"No, and Heather didn't know very much either, so she and I will have to figure it out. It shouldn't be too hard," I said dismissively.

He seemed slightly pleased. "Maybe I can help."

"With what?"

"I'll . . . I'll . . . I'll have to bring you some documents I have got hanging around my office—you know it's important to me that you get plugged back in to the swim of things without any big problems. Listen, to change the subject, I've been thinking about supper?"

"Well since I am staying with you, I'll be doing whatever you are doing."

"Okay, we are going out about seven o'clock to reintroduce you at Rock Earle's—you'll remember when you get there."

When Wiley turned the corner, I sprinted and limped up to my office and called Heather on the phone. "Get ready, Heather. I told him you didn't know much, and he offered to provide us some documents—whatever that means."

"Got it."

I then told Lisa, and she locked the door again and led me to our secret files. "I think what you want is all in there." The files were called "Notes on Putnam." It was a thick file, nestled in between all the others. All of them seemed important. They seemed to hold the key to who I used to be, but like all things in the legal world, which is a crisis a minute, now I was in a crisis. I could not afford to explore my old self in a leisurely fashion. I had to do this part as fast as a fifty-yard freestyle.

"Lisa, thank you. I believe we better keep these files behind your secret door, or I think Wiley will come around to snoop." Before I left that day, I put some invisible tape—a thin sliver—on all my drawers. I remembered that from a spy movie. It's more reliable than a hair stuck with spittle.

At six forty-five, we got dressed and swung by Travis's house.

She came out radiant as always—a slit in her dress, secreting perfume, her hair twisted off to one side in a perpetual wind—the romantic sea-breeze look—glamour, glamour, glamour.

I gave up the front seat. "Thank you, honey," she said and dragged her fingers across my cheek.

We drove to Rock Earle's through the late summer dusk. Still hot but with a glowing promise of autumn in the way the sun slanted across the treetops and into the second stories of downtown buildings.

Downtown traffic was picking up. We got in line for the valet parking just in front of the restaurant. A Mercedes with blacked-out windows was there before us, and when the door opened, a rather fat man fashionably dressed with a big honking diamond ring on his right hand and a Rolex watch on his left, got out. I had on Weejuns. This man sported Italian loafers, and his salt and pepper gray hair curled over the collar of his silk shirt. The valet boys treated him like a regular, and he tipped generously.

I don't know why I paid such attention to this character.

Travis got a salad with a medallion of beef, Wiley a thick steak, and I ordered some seafood—a grouper I think, something from the sea, something that swam for a living. I have to swim, and so did my supper.

The character we had seen at entry made his way over to our table, greeting everyone in between. It was, of course, Butch.

Rock Earle's restaurant is like a splinter of New York stuck into the heart of Old Greenville. Fancy wine list, fancy steak, fancy salads, fancy seafood, and fancy people. Low lights all aglitter with waiters and waitresses who are too polite.

Along one side is the bar in town where everyone appears once or twice a week—chiefly old men and young women. The old men are buying. The young women are mooching. Occasionally, they leave together, and the girls keep showing up in tight little dresses.

It's the kind of place that generates quiet gossip—little secrets that swirl around in fancy cars. What happens at Rock Earle's doesn't stay there very long.

Butch arrived at our table. Wiley and Travis paid close attention, wary even as they grew cordial.

"Fred, good to see you. I wanted to see how my man was doing," he said and put a beefy hand on my shoulder. He smelled like heavy cologne.

Suddenly I remembered. This was *the* Butch, the very same Butch I had bailed out several years ago—I couldn't remember details. My heart started beating like the start of a medley relay.

"I still can't thank you enough for the last time you helped me out. Are you back in the great game yet?" He said all this looking directly at me.

"Well, Butch, you are welcome." I could think of nothing else to say.

He greeted Wiley and Travis, gave her a little hug, and then turned back to me. "Have you been up to your cabin yet?"

Before I could think, I said, "What cabin?" He turned to Wiley and Travis.

"Didn't you tell him?"

"No, we haven't told him yet."

"Well, I'll have to take him up there myself then—that's it. I am going to take you up there tomorrow so you will know what a grateful client I am." He looked at them, and I thought I saw a wink.

"Well, Wiley is kind of running my life now at the firm, so we will have to clear it with him."

He nodded assent. "Sure, Butch, why don't you come by eleven thirty or so? Maybe we'll all go to lunch up at Travelers Rest."

"That sounds like a deal."

Butch shook hands all around and then went over to the bar to greet more friends.

Wiley and Travis said nothing, but it looked like they were figuring out some problem in a mystery calculus. I was full of questions. Suddenly, the plot had become thicker than the shrimp and grits at Rock Earle's.

Now I did remember Butch. I did remember the scene at Paris Mountain, and I remembered that he left town. But he was back in town now, and his presence in Rock Earle's indicated a familiarity with the town and a reputation that was acceptable enough for anything to happen.

Rock Earle himself greeted Butch with a manly hug. They looked like old friends.

Butch looked back at me over the shoulder of his new acquaintance, a buxom fortyish woman with a little black dress. One of many scattered in the room like black orchids in a Mexican jungle. I felt like a pawn again, but I was definitely curious about "the cabin." It sounded nice. Maybe a pond to swim in? I'll wait and see.

CHAPTER FIFTY-TWO

Reach, pull, roll. Reach, pull, roll. The water was my element. Next, I was plowing through the water like a wave free of the bonds of memory and thought. Faster, faster, faster. Like an airplane gathering speed at just the right moment, I took off in flight from the water into the air like a night bird soaring through night sky with a bird's-eye view of the dark landscape below me. Barren woods and rolling hills came and went. It was winter time in the South. I was so quiet in flight that a herd of grazing deer below failed to raise their heads as I passed over them.

In the distance, I noticed flashing lights—blue, red, and white. The splendor of the lights drew me closer. I was drawn to the glow like a mosquito to light, and I could not change the direction of my flight. As I moved in to inspect the source of the flickering light collage, I passed over a ridge and saw the illumination of an ambulance and several sheriff's cars parked in front of a large white farmhouse. There was a circular drive and a barn a short distance away. Something terrible had happened. I felt it. I was afraid and filled with horror. It's time to get away!

Damn those flickering lights! They are going to make me have another seizure even on this new medicine. Some powerful force was forcing me down. All I could do was land where it directed me.

I landed among five sheriff's deputies. At least three EMS techs were walking around the driveway in front of the house. They didn't seem to notice me. Am I invisible? A whining German shepherd was leashed, muzzled, and pacing with a sheriff's deputy who was attempting to calm the dog down. "What's going on?" I asked one of the EMS techs. He was huddled over a case with all sorts of medical equipment. Could he hear me?

I was distracted by a man with a rugged weather-beaten face dressed in farmer's overalls talking to one of the deputies who was intently writing down every word from the old man's mouth. "I am Louise's neighbor one hundred yards up the road. I heard Doc barking and whining, and he just wouldn't stop, so I came on down to see what was wrong and found her here under the tree stiff, naked and frozen to death. Old Doc was lying across her trying to keep her warm, but he couldn't save her. He was her favorite. They were never separated. Poor Doc can't stand it." I heard his voice catch, and he said to the deputy, "We were neighbors for thirty-five years. I never in a million years expected this to happen."

A plaintive frail voice cried out faintly from under a nearby magnolia tree. "Help me, help me, please! Somebody, please!

I rushed to the EMS tech still huddled over his case. She's still alive! "Get over there and help her, please," I begged him. "You moron, a woman is dying, and you do nothing?" He still ignored me. "Give me a blanket, you idiot, I'll cover her up!" Stooped down and refusing to turn around, he still paid no attention to me. A blanket appeared in my hand. I rushed toward the magnolia tree with stakes around it and yellow crime scene tape circling the bottom of the tree about ten feet in diameter. A crime scene. The air was freezing cold. I took a deep breath of the frozen air, and my chest began to hurt. Still, I ducked under the yellow tape with the blanket to save the helpless, desperate woman.

There under the huge magnolia tree, lying on the ground facing away from me, was a pale naked body. The women's head rested on her left arm above her head. She looked marmoreal, like a statue in repose. I noticed that her short white hair was standing on end completely frozen into a crown of icicles. Her vacant blue eyes were wide open, bulging out of her head in a frozen stare. Only her mouth moved. In a melancholic, high, raspy voice, she wailed, "Fred, Fred, you are the only one that can save me now!"

How does she know me? I reached down to cover her body with the blanket. Suddenly, she reached up and grabbed me with a frozen hand with fingernails as sharp as the icicles on her head. She clamped onto my wrist, pulling me down to the ground, now screaming, "Help me up, please! I am pitching forward, losing my balance, and going down. I start screaming . . .

Wiley is standing over my bed shaking me. "Fred, Fred! Stop yelling! You are going to wake the dead! Please calm down, buddy. It's going to be okay. It's just a bad dream, a nightmare."

My heart was racing, and I was sweating. Stop the panic! I started deep breathing. Finally, after a few minutes, I asked Wiley, "Did Louise Putnam have a dog?"

Wiley said, "Yes, a German shepherd. Why?"

My heart is still racing, and I swing my legs to the floor to sit up. "Dear God, please don't let me have another seizure," I pray out loud. "Sorry, Wiley, I think I just did wake the dead. I walked through the whole death scene of Louise Putnam. She was frozen in place but wailing and trying to get me to help her. No one else would. What a horrible way to die! It was so vivid . . . I think I'll just get a drink of water and then go back to bed."

Wiley just yawned and said, "Fred, I'll share a drink of water with you. Then we both need to get some sleep."

Whatever Butch was up to, I would have to trust my own flawed powers in this—plus, of course, maybe Lisa and maybe Heather . . . and now, the ghostly intentions of Louise Putnam.

At the office, I felt fresh as a fish just caught. I was not gasping for breath yet.

"Lisa, tell me about Butch."

She rolled her eyes. "Oh yeah, he's back again."

"Have you read my notes?"

"No," she said.

We went into my office. The slivers of tape were gone. "Did you go through these, Lisa?"

"No, I have already told you, no."

These papers had suddenly become valuable . . . to somebody besides me. This would have to wait until later.

"About Butch, long version or short version?"

"Tell me, and let's stick to the facts and any documents we may have. I'm a lawyer. Nothing exists unless it's written down. Butch mentioned a cabin last night." I congratulated myself on remembering that detail.

Wordlessly, Lisa went to her desk and came back with a file marked deed. "I think you mean this." Inside the file was a record of property on Cliff Falls Road and the deed itself conveying property from a corporation to me.

There was also a note attached from Butch. "This is yours free and clear buddy. Thank you for saving me. You are my favorite attorney. I'll always come to you for help." Something wasn't right. Had I also wiped from my memory the rules of ethics for South Carolina attorneys? Why would I accept such an extravagant gift from a client instead of a fee?

I looked up at Lisa. She was shaking her head. "So you didn't really remember this, did you?"

"I guess I did at one time, but now it belongs to those memories that were burned in the wreck."

"You, poor man." She shook her head.

We put the file back, and I asked her to arrange all the other files in chronological order. "Well, on the brighter side," I joked, "I know who Louise Putnam was. I met her in a nightmare last night." Meanwhile, I am going to find a hiding place for my papers.

CHAPTER FIFTY-THREE

Wiley came to get me at eleven thirty from my office and walked me down to the lobby. "Butch said he wanted to go just with you, so I'm passing you off. Don't tell him anything—the firm is still suspicious of him." Wiley's voice was clipped and strained like a spy whose plot isn't going as planned. "I'll work on those documents for the Louise case and put them in your office with Lisa."

"Please make a copy for Heather."

"Good idea." Wiley then put on his big smile for Butch who stood in the lobby.

Butch reeked of expensive cologne. We all walked outside to his waiting car. It was as plush as a honeymoon suite.

I thought the front license plate on his car said "Me and God," but I just caught a glimpse of it as Wiley urged me into the car. "Butch said it's about an hour up there, and you've got a lot to talk about."

"Well, Butch, I'll be interested to hear it. I hope you realize I can't remember anything about this, and I barely remember anything at all—even exactly who you are."

He looked puzzled but recovered quickly. "That's fine, Freddy boy, we are going to do just fine—the ride up should jog your memory. Wiley said you were doing just fine."

Hmm. Wiley shut the car door on my side and retreated back into the law firm, leaving me alone with Butch. This is just great, I mused cynically.

Even at the speed limit, his car had a roar. Butch's hair looked like the shaggy mane of a great jungle cat. We were on the Serengeti Plain in search of wildebeests.

But Butch's belly looked more like a big bear or boar hog after an orgy on acorns.

Why would I have accepted such a gift from a client? Had I even known about it before the wreck? I had read the deed that morning, so I knew the address of the place, but I couldn't remember how to get there. So I tried to memorize landmarks as we drove up to the cabin. Highway 25 through Travelers Rest outskirts, Wal-Mart, Dunkin Donuts, and just past the town, the Cider House. Butch pulled in.

"Hello, Dave! I'd like some of those hot pickled okra, some peach chutney, some hot dilly beans, and a couple of those barbecue sandwiches. Oh yeah, don't forget the Happy Cow cheese. I like the mild flavor of that farmer's cheese. The ten-year cheddar is good too. Hey, Kenny."

Dave was behind the counter with his glasses perched on his nose and the Monavie bottles on a shelf beside him. "You sure you don't want anything else, Butch? The tomatoes are good, and that cantaloupe is all about to go to waste. Here, let me toss in a couple of onions too." Then outside, we got two bags of fried peanuts from Kenny.

Butch laid down a hundred-dollar bill and told them to just keep the change. They said there wasn't any change. In fact, he owed them ten dollars.

"I knew I couldn't run one past ya." And he forked up the ten bucks.

He quickly went back in for some apple cider, and we took all this to the cabin. More landmarks. The big boat on the hill at the entrance to the Foothills Racetrack—races every Saturday night. Two produce stands—one on the left, two on the right. A big firecracker store—I concentrated hard to try and remember these things so I could find it again without Butch.

We rolled under Highway 11, about a half mile after that took a right on old 25, headed up toward Saluda, North Carolina. The road curved around past a small resort hotel that serviced visitors to the Cliffs. Butch said, "Yeah, ever since the Cliffs came to town, real estate ain't been the same. Bubba Dog has control of this end of the county so tight that I can't even build a gas station," he spit. "At least he hasn't got the other side yet, but he's coming fast."

We kept rolling around curves, little houses, and thick woods. Finally, we broke out running down a ridge on our left and on our right fields full of eggplant, okra, and tomatoes. A few long haul trucks and ridges on the right behind the fields. Butch started to slow down, and there it was—"Cliff Falls Road." Butch said, "Hell if I know what waters it divides, but there is a little hill, and the water runs one way down and one way up. I keep meaning to find out whether one side runs to the Pacific and the other side to the Atlantic."

Did I used to laugh at his jokes?

I had been quiet the whole time.

Butch started in a sort of formal way. "When you helped me that last time and I had to leave town, I knew you were the only lawyer who would have gone toe-to-toe with the solicitor the way you did. With your contacts and reputation for honesty, I knew you should be my only lawyer. I was a mess back then, but I fixed myself up and earned a little money, so my real estate has done well. I wanted you to have this land and this little cabin. I got it from an old widow lady who didn't want it any more. It's just my way of saying thank you. You got your head knocked around right after I gave it to you. In fact, you were on your way up here for a meeting with me—the first time you'd been here—when you had your wreck."

I felt eerily at home somehow, and I asked him to stop the car. There was a sign "Garrenterra," and right between that and a little pond was a scarred-up place on the road—tree trunk knocked over, burned grass, broken bushes heavy with green leaves now but twisted and broken still.

"Is this it, Butch?"

"Well, yeah, I think this is where they found you."

"Do you know who found me?"

He looked away. "I think it was the EMS. In fact, I think it was my niece . . . Eva."

I said nothing. I could barely breathe. Eva was Butch's niece!

I must have looked shocked. "You didn't know that, Fred?"

"Well, I can't remember anything, Butch. I'll be double-damned if I remember that. Eva, your niece?"

"Well, I kept telling her that she needed to tell you the whole story, but she was in love with you, boy, and she didn't want to spoil it." He let that sink in.

I felt myself brooding.

"In fact, I have called her, and she is coming up here later."

"You shouldn't have done that, Butch." I didn't know what to think. Did Wiley know this? Did Travis?

"Well, look, don't say anything right now. Let's just look at your cabin."

I was silent like an owl. Who, who, who? Who could I trust?

CHAPTER FIFTY-FOUR

The rest of the road was covered in a dark green canopy—poplars and tall oaks, magnolias, dogwoods, elms, birch trees, any kind of hardwood you could think of reached up to the sky. The understory clean, vines dangling, muscadine with clumps of grapes. We saw the small glimmer of water on the right. "That's your pond," Butch said. Glassy Ridge, the sign read.

Here was a little dirt road, and we took a right, climbed the hill about twenty-five or thirty yards, and there above the pond was an A-frame structure with a screen porch. Decks and a driveway all graveled in. Surrounded by the forest. "Here it is." Butch reached in his pocket, got out a set of keys, and handed them to me. "Let yourself in."

I was skeptical. "You say this is mine?"

"Yes, Fred, I gave it to you as a fee and a present."

"Fee for what?"

"Well, we need to talk about that. Let's say it's just a present for right now." My mind was bouncing around like a pinball on fast forward. Wiley, Travis, Butch, and Eva. Now this.

First this—the cabin that supposedly was mine, but I had never seen it. I have seen the deed, and the property is in my name if all those documents are accurate, and they are properly filed. I didn't put it past Butch to just do one part so he would have an out.

Next, the news that Eva is Butch's niece . . . How strange! Can a man trust love at all? The answer is no.

Butch is a mystery too. Exactly what is he up to? Mysterious, as well, are Travis and Wiley. Was there a relationship between Louise and Butch? Did he leave her to freeze that night? Did Louise give him this cabin?

"Now I had the hardwood floors done over for you and a couple of rugs dragged in, but there is only one bathroom, and the kitchen needs some work. I think it will be good for weekends though, and you got the pond to fish in, and I understand you like to swim, so—it's a little muddy sometimes—I hope you like it."

Butch did seem genuine with a wave of his big fat arm over his belly. I couldn't help but feel a kind of guilty pleasure—whether I could trust him or not, this house hanging on the side of a ridge thick with trees gave me pleasure. Was the water any colder than Butch's motives?

He had mentioned a fee—fee for what?

He brewed a pot of coffee, and we sat down with the barbecue from Dave.

"Now there is a matter of some land here and in Pickens County. It may come as a surprise to you, but I loved a widow woman who lived on a big farm near Travelers Rest named Louise Putnam. She was a beautiful woman and had the misfortune of marrying old crazy Robert Putnam who ran the grocery store in T.R. We were close friends for many years." This was all sounding familiar.

"He used to have a little bit of everything, and he was almost as shrewd as me when it came to real estate. He also had a poker game every Saturday night that dragged in boys from Marietta, Travelers Rest, Pickens and Anderson, and Walhalla and Williamston. There were even a couple of boys from Georgia. I played down there a couple of nights myself until I started getting nervous about all that cash. That was back when the sheriff's deputies had a gang that stole from poker games.

"Anyway, Robert liked to collect old school buses, even traded land for 'em. He had on his property every vintage school bus there was. Thing was, he didn't care about keeping 'em nice. He wanted 'em as homes for his critters."

Butch went on to tell me a familiar story of Robert Putnam and how he kept farm animals along with cats and dogs in these buses and how he and Louise would feed and shelter them.

"The buses were covered in kudzu and morning glory, honeysuckle, and muscadine. He even had one called the blackberry bus with blackberry bushes all over it."

"A couple of times Greenville County Council wanted to condemn the land, but all the councilmen played poker with Robert, and that movement stopped as soon as somebody brought it up. Well, Robert up and died one day of a heart attack, and Louise, who had put up with Robert for years, inherited all the land."

I thought to myself, *he has omitted the part about Louise loving her husband and being grief-stricken to the point she was totally devastated by his death, and what about her commitments to the mental hospital?*

Butch continued, "It seems that Robert left everything to Louise in his Will. They didn't have no children, you see. Louise got everything, including the buses and the farm animals.

"So," Butch says, "yeah, I started seeing Louise right after Robert died. In fact, I took her to Sunday dinner at the Golden Corral a week after he died. She just loved their fried chicken and pecan pie. Since I was one of his best friends, I knew that I could do a lot to comfort her. She cried a lot, but I made her laugh. In fact, I think I was the only one that she ever had a good time with, and I taught her how to party. I introduced her to Southern Comfort—I mean the sweet whiskey. Sometimes it seemed like she couldn't get enough of it. We went out a bunch of times though, and one night she got drunk. We were, you know, trying to do it. My belly got in the way, and I had forgotten my Viagra. She kept getting drunker and drunker. Finally, she got mad about me not being able to raise the flag. Blamed it all on me! She jumped out of the bed stark naked, said she'd find somebody who could, and ran outside. She went plum crazy. That was two winters ago."

I tried to picture all this, amid kudzu, covered buses, cats and Doc, Louise's German shepherd as the helpless witness. *Butch,* I asked myself, *did you lock her out of the house?* I was getting nauseous, and anger was making my face flush. *Keep a poker face,* I told myself!

Butch continued, "I went out to look for her, but she couldn't be found. I even went in one of the buses that was close to the house, but she wasn't there. I hollered and hollered. She was nowhere. Thirty minutes before that, she had said she loved me madly. Women, so damn fickle, so I had to leave. The next morning they found her frozen under that big magnolia tree in the front yard—alcohol still in her blood. She must have been hiding before she landed under the tree 'cause I sure couldn't find her. Mind you, I tried! With my history of ugly romance, I thought it best I lay low and say nothing.

"Now it turns out that Louise owned all of Robert's land, just like I said. She had had a will, but it left everything to Robert, who was already dead. So she had no good will at all. I have learned from the law firm that Louise's estate passes to her cousins who are the children of her dead aunts and uncles. It passes by state law this way because Louise's folks are also dead. But I knew what I had to do to preserve her memory based on what she told me time after time—'Butch, I love you, I want you to help take care of things should something happen to me.' I shoulda made her write it down."

Finally, I spoke. "Butch, as you obviously know, I am the named and appointed personal representative of Louise's estate. Now both Louise and Robert are dead, and I am trying to finalize her estate for the Greenville

County Probate Court. Since the cousins are the intestate heirs, how could you possibly be of assistance to me in getting this estate probated and closed? Louise's estate seems to be going in equal shares to the cousins."

Heather had coached me well. But I knew it couldn't be that simple, or he wouldn't be going to this much trouble.

"Well," he said, "I know all the cousins, and they want me to sell the real estate for them. I got a very big deal all put together. I can make a big commission. You are in charge, and you need to grease all the wheels. I am going to need contracts that secure the land and my relations with these blood-sucking relatives." His eyes got narrow. "You see?"

Obviously. For some reason, I knew that I had not entirely come to the same conclusion as Butch, but I could not grasp why. What was I forgetting?

"Well, for one thing, Butch, in an intestate estate, I have to get court approval to sell all the real estate," I said, trying to stall him. "I have to bring an action before Judge Poe and the Pickens County Probate Court as well to get court approval to sell the real estate in each county. We have real estate in two counties. In the meantime, I am behind the eight-ball with Judge Poe. She is pushing me for answers. I still have to report to her the status of the case which I am still unable to do. I don't know everything yet . . . Also, the big land deal sounds great, but the cousins don't have to sell the property. They can just inherit the land as tenants in common, and each own their individual shares without selling it." I am relieved that I can actually remember probate and real estate law without having to look it up in the statutory code books. Heather to the rescue again.

"You don't seem to understand, Fred! They want to sell, and I've got a buyer who wants all of it. He will pay top dollar for it. You and I will make millions in commissions!" Apparently, the greedy Butch is also familiar with the provision of the probate code giving a statutory commission of five percent to the personal representative for the sale of any real property from Louise's estate. "Butch, you do realize that all my commissions go as fees to my law firm, right? Not to me."

"Well, Freddie Boy," he replied, "we'll just have to see about that!" Then he winked.

All of a sudden, things started to get clear. Louise—Butch—Wiley—and Travis. Louise was probably tricked and murdered, and I have been set up by Butch. I gritted my teeth and calmly inquired.

"Butch, what have you promised Wiley and Travis?" Tit for tat . . .

"Well, let's just say they are helping me with this land transaction and how to deal with you, being as how you have hurt your head and can't remember anything. They are keeping me posted on what the judge thinks and how much you remember." He tapped my head at this point. "You see, I've got a big investment already." He kind of bulked up in a menacing way, like some kind of threat posture for a big bug. I felt defensive and guilty over his assumptions about my obvious lack of professional character in the past and his history of manipulating me. I also feel a sense of great relief! My memory is coming back in bits and pieces.

At the same time, my mood is saddened with empathy for the poor little girl from the mill hill. She grew up to be a materially wealthy woman, but she died alone and frozen from a broken heart. No wonder a force from my subconscious came to me in a dream to help me dust off and charge the battery of my stalled brain. Butch was a conniving greedy criminal conspirator who also had an endless network of contacts throughout the upstate to achieve his goals. How did I ever get mixed up with him? He had set Louise up too, I was sure. I felt sick to my stomach, but at least a part of the mystery of Wiley and Travis was clear. Even so, they knew the complexities of the law. They also knew things that are conspiratorial don't necessarily work out in the courtroom. The courtroom is a place of unpredictability. Even an old hand like Butch knew that. Plus, Travis had no use for Butch. At least that is what she told me. She had emanated animosity describing Butch's legal entanglements with me and the law firm. So was it all so neatly arranged as Butch thought?

He growled, "The judge has told you to finish this case. We are ready to go! You got 'er almost all done, boy, and I've already done all the work, including finding the buyer. The cousins are ready to sell, so all you need to do is schedule a hearing! That's your job, Fred. Before your accident, you were running all over the countryside doing who knows what instead of sitting in your office and getting the paperwork ready to file with the court. You wouldn't even answer my phone calls. Then you had your wreck. Now you're better. I want to know right now when you're going to get this case heard, and what you're going to do to get things rolling the right way. Got it?"

With this, he turned to look me squarely in the eyes.

CHAPTER FIFTY-FIVE

Well now I knew more. But I still had big holes in my memory. I knew I couldn't reveal anything to Butch—or for that matter, Travis or Wiley. My instincts had been correct, so I just said, "Butch, I'm working on it again. I just don't remember everything . . . but thanks for telling me your side of things."

"Well you have to remember something or pretend you remember something so you can get the petition ready and filed. Like tomorrow. I think you can figure out how it should read." He went out to his car and dug around in the trunk, came back with a file folder full of notes and a file of legal documents. "Here—there are copies of any document you might want. I've got stuff about every relative and all the property descriptions for Greenville County and for Pickens County. Here." He put his hand on my arm. "I want land deals to go through. Now!"

"Well, Butch," I said, "I am sure it will all work out for the best." He frowned.

"There you go—getting all idealistic and noncommittal on me. Oh, by the way, Louise gave me this cabin before she died. After she gave it to me, I transferred it to one of my shell corporations. It's not in her estate. It's all yours, buddy. Here is the certified copy of your deed."

He looked down at his Rolex. "It's two thirty. Eva should be here in a minute. I'll tell you what . . . I'll leave ya'll alone." He winked. Then he added, "She really loves you." And he rolled his eyes.

Just then, I heard the gravel crunching, and sure enough an EMS vehicle was rolling up the hill, no sirens, no flashing lights. Eva pulled in the driveway beside Butch. She got out in her uniform, crisp and pressed, although there were dark stains under her armpits—she must have been working. "Hey, uncle," she said brightly without looking at me.

"Hey, baby doll," he said. "At last Freddie boy here knows now. It was high time we told him."

"I agree, Unc." Eva looked trim and fit. No longer pregnant.

"Now, honey, can you take him back down to town? Please."

"Sure, Uncle Butch."

"Good." He looked at me, shook my hand, and patted me on the back as he left. "I'll talk to you later." The tires on his big car crunched on the gravel as he drove away in departure.

On the one side—corruption. The greed and driven power of this rich man. On the other side—the power of lust and love. Like two pincers of a scorpion.

There was even electricity as I looked into Eva's eyes, more power.

The only power I felt in me was swimming—right here in this moment I wanted to dive in the pond.

Maybe Eva would like to skinny dip?

"Why are you laughing?" she asked, as she began to disrobe, unbuttoning each shiny button on her EMS uniform, her armpits still wet and stained, and her hair loosened from the tight bun for work.

"Well, I just thought we might go skinny-dipping," I said, feeling myself start to swell.

"Now that's not a bad idea." And she began to hurry—shoes off, socks off, pants off, shirt off, brassiere off, panties off.

All draped over available furniture—half-finished antiques and a tabletop.

My clothes mixed in there too.

Towels thrown over our shoulders—we held hands down to the pond.

I hesitated. I knew nothing about this pond.

She dove in without hesitating. When she came up, she said, "I used to swim here—skinny-dip in fact. It used to be a swimming lake in the daytime and a fishing lake at night. Come on, the water's nice."

I jumped in and could feel no bottom. The water was cool, enveloping me in the basic element—water. There was an odor of pond—eau de mud and leaf rot—with a whiff of fish, another element is earth. She looked more beautiful than ever, sleek and shiny as a bass.

We swam for a while, bumping up against each other. I felt the smoothness of her side and her leg. She swam against me, nuzzling my neck with wet kisses, doubly wet from the pond. I felt her legs, and she lay back in the water staring at me seriously like a mermaid in heat. The third element is fire.

I felt like a tree trunk.

We made it only halfway up the bank, and I dragged her down onto the towels. Just then, she screamed.

"You're not supposed to do that yet," I said, so happy to frolic surrounded by light dappling us, green leaves, black tree trunks, bird song, butterflies, frog calls and chirps.

"No, there's a snake!" she yelled. Sure enough right there about three feet away was a big copperhead sunning himself just off the path to the pond.

I became limp as a rope or a sunning himself.

"I'm . . . I'm . . . I'm afraid of snakes," she said.

"But you're the EMS tech."

"So what—I'm naked right now, and I really don't like copperheads."

"Okay, let's go real slow. He is not moving." So we slowly . . . slowly . . . slowly . . . came to our knees and then to our feet. The copperhead hadn't moved. There was traffic on the road down below. The magic of the scene had slithered away like we wanted the snake to do. I looked for a stick, but there was nothing that didn't look like a snake, so she walked ahead, and I walked behind, both of us keeping our eyes on that patch of sunlight where the copperhead lay. When we finally made it to the cabin, we were cold and cautious. We bathed separately, as if the pond had baptized us in unholy water. I suddenly felt miserable as she began to put on her clothes. "Wait a minute."

"Why?"

"Well just a moment ago, we were together. Now you seem to be ready to leave."

"Well, honey, we've got to get back. We used up all our time on that damn snake."

"Yes, yes, I can see that. But now I'm full of questions. As long as we were in the water, I couldn't even think of them. Now they are flooding in."

"What do you mean?"

She continued dressing. I started to dress too, reluctantly. "Well, I didn't know that Butch was your uncle, for example, and now I'm not sure what to believe. I still can't remember very much, although I do know we had a passionate affair, and it is still with us. What about the baby?"

She looked me in the eye and held me. She was still half dressed. "Oh, honey, honey, honey—if you only knew."

"If I only knew what?"

"If you only knew how complicated my life has been. They told me not to love you, but I couldn't help it." She started to cry.

Oh my god, another mystery? This one crying in my arms. Aren't all women mysteries? I would have to postpone any interrogation. I held her close to say, "At least let's agree to have some kind of meeting. With you popping in and out of my life like this, I can't stay focused on what I'm supposed to do. I can't keep looking for who I am."

She stayed quiet and just kissed me. Her clothes fell to the floor again like magic.

On the way home, she volunteered that she didn't know Travis and Wiley, that they had discussed nothing together, and that she had never been close to her uncle Butch. She swore this—"Cross my heart and hope to die!" and she gave me her card and wrote her cell phone number on the back. "Here's where you can reach me anytime you are free."

"What about Jason?"

"I'll take care of Jason."

"What about the baby?"

"He's no problem either."

"Can I trust you?"

"Yes."

She let me off a block before the office. I had to walk past the coffee shop and a sushi bar. Somebody called me from inside. I just waved and kept walking. Whoever it was would have to wait.

CHAPTER FIFTY-SIX

When I got to my office, Lisa had a stormy look. "Wiley left this and told me I'd better give it to you or else."

"Well, Butch gave me this," I said, showing her the file of notes and deeds Butch had left with me.

She had a similar pile of papers.

Just then, Heather came to the door. "Why didn't you come have some coffee after that EMS truck let you off?" she said, her eyes twinkling. She was the voice from the coffee bar.

I ignored the question. "Look, Heather, we've got some documents now." I pulled out my notes, and lo and behold, it looked like Wiley had copied my notes, and Butch's notes were the same as Wiley's—three whole files full of the same information. What did they mean? We were supposed to draft a reply to the judge's questions out of all this. How were all these the same? Did Butch get Wiley to pilfer my office? Did the judge know we had all this?

Heather, crisp and efficient as ever, took one of the files, gave one to Lisa, and let me keep one. "Can you work here tonight?" Heather asked. Before I could reply, she said, "I can't work at my house because of my children and my husband. I'll be here tonight. We can work together, but no monkey business—I know your reputation."

I was shocked. Me, a southern gentleman. "Heather, look, you are fetching and much prettier than the Gaffney peachoid—but I can . . . I can control myself—and this work must come first." I couldn't tell if that reassured her or insulted her. Come to think of it, the Gaffney peachoid is a big water tower and isn't very pretty any way.

"Lisa, will you please organize these materials as best you can?"

Everybody nodded. "What time, Heather?"

"Seven fifteen sharp."

It was four o'clock. Wiley wouldn't be looking for me for another hour or so. I wanted badly to go swimming, distract myself, let this situation dissolve in the blue water of the pool. The day had gone from skinny-dipping in a mountain pond to diving into documents with all your clothes on. I needed a swim.

But I had work to do. Which, by the way, is always what happens. Whenever you need to be baptized again, there is work to do. Whenever you need to discover yourself again, there is work to do. Whenever there are questions about love and longing, there is work to do. Here I was, a brain-damaged lawyer, stuck between three lives—my life before all this; Butch, the firm; Eva; and in the way past, Travis—and wasn't I supposed to be married before all this? Now I have to sort through legal documents.

During the last eight to ten months, after I woke up, I did kind of understand and kind of remember many, many things that had happened but not all. Now Heather and I would work to add more things.

As for my life after this—that kind of question about the future is never sure for anyone. Who knows what tomorrow will bring or the day after that or the week after that or the month after that.

I had been a healthy man until I was trapped in the flames of a burning car—at least my skin had grown back, and I could work on my neurons and my memory pathways now. I could swim, even swim fast.

Now it looked like I was going to be a real lawyer again.

I picked up the files. I put my notes on the left for tonight's meeting with Heather. I had seen the deeds earlier, and now I understood the notes from Butch. I also knew what he wanted me to do, essentially petition the court to have all his land deals approved assuming that Louise's cousins inherited all of her property. The two of us would benefit financially from the huge commissions. Whether the law would support that or not is evidently in question, or Butch would not have gone to such lengths to influence me— even though I was his old advocate. I was to report to the court so evidently the judge trusted me. The deeds, even though in slim folders, were piled high with questions.

In my secret drawer, there were two other folders—a slim folder, well ordered, that said divorce decree on the outside. The other folder was fatter and looked disordered—that was my journal. I didn't remember either of these files. From the looks of it, I had tried to write a lot.

The divorce file went as divorce files usually go . . . plaintiff and defendant . . . list of assets . . . marital property . . . dreary and cold. So sayeth the court.

I remembered nothing. How curious. I loved this person enough to marry her, live with her, share her sweat—maybe we brushed our teeth together. Maybe we bathed in the same shower. Maybe we liked the same food.

Maybe we didn't. Maybe we took evening walks—maybe we drank coffee in the morning.

Who knows? I couldn't remember a single thing. But isn't it like that with most divorces as people "get over" old romance, try to find new romance to get swept away in the torrent of sex and longing?

All these things flickered through my mind like scenes from a movie, not put into words.

For a lawyer, nothing is real until words are put on paper and signatures are fixed and notarized. But for this divorce, I couldn't remember it, and I couldn't remember my marriage either. The paperwork didn't matter, notarized or not.

Maybe the fire and the wreck were actually good for me.

My past burned up on the side of a mountain.

The journal was easier. Fragments of observations on Greenville, halves of halves of introductions to short stories, notes for poems, random thoughts.

I couldn't tell where or when I had written these things. There were only occasional dates. Some were on note cards, some on legal pads.

It was a collection of thoughts without structure, no outlines, no clear logic until I came across this—Easter time 2000. Everyone worried about Y2K. It's all over the place, even as we celebrate the triumph of Christianity over paganism—blood, grapes, rebirth, and the new green world of spring.

Usually, I wonder about thinking of these things; but according to my journal, this particular Easter I was occupied with the law:

"Let me tell you about the Law. It is, above all else, a fiction. At times, a very inconvenient one. I compare it to the rules governing Olympus, with Apollo and Aphrodite, Zeus, and the whole divine lot settling their grievances by courts like our own, full of whim, rage, and capitulation. Imagine due process for Hephaestus or habeas corpus for Prometheus. They had rules, I'm sure, even if Virgil or Homer never said so . . ."

Most people think of the law differently. If you are a client or consumer of the Law, you think of it as a somewhat shiny body of rules that either inconvenience you or safeguard you and reflect the Ten Commandments in a vaguely derivative way. That is, in most of the western world.

In Greenville, we pretend the biblical base of the law is stronger . . . in public. The Law keeps you honest or makes you do things right or prevents somebody else from doing things wrong to you. The subtlety of concepts like right and wrong, justice and truth, due process, interpretation—these never enter your mind.

A lawyer knows something different though, for he or she has studied these rules as they were applied in real life. Furthermore, the lawyer uses the fundamental tool of the law—the legal fiction. What is that? The legal fiction is "the piece of a platonic ideal that keeps the rule understandable and tied to a generally agreed-upon standard." The greatest legal fiction of all is "The Reasonable Man." What would a *reasonable man* do? Let's say, for the sake of argument, "that your car is stolen with a passenger asleep in the backseat. You are watching, and you have a gun." Let's say, further, that you are trained in skillful operation of said gun. So you drop to your knees, fire several rounds, and stop the car, having flattened the tires and frightened the thief. He escapes; however, one of your bullets has hit a bystander, who decides to sue you.

"Your Honor, ladies and gentlemen of the jury, as we have discussed today, the facts show that my client was not acting recklessly but protecting his property and his passenger. As a reasonable man, he had the right to save his car from thievery and protect the life of his sleeping passenger." So said my journal.

And we got the man off. The man was Butch, and we managed to exclude the fact that Butch's car was a gift from a widow he had seduced. The bystander was the widow's son and friend of the thief. Butch was on his way to a rendezvous with the son's wife, who was the passenger who passed out from drinking. All this is a good day's work for the great evangelist. Now, none of this is very reasonable, but it doesn't have to be because the reasonable man is only an ideal that hovers over the facts of any case. There is no such thing as a *reasonable man.*

I must confess too that I had tried to be the reasonable man for many years. I saw, in the law, the perfect expression of Plato and Aristotle, my heroes. Grinding out justice by the eternal debates over ideals and realities. I saw myself as a gatekeeper for reason and all my passions were subordinate to it. Not swayed by anything save honor, truth, duty, and logic. I brought reason to bear on my clients' problems and left all the passion to someone else. That is a real lawyer.

This case was so blatantly unfair. I had tangled up the arguments and the facts with trivial technicalities that prevented all of the truths from emerging. I was disgusted by the outcome, for, secretly, I wanted Butch to lose. His seduction, his unfettered lust made me sick, but he was my client. I had taken the case, and even as it unfolded my own desire to win and defeat the forces against Butch took hold. One more swimming race to win. One more competition.

After the verdict, though, I just walked back to my office, closed the door, cursed, and cried.

Now this was interesting. The journal had summoned a memory up. It had a date—close enough for this to be an event that might have some bearing on Louise's case. This could be important. There was a short note on the adoption of Louise by the Smiths and her childhood with them.

I reread it several times until I thought I could remember. The adoption of Louise was so important in this case. It was the tie that binds or not, so important in the law. Did the Smiths really adopt Louise? If so, did I have a copy of the adoption decree? Where did they live when they were raising Louise? Did the Smiths live in Greenville County? If Louise had not been legally adopted by the Smiths, wouldn't Tammy, her biological sister, inherit Louise's estate as her biological heir rather than the cousins who would not then be considered heirs if there was not legal tie by adoption? Did the Louise have a legal name change? Had Louise kept a copy of her adoption decree? Did I write all of this down correctly? I had been trying to avoid Butch because I was doing research in the surrounding county courthouses to locate the adoption decree. He didn't want me to be so thorough.

I seemed to be thinking clearly back then. I had concluded that it was not entirely clear that Louise's cousins through her adoptive parents would inherit her estate. What if the legal adoption by the Smiths never took place? If it never happened, Louise's younger sister would get it all!

I hid the files again. Wiley had called me and said we were going out. He didn't say where.

"All right," I had told him, "but I have to be back here at seven fifteen. We can't stay out long."

Wiley sounded disappointed. "In that case, we'll run by the Pita House for some grub."

The Pita House was on the way home. It was run by Palestinian immigrants. Something about the name tickled my palate, and I remembered hummus, zatar bread, falafel, and shawarma. Food from the Holy Land, right here in Greenville, a Baptist Jerusalem.

"Fine," I said.

That's what we did, and I felt fortified for the evening. Damn, I had not had time to review my notes at all, but at least I wasn't hungry.

Curiously, Wiley had asked no questions.

CHAPTER FIFTY-SEVEN

At seven fifteen sharp, Heather was there waiting for me in the lobby. We adjourned to a conference room down the hall and spread our files out on the table. She was diligent and all business. No perfume, no makeup, no slits in her dress.

I couldn't help thinking that Heather was, in fact, a reasonable woman, crisp and logical, ready to get to work. A woman lawyer, through and through.

She did wear nice nail polish, however.

First, we compared our files, and they matched document for document. This meant that someone, somehow had copied my file—snuck it out of my briefcase, copied it, then snuck it back in, unbeknownst to Lisa.

Maybe it was Lisa. I tried not to be paranoid.

It didn't matter anyway because this was our starting point—maybe our finishing point as well. The documents would speak for themselves.

"Okay, Heather, do we divide this by chronology, by category, by relevance, by admissibility?"

Heather pondered this for a moment. "I believe we should start with chronology but then make notes as to potential relevance." She whipped out a huge yellow legal pad and three sharpened pencils. "Okay," she said as she leaned over and touched my hand, "are you up for this? I learned this afternoon from Wiley how damaged your brain had been, and I don't want to overstress you."

"Well, isn't Wiley sweet? If I get stressed out, I will tell you, and you can tell me later everything else he might have said."

Heather pulled her hand away and resumed her legal efficiency. All business. "Okay, let's see the events that occurred from 1998 to 2002. First, we have an obituary for her husband—apparently a fine man who, despite or perhaps because of his eccentricities, was a town favorite. There was an annual concert at his grocery store, and early on, he gave tours of his bus collection. Later, the cats, dogs, and farm animals ran people away."

There were two large glossy photographs. One of the buses before they had been overgrown and the second after the vines covered them—honeysuckle, kudzu, confederate jasmine. You could see cats in the shadows. The obituary mentioned a sudden illness, and there were medical notes appended.

The description of the property took me aback. There were one thousand acres that encompassed the family farm and the bus collection. Then, there was another hundred fifty acres a couple of miles down the road. Then, there were three hundred acres next to the interstate and four hundred more acres in little batches of five, ten, and twenty-acre plots—all of it, by the county map, prime land for multiple kinds of development. More acreage near Highway 123 in Pickens County. This was Butch's dream. There was even a sketch of a housing development and another sketch of a large Bi-Lo grocery store. Neither Heather nor I knew the origin of these sketches.

The next set of documents discussed Louise's prolonged slide into death following Robert's demise. It detailed psychiatric hospital stays with medical notes, drinking bouts, pancreatitis, DTs, and this was all very predictable—her alcohol abuse having begun following the death of her husband and then progressing ultimately to her death.

Heather sounded very sad. "She must have really loved him."

"Well, I am sure that she did," I said. Butch sent her right over the edge, I thought. Alcohol is a depressant, and she was already diagnosed, and he just accelerated her death or caused it. "The point is that Louise was the sole heir of Robert's estate, and that estate has already been probated in Greenville County Probate Court," I said rather abruptly. "So it is, and has been, all in her name."

Heather looked at me in a way I had not noticed before. She seemed pleased that the intricacies of the law were coming back to me.

Just then we got a call from her husband. She looked at me and motioned to the phone, mouthing, "That's my husband," and I motioned with my head for her to go ahead and take it. "Oh, hey, honey," she said, "yes, we're making progress. I'll get home as soon as I can. No, he hasn't attacked me yet. I promise I won't let him. All right, I'll call you before then." She rolled her eyes.

She turned to me and said, "Fred, I don't know everything that you've done to make your reputation as a rogue, but it's out there. Hopefully doing a good job this time will rescue it." She touched me again.

"Wait a minute," I said, "I thought I wasn't supposed to touch you."

"Well," Heather said, "there are just different rules for boys and girls. I can touch you. You can't touch me, got it?" She grinned and winked at the same time.

"Yeah, right." Why does everybody wink?

As we kept trudging through these documents, I was struck that there were too many of them. "Me think the lady doth protest too much." They were an invitation to get mired in detail.

The practice of law is often like that—motions, countermotions, objections, interim rulings, postponement, continuances—etcetera, etcetera, and etcetera. A simple matter of who gets what can degenerate into a battle of dictation and transcription. She who has the best transcriptionist wins.

The strength of the law is its masculine reasoning—like Alexander the Great cutting the Gordian knot. The search for the rule that applies the most simply and cleanly and the arguments in favor of that are what should determine the outcome of the case. This is not always clear. Especially in Corporate Law. However, Probate Law did have a fairly clear set of rules and interpretations to apply to any given circumstance. Judge Poe was a master of this. Solomonic in her grasp of relevant detail.

I think I finally knew that I had to find the simple key to all this.

We plunged on through the gruesome details of Louise's last days. She was the prey. Butch was the predator.

One night, Butch created a deadly cocktail for Louise of alcohol, seduction, sex, rage, and freezing weather. It felt like a plot. He must have waited for months for just the right moment to set it in motion. There was the sheriff's report of finding her naked and frozen under the tree outside her house. No foul play presumably—so what exactly did Butch do? There was no mention of Butch in this report, but it wouldn't have surprised me if the reporting officer was a friend or relative or relative of a friend. I saw no mention of Louise's dog. The one in my dream.

"Heather." I put my hand across the files. "How much do you know about Butch?"

"You mean Butch Canal?"

"Yes, the person we just spoke about."

"Well, I understand he is interested in all this property—so what? Besides wanting to make a big commission on the sale of the property, there is nothing special about that."

"Did you know that he had an affair with Louise right to the end of her life?"

Heather's eyes darkened. "Do you have any proof of that? Was he there when she died? Did he make up any of these documents?"

"He was there at the farm that night when Louise died under very questionable circumstances. He said he left before she was found. He said she ran outside in a fit of crazed and drunken rage, and he could not find her himself. Stark naked, mind you, when they found her. Now he is so involved with this probate case that he is trying to orchestrate everything that happens. I think Wiley and Travis are his spies." He must have bigger plans than just commissions.

Heather's head shot up, and she stood straight from her chair, no longer hunched over the file.

"Why that tricky little . . ."—she pointed a finger at me—"Travis—Travis has been pumping me for information about this all week long, and I promised I would call her tomorrow." I stood up too and tried to calm her down, but she was fuming. She had to march around the conference table, long and glossy, several times before she could sit down again.

"I can't remember everything I told her."

"Well, don't worry about it. What's done is done."

"We are still in the last game of this chess match. They have surrendered all the documents that exist and will be submitted to the court unless we find something else. It strikes me that there is too much fluff here. Let's sit down and plan what needs to be done now."

"Yes, I believe there are too many uncorroborated affidavits, too many declarations of intent without Louise's signature. And of course, there was her will leaving everything to her deceased husband—a will of no effect because he was already dead. No children either."

"Okay, let's keep going, I think I can clarify all this."

Next, there were a series of affidavits about Louise this, Louise that. The gist of all of them—from the grocer, the school system, her colleagues, tax records of her parents—was that Louise was the adopted child of the Smiths, and she had the same legal name—Louise Smith—as her parents.

In this little collection of affidavits, Heather found one that stood out.

It attested to her parentage in a peculiar way. It acknowledged that she had been born Louise Gentry but that early in her life, her birth mother had given her to another older couple to raise. There was no mention of a legal adoption. She had taken their name and had gone by that same name, Louise Smith, her whole life until she married Robert. This was the first clear mention of a potential complication.

"Read that to me again," I said. Heather did. "Is there a mention of any siblings?"

"No, but we know that Tammy Gentry was definitely a younger sister raised by the maternal grandmother."

"All right, put that down on our yellow legal pad—'Did Louise have any other siblings? What do we know about Ruby Gentry, the mother?'"

"As far as we know, Ruby had no other children besides Louise and Tammy. She, uh, I think she had a reputation for being, well, being popular with the men on the mill hill. But she also had a good work history as a doffer for Judson Mill for thirty years," Heather replied. "We would know if there were other children. Apparently, there were not. Also, there was no father listed on either one of the children's birth certificates."

"Good," I said. "At least we don't have to worry about Louise's Baby-Daddy or his kin out there who might have a claim to her estate." Heather laughed.

The cousins who were kin to the Smiths were another matter. Both of the adults who had raised Louise had multiple brothers and sisters who were now deceased. They had multiplied like rabbits. Their children, the cousins, were numbering almost fifty relatives who would take their parents' proportionate share by intestacy. Locating them and obtaining all their addresses and information was a tedious, but very important task. Fortunately, Heather had accomplished this mission in my absence, and she had even done a spreadsheet. I was impressed, but I wondered if . . . "Heather, I think Butch got a copy of your research. Do you know how he got it?"

She looked shocked and shaken. "No, absolutely not! You know I wouldn't give it to him," she replied. "There are certain things I do not do, and one of them is ignoring my duty of confidentiality as an attorney. My license to practice law is too important to me. Who in this office would do such a thing?"

"Travis or Wiley, I don't know," I replied. "But Butch has it, and he has herded the cousins into his corner to act as their agent and sell all the real estate to the highest bidder . . . By the way, I believe you."

"Thank you," she said with much relief.

I was becoming a lawyer again. There was even an affidavit from a nurse during Louise's various hospital stays stating how loyal Louise's sister, Tammy, had been. She had visited Louise every day and stayed with her at night on occasion. The cousins barely knew Louise. There was a final affidavit from the woman who claimed to be her sister, stating simply, "I am

Louise's younger sister and only living relative. We never knew our daddies. I loved her. I was loyal to her throughout her life. We stayed in touch. Our mother was just too poor to raise us both. Our grandmother raised me." Signed, Tammy Gentry.

"So, Heather, what do you think?"

"Well, Fred, it looks fairly straightforward to me. One side—the cousins— may be heirs by intestacy through the adoptive parents. Then on the other side, there is a claim of biological sisterhood. I am very tempted to report this to the judge as is unless you want to track down all these affidavits and records that might show whether Louise was actually legally adopted or not. It all seems to hinge on that question."

"By the way, Fred, here's another wrinkle," she said. "One of the cousins mentioned to me that he remembered visiting young Louise and his aunt and uncle in a house outside Easley. You know what that means. The adoption records are probably in Pickens County."

I had retrieved the simple key to the case. Obviously, I had been looking into the adoption issue before the wreck, but I had no memory or documentation of this.

"You're right. We have no choice. We have to look for the adoption decree," I concluded. "Just to be thorough, since we don't know a lot about the Smiths who adopted Louise, we need to check the records not only in Pickens County but Greenville and Anderson Counties too. Hold off on informing the court for now."

There was a knock at the door.

"Just a minute," I said, turned to the door, then back to Heather. "Well, Heather, I knew I could depend on you to clarify all this with me. I am still not thinking clearly, but this is lucid, and I think we can put it to rest for the judge if I can locate the adoption decree." We both stood, and I gave her a friendly hug. "Thank you so much."

Just then, the door burst open. Heather screamed, "Ronald!"

Ronald screamed, "Don't you touch my wife!"

I just sat down. It was nine o'clock. They didn't let me scream.

CHAPTER FIFTY-EIGHT

We spent thirty minutes calming Ronald down. Ronald was, of course, Heather's husband, and it turns out Wiley had warned him of me and my reputation. Travis had warned Heather the same. "You can't trust him . . . You know how he is with women . . . Ever since he hurt his head, he can't think straight, and he is impulsive . . ." Ronald was a member of our firm himself, over the corporate division. We had never crossed paths. That section of the law firm deemed Butch's dealings so dirty they wouldn't let him in the door. Plus, he wouldn't pay his legal fees. That is very important.

But after all this was aired in a tortuous conversation, I swore my innocence over and over, and Heather backed me up. It became clear—all three of us had been set up. Heather said, "We've got to help him get his reputation back. The judge would have not appointed him personal representative, despite the terms of the will, if she had not trusted his integrity."

Ronald said, "Well, what about Butch?"

"What about him? That has nothing to do with this in a legal sense—his name is on no document."

"Let me look at this," Ronald said, and he started to burst into the organization of the file that Heather and I had so meticulously prepared.

Both of us stopped him. "Now, wait a minute, Ronald. Let's be more productive."

"How is that?" he said, his eyes still pouring venom toward me.

"Let's pretend you're the judge, and we'll present what we have to share with the court."

He liked the idea of being the judge.

Ronald was a corporate lawyer and accustomed to arcane rules involving many pages of legal reasoning. "Oh, the widget had a patent that lasted a full two and a half years as opposed to two years and five months, three weeks, two days, and twenty-three and a half hours. The statute allows for no legal or persuasive extension of time in this case, therefore, the licensing agreement in place for the last five years is null and void, and the defendant owes five million dollars or something like that."

In a way, I liked Butch's methods better—sneak around, and when you finally get to the point where you shake your hands, the deed has already been transferred and snugly recorded. No fighting in public.

But Ronald made an excellent judge. Somehow, Ron, Heather, and I had come to the same conclusion.

We were ten minutes into the presentation when Ronald just stood up and said, "I agree, either there's some sort of adoption decree out there, or there's not. You have to find out whether Louise was legally adopted. That's it, and that's all of it. There has to be more leg work, but it should be simple. This case will have a fair resolution . . . if we answer the adoption question."

I thought for a moment—Ronald had confirmed our plan of action. But then something crossed my mind. Call it a suspicion.

"Ronald, did you agree to report back to Wiley on all of our deliberations?"

His face got red, and he lowered his eyes.

Heather shouted at him. "Ronald, I thought you were a better person and lawyer than this!"

Ron just mumbled, "I'm sorry."

I said to Heather, "He helped us to get to this point, and now we all have to agree to keep this secret." Everybody shook hands firmly. Ron too. I added more ominously, "Look, I think my car wreck and the burns I suffered had something to do with all this. When Heather and I go to Pickens County Courthouse to research the issue of Louise's adoption tomorrow, we must go in separate cars in case they follow us." Heather's eyes grew wide, and Ronald's did too, even though he was familiar with dirty tactics, bribes, and corporate corruption. "In fact," I said, "Ronald, you drive with Heather. Then they will think—that the whole situation is under control. We'll meet at nine o'clock tomorrow, okay?"

"Yes," everyone agreed.

In the meantime, I said, "I have changed my mind. I am going to draft a status report to Judge Poe presenting our present conclusions and planned course of action. I'll have it hand delivered by Lisa to Judge Poe in the morning. Just in case something happens to me again . . ."

As Ron hurried out the door, Heather turned around and grabbed my shoulders. "I am not afraid. You can do this!" she declared. "Also, once we figure out how to research the old records in Pickens County, I'll sneak over to the Greenville County Courthouse, get it done there, and then head to Anderson County. I was a title searcher before I went to law school."

Thinking back on this scene, I was amazed at how well I had thought through everything. I had understood what Heather said, I had understood what Ronald said, and I had contributed thoughts of my own. But now I also knew why I felt uneasy. Now, I had to worry about the trip to the Pickens County Courthouse.

There was a lot of property at stake. Louise's husband was one of the largest landowners in the state, and Butch wanted to broker control of all of it with the cousins, every last red clay mud ball. The only thing he didn't want was the cats in the bus. He may even have tried to kill me over it. Did he know I had been looking for the adoption decree? Pickens County was his territory, and we were going to search for an adoption decree there or rather, a lack of an adoption decree, that could stop him in his tracks. I had wrongly assumed the Smiths had only lived in Greenville County their whole lives and if there was an adoption decree that's where it would be. However, Pickens County now was the most logical place to look first. But Butch probably knew that too, and I wondered to what lengths he would go to make up evidence of an adoption by the Smiths.

We were definitely going in two cars.

When we got back from our search, I was going for a long swim.

CHAPTER FIFTY-NINE

I tossed and turned all night. Wiley came in late and checked on me, but I pretended I was asleep. Who knows what he wanted. My dreams were chaotic fragments of women, mountain cabins, Butch, real estate, women, Eva, legal documents, Travis, affidavits, women, Travis, perfume, Eva, Butch, legal documents—stitched together as some crazy narrative that woke me up hour after hour. It was a long swim—through the river of night.

I got up and took an extra pill from my seizure medicine—the doctor said I could do it. The dreams got softer and didn't wake me up. They were still there, still stuck to my mind when I finally woke up for good. I was tired.

Six o'clock. Much of the world was already on the road, and the Pickens County Courthouse wouldn't be open that early, but I needed breakfast.

Heather and Ronald and I met at my office—there in the labyrinthine pool of law as I had begun to call it.

Ronald said, "Labyrinthine, that's not bad. Sorry, Fred, you know, about last night."

I looked at him carefully. "Ronald, you don't need to apologize. Heather is a treasure, and you were just protecting her—I believe that, but I also believe that you were sent there by Wiley and through Wiley, by Butch. So are you truly in with us or not?"

Heather looked at him with her lips in a thin line. "You'd better be" was written all over her face, although she couldn't say anything because she clenched her jaws so tightly. If she had tried to talk, she would have broken her jaw.

Lisa, of course, said nothing.

Ronald nodded and then said, "Look, you guys, I didn't know the whole story. Now I do. Let's get on the road." He assumed his corporate lawyer, take-charge manner—yellow tie with a thin red stripe, Brooks Bros. shirt, and Italian loafers—come to think of it, he dressed like Butch without the cufflinks and the big rings, and he wasn't so fat.

Heather was in a power suit—navy blue colored, modes-length skirt, striped blouse.

I never wore anything but a blue blazer and khakis—and after all, we were going to Pickens County, not Manhattan.

I reached over and messed up Ronald's hair to the glee of Lisa and Heather. "Look," I said, "we're going to Pickens County. You guys look too good." I grinned, while Ronald, flustered, tried to comb his hair back in place with his fingers. "Let's go. Ya'll lead the way . . . on second hand, maybe somebody better ride with me. I don't remember how to get there." Ronald said he would take me. Heather would go up Highway 8.

As we were leaving, Lisa said in a whisper, "Tell me what happened last night when you get back." I winked this time.

Ronald wasn't bad on the trip up and, in fact, proved to be helpful as he dissected, in legal fashion, the various points of corruption that Butch had set up in all of this. The seduction of Louise, the gift of the cabin to me—from Louise's property—the supposed oral contracts, maybe written contracts with one set of heirs—the "affidavits" that smelled like Butch dictated them. Now we were headed into Butch's home territory—Pickens County. He was behind every tree here.

His cousin was the sheriff; another cousin, through marriage, was the register of deeds. He had a couple of in-law cousins who were magistrates. He had the whole place sewed up in blood kin. Three or four deputies as well. They might be dangerous.

Two cars was a good idea.

Pickens County—mountainous and rugged—they won't let you live there unless you've been shot at and hit—at least I heard that once.

I, of course, couldn't remember it that day, but I can now. The land is tawny and rugged with trees, curvy roads, and lonely house trailers.

Ronald had driven his BMW. Heather had hers. One of them was a convertible, but this wasn't the kind of trip to take with the top down. Heather went up Highway 8. Ronald and I went a more leisurely way through Easley. It was a beautiful day—full of sunshine—and for me, portent. What would we find? All of us thought it could be the key to this whole sordid mess.

Greed, land, money, seduction—the only thing not present was whiskey and wild women—but Louise was naked. Maybe that qualified. Butch was there—a drunk, and he was a walking scandal all by himself.

When we got to the parking lot of the courthouse, we stood out like sore thumbs among the pickup trucks and SUVs. Two fine Euro sedans, obviously from Greenville. Pickens County had plenty of lawyers, but they didn't look like the ones from Greenville, and they didn't drive the same kind of machines.

We got out of our cars first. Heather looked slumped over in hers. "Oh my god," Ronald said, and he rushed up to her.

She unfolded herself, having just been applying fresh lipstick. She rolled her window down. "You guys calm down. Nothing's going to happen. My mother taught me to never go out without my lipstick."

CHAPTER SIXTY

The Pickens County Courthouse was majestic and modern with brand-new security systems and metal detectors. The clerk of court had worked for years lobbying the state and the county delegation to the legislature. We need a new courthouse—we need a new courthouse—we need a new courthouse. That was her mantra every year, and every year she was elected she pursued it obsessively. Well, she finally had won, and she had accomplished a great thing. The courthouse in its gleaming marble and brick glory was a monument to the ideas of justice, truth, and the law. It was worthy of the Acropolis itself, a temple with columns gleaming in the sun. The only thing lacking was Apollo himself.

Inside, we went straight to the clerk of court's office, where the records of old adoptions were kept—or so we hoped.

"What ya'll want?" the secretary said. We all looked impressive—Heather in her power suit, and Ron and I dressed in lawyer blue with yellow ties.

Heather spoke up first, as is her habit. "We've come to look at the old adoption records."

None of us knew or could remember the exact procedure, especially on old adoption records, and nobody at the firm had done an adoption in many years. Heather reminded me that all adoption records were now filed with the clerk of court in the family court division. Older adoption records were probably filed as judgments with the Register Mesne Conveyances in another part of the court house. "Well, show me your judge's order, and we'll try to arrange that. All those records are confidential. If you're a lawyer, you ought to know that," the woman said dismissively.

Heather once again surprised me with her knowledge of the law. "Thank you for pointing that out to me. I know that all adoption records must be kept confidential after the statute was passed in 1976, except by order of the court," she said smoothly. "However, we are seeking records prior to 1976. In fact, we need to research adoption records prior to 1950. As you know, those records were not kept confidential. In fact, adoption decrees before 1950 were recorded as judgments from the circuit court. Of course, you, as an official of the court, already know all this," she said and smiled sweetly to the clerk, looking her right in the eye.

Ronald and I looked at each blankly—but approvingly—at Heather's knowledge of the law and adoption history; plus she was not cowed by the clerk's attitude. Obviously, no court order was needed from a judge in Pickens County, so we might be able to keep this a secret from Butch. The woman seemed unmoved.

I stepped up—let's try. "Thank you so very much, ma'am. However, as Heather pointed out to you, these adoption records are public if they are not sealed. They are not confidential and would not need a judge's order." Without waiting for a reply, I shoved the list at her. "Here are the names we are looking for," I said. "We would appreciate it so much." We stood before her arrayed like soldiers with machine guns.

The woman looked at us and then the list, then at the list and back to us. Finally, she said with a resigned expression. "Okay, go help yourselves then. You've got to go to the other record room—it's probably even on microfiche by now. The way you do that is go down the hall on the left, turn right, then go down that hall, and then the first hall on the left after you've passed the hall on the right should be a little sign. It's just past the restrooms. Turn left there, and you've got about a twenty yard walk. There are three or four doors—all locked—and a couple of bathrooms in there. Turn left, and there is a little sign on the wall that says "Records Prior to 1960."

Ron said, "Excuse me, could you repeat that?" The secretary looked at us blankly. "Just go down the hall until you find it. Ask somebody out there." She returned the list of names.

Even without the potential menace of Butch, things were getting complicated enough.

We trooped out into the hall after fighting our way out the heavy door—clearly the product of a berserk architect and a maintenance man who thought door springs should be tight as Speedo bathing suits. This thought swam into my mind just when Heather began to walk in front of me. She looked like a swimmer, with broad shoulders and a narrow waist.

We eventually found the door to the records. I tried the door. It was unlocked. I entered, and we began the research for the adoption decree by the index to names for the older judgments from the circuit court. Indeed, they were on microfiche, and there were only two computers. Ronald and Heather sat down at the computers, each dividing up the search by name and decade. I was relieved. They probably surmised that my brain had already been taxed enough in the last few days. They were right. I watched for Butch and busied myself browsing through the multiple volumes of indexes. I found nothing pertaining to Louise, Ruby Gentry, or the Smiths. By then, it was lunchtime. Heather and Ron found nothing of interest in their research. They both concluded that a legal adoption had not taken place in this county because, if it had, it would have been legally recorded here. The courthouse was deserted. Time to go. We had made a thorough search.

We headed down the long hallway. Well, at least we haven't seen Butch—yet.

That is until we looked down the end of the hall, and there he was—shiny gray suit, slick shiny hair, and fancy shoes. I thought I could see myself in the gleam from his fingernail polish.

"Why, hey, ya'll," he hollered from the end of the hall, "what ya looking for?"

Well, we had been caught red-handed, but Ron had an inspiration.

"Butch, Butch, we need your help. We can't get in this record room. We are looking for some of the records that . . ."

"You asked me for," I interjected.

"Oh, you mean stuff on Louise."

"Yes, of course."

He pulled out his cell phone and muttered something to somebody while he watched us—his eyes merry with our predicament.

In about ten minutes, the clerk of court herself came around the corner.

"Oh, hey, Butch." She gave him a peck on the cheek, and he hugged her. "Are these those lawyers from Greenville you told me about last week?"

Heather and Ron went white. I felt fire in my face. "Why, yes, Sarah Beth. They need to do some research."

Now this presented a real predicament—much more real than the fantasy wreck that we had all imagined or the ambush, with Pickens County sharpshooters mowing us down. All that had been fanciful and frightening, but it was all in the mind of a tortured, brain-damaged lawyer who had wrecked his car, and now couldn't depend on his memory.

What was real is the reality of the law and the importance of uncontaminated documents. What if Butch had managed to get Sarah Beth, the clerk of court, to produce documentation or an adoption order in the old county records to accomplish his ends to prove his point and finally get his hands on Louise's land? Had we missed something in the records? What if he had promised land to the clerk of court—he swore he had already given me a cabin, and I had even seen the deed, made love there, and had been interrupted by a snake. Surely, as an elected official, she would not want to take that risk—even for him. What else could he have done? Was I too paranoid? So far, no adoption decree or order in Pickens County. Any more tricks, Butch?

All these thoughts crowded into my mind. I couldn't think clearly and systematically the way lawyers are supposed to.

"Ya'll come on in," Sarah Beth said.

"Mind if I join you?" said Butch.

I thought we'd better get in the door first. If we objected to Butch, Sarah Beth might not let us in. I looked at my watch and calculated quickly.

"Butch," I said, "I think this is going to take a long time, so let's let Heather and Ron work on this thing, and you and me go to lunch. Madam Clerk, do you want something?" She said no. I knew Heather wouldn't eat with all this commotion going on, and Ron didn't think very highly of any food outside the Poinsett Club. "Come on," I said and motioned for Heather and Ron to go on in. "Butch, I need some help navigating out of this place." Butch hadn't fully anticipated this I don't believe, so he went along without a fuss. The clerk of court could be his eyes and ears. I got him about halfway down the hall then ran back quickly to Heather and Ron. "Just pretend you haven't finished. I'll be back in forty-five minutes," I said. Heather seemed to understand. Ron was just there for the ride. He was more comfortable in corporate boardrooms.

Butch had two hamburgers, and I ate his french fries. Downtown Pickens within five or six blocks of the courthouse was a ghost town. Empty buildings, spaces for lease or rent, empty sidewalks. A café served the lawyers, judges, and courtroom personnel. There weren't any other cafés.

Pickens, just like many towns in South Carolina, had succumbed to death by Wal-Mart—first the bypass was built, then the chain stores came in, and finally, Wal-Mart happened. Any downtown commercial traffic that had existed vanished—stuck in the huge parking lots of big box development. I looked at Butch and wondered how much of this he had done.

"Well, Pickens is sure making progress now. We got all these empty buildings, and we got the Pickens Development Commission going last year. You know, I've got a dream for all of Louise's land. I have even had an architect draw up some green roads, green parking lots, and green house layouts." He reached over and grabbed my hand. "It could be beautiful, son."

I detected a kind of missionary zeal that I hadn't seen in Butch up till now—a higher purpose. If he could get the land, he could make changes—schools, indoor plumbing, sewers—the whole crazy vision of progress that animates us like a Greek ideal, like a software update of General Lee himself.

Lucri bonus est odor. Sweet is the smell of money.

I had to play the lawyer a bit.

"But, Butch, what if you don't win this? What if Louise was never legally adopted by her other family? My research says that her biological sister would be her legal heir."

Butch suddenly turned red and angry. "But Louise was adopted," he said loud enough for the whole café to hear him. "I don't know why y'all are lookin' over here anyway. She and her family always lived in Greenville."

A skinny old man in the corner perked up his ears and shouted. "That ain't right, Butch, and you know it."

"Whoa!" Butch almost came out of the booth flinging hamburger. "Shut up, Davey Don."

"You shut up yourself," the old man said. He was about a third the size of Butch, wiry as hair on a boar hog. He had that kind of build that says "stay away or I'll hurt you." The kind of skinny little white man that likes to fight and has been fighting ever since he was a little boy. One pound of those guys is worth ten pounds of anybody else.

Davey Don started to come out of his seat, and I pulled Butch back. "Butch, sit down. Everything depends on the records. You know that. Finish your hamburgers, and let's get back." I had lost my appetite. The french fries lay in the ketchup like the remains of Butch's face if he and Davey Don had come to blows.

I didn't tell Butch this, but I made a note in my mind and hoped I would remember it . . . Hmmmm . . . Davey Don says Louise wasn't adopted. This is exactly what Butch feared and Ron, Heather, and I suspected. What inspired Davey Don to make that statement? Did he know something we could use to sort all this out? Did Butch have no knowledge that the Smith's had probably lived for a time in Pickens County, and that's where the adoption most likely would have taken place?

Butch left me at the door to the restaurant.

Davey Don had disappeared.

Suddenly, it dawned on me. If Butch was going to drum up a counterfeit adoption decree with all his power and influence, he would have already done it. There was no adoption decree for Louise in Pickens County. With a little help from my friends and colleagues, was I finally ahead of his game?

In South Carolina, the Rules of Wills have existed for years. The primacy of real and personal property is sacred. Sacred to the point where cities and even the state go after private property very reluctantly—the legal fees involved are substantial, and many times the state or the city will lose the case—thus, you see, even the most progressive towns like Greenville and Spartanburg and Anderson are hemmed in by pockets of private property that they cannot annex and won't try. This same reverence for private property extends to estates of the deceased.

The last legal competence allowed to a person is on his or her deathbed. All you have to prove is that you know your real and personal property and know who you want to give it to—not a very high standard for most people. With her last breath and a witness, Louise could have given it all to Butch; but in her whiskey-soaked naked state, she didn't. Butch should have thought a little faster, but maybe she didn't want to give it to him. Especially if she knew he was going to shut her outside and freeze her to death!

When we returned to the courthouse, Ron and Heather had done their work. Sarah Beth had abandoned them after Butch left, and they'd found no other record of Louise's adoption. Butch was in the dark on this one.

I told them about lunch and about what skinny little Davey Don had said.

We looked in Anderson County and Greenville County as well—no legal adoption decree or judgment was found. We had done our due diligence. Therefore, we had to conclude that Louise was not legally adopted by the Smiths. Now I needed a finding and final order from the probate court to that effect. It was not enough that Louise had taken the Smiths name, acted as their beloved daughter, enrolled in school, and named them as her parents. She took care of them in their old age, and she also inherited property from both of their estates when they died. However, by law, she remained forever attached to her original biological family. Therefore, Tammy, her biological sister, was the rightful heir. Butch's plans had fallen apart.

CHAPTER SIXTY-ONE

Friday afternoon, just as I was leaving to go swim, Travis slithered into my office, looked around, and closed the door. Fragrant with the opiate of musk.

Cave quid dicis, quando, et cui. Beware of what you say, when, and to whom, *I muttered to myself.*

"I understand there is no record of any adoption of Louise. This means it's all over." She looked at me with a faint question in her eye, breathless.

"Not exactly. I still have to petition the probate court for a final hearing. I am sure the cousins will protest my findings and conclusion," I said. "But yes, it's getting there. They burned me for nothing."

"I have known it all along," she blurted out.

Then she burst into tears. "I . . . I . . . couldn't keep it secret anymore," she said and blubbered out an apology that took us out of the office, into her car, out to her house, and finally to her bedroom. She rambled on for hours, as if she was confessing mortal sins to me and needed forgiveness.

When we finished making love, I knew she and Wiley had protected me from Butch the whole time, watching my back, easing me into the firm and back into the business they knew would await me . . . They had told no one everything and told Butch just enough to get a hold of all his documents.

They even had to keep Jason away from me because he was so mad with Butch. He was watching Eva for me. All this between hugs and kisses.

"This was so hard for me, darling, but I knew I had to let you do it—please stay here tonight. Butch is so dangerous," she said this holding my face to her breast.

We called Wiley, and I told him what had happened. He said, "Oh, buddy, I am so happy you have made up with Travis. It was killing both of us to keep you in the dark, but we knew how wicked Butch could be. We have watched your back the whole time. Make sure you lock the doors. I will see you at the office in the morning . . . And keep your Speedo on."

In between kisses, I thought to myself, *well that's three down—Jason, Travis, and Wiley.* This is starting to make sense, but I can no longer trust Travis in the depths of my heart. *In cardio profundus* or something like that.

"Lisa," I said the next morning at the office, "I think Wiley and Travis are all right."

Lisa scowled and said, "I still don't trust them, but if you want to keep swimming in this pool, as you say, then we will have to stay with them—so okay."

"Yes, and please get Heather on the phone." A new surprise—Heather was at home quarreling with Ron, and I told her I had to draft the petition and request a hearing.

She said, "Fine, let me finish here, and I will be at the office later. Go ahead and get started." Ron was yelling something, and I didn't ask about that. It just made me sad for Heather and Ron.

It's hard enough for a lawyer to stay married, much less two lawyers. One says, "Pass the salt." The other says, "Under what circumstances," "make that in writing."

I began work on the petition—first draft. In the matter of the Estate of Louise Putnam, as ordered by Judge Poe in the Probate Court of Greenville County. I am the petitioner, with Tammy Gentry, cousins named as the respondents . . .

I gave a brief summary of the case. Louise had died with a will, but it was of no effect since her husband, her testate heir, and her parents were deceased. The only thing the will accomplished was the appointment of me as the substitute personal representative in the event of Robert Putnam predeceasing his wife. Thus, the disposition of her property passed by intestacy to her statutory heirs, and therefore the judge had charged me with the task of determining the proper beneficiaries of Louise's estate.

I summarized the case of the cousins; the claim made through Louise's presumed adoptive parents. Would they raise the argument of equitable adoption? Probably so. Would they probably try to rely upon legal documents that supported their case—the school records, the tax forms, and the probate references to receiving estate property from the Smiths, her parents?

Next, I summarized the opposition case made by Tammy's lawyer. Several affidavits by her and her friends and remaining members of her immediate family. Finally, I got to the bombshell. "After an extensive search made in the court records at Pickens County Courthouse, Anderson County Courthouse and Greenville County Courthouse, I could find no adoption records to substantiate the claim of legal and valid adoption by the Smiths.

"Therefore, I must conclude that Louise Putnam was never adopted away from her original biological family. There are no actual adoption records to substantiate the cousin's claim of severance from Louise's biological heirs by adoption. I have concluded that Tammy Gentry, her biological sister, is the sole beneficiary of Louise Putnam's estate.

"Therefore, I respectfully request that the court order that all the real and personal property of Estate of Louise Putnam be conveyed and distributed to Tammy Gentry, her biological sister and legal."

Lisa typed this up, and as I contemplated it, Heather came in looking flushed and muttering.

I touched her forearm. "Heather, it's going to be all right. Let's finish this up."

She looked at me, and there was a hint of a tear—but female lawyers don't like to cry, and I wasn't going to ask any questions. "Thank you," she said in a formal manner.

She reviewed it, made some corrections to the format, and looked at me. "I think we have got to go to the judge now." We hand delivered the original petition and the notice of hearing along with fifty copies over to the Greenville County Probate Court that afternoon to be filed, the hot August sun baking the pavement, making the car shimmer. The final hearing was to take place in forty-five days.

"Heather, please just drop me off at the Y. I need to go for a swim." Before stepping out her car, I said, "Thank you so much . . . I couldn't have done this without you."

"I know," she said. "Now go get into the water. You're a real shark again," she teased. "I'll get all these pleadings served on the parties." Then she drove away, a shark as well.

CHAPTER SIXTY-TWO

We were all present for the hearing in Greenville County Probate Court, except for Butch. Twenty-five of the first and second cousins strode into the courtroom with their legal multiple representatives, mostly younger, but well-respected Greenville probate attorneys. For the most part, the cousins appeared resigned and unhappy. There was no sign of Butch. Tammy Gentry was also present, represented by an older revered Pickens attorney, who was said to know the South Carolina Probate Code by heart. Tammy appeared in a simple shift, with her hair pulled back in a bun. She appeared younger than her fifty-five years. She wore no makeup and flip flops. She spoke politely to some of the cousins who, for the most part, just ignored her.

Tammy, who grew up in a mill village in a shotgun house, was about to become one of the richest women in South Carolina. She was full of kindness, humility, and a sense of family even after her sister was taken away from her poor little family by the Smiths. She remained connected and comforting to Louise even as she was hospitalized for mental illness.

I had visions of her soon pursued by churches, charities, nonprofits, and financial institutions with their hands held out. I hoped she would be able to resist and remain the simple, fine person that she had become without material riches.

I had decided to bring Heather with me in case I got irreversible jitters and lost my concentration or had another seizure. All the attorneys, including Heather and myself, took our respective places at the front of the courtroom and sat down.

As Judge Alexandra Poe swept into the courtroom in her black robe from a door behind bench, we all stood. "You may be seated," she instructed. Then she proceeded to read into the record for the benefit of the court reporter sitting beside the bench, the name of the case, caption, the date, the names of the attorneys, myself as the personal representative, and the purpose of the hearing.

I was mesmerized by Judge Poe's beautiful face. Was that her sexy musky scent that was drifting toward me? Her long black hair and black robe flowed together like a waterfall. My mind began to drift in the direction of Judge Poe's allure that was so distracting. Suddenly I began having a sense of déjà vu. Was I going to have another seizure? My heart was pounding. *Focus, Fred, focus!*

I had been practicing for this moment for a few days with Heather's instruction and critique. I wanted to say the right thing, be procedurally accurate and concise in my argument to the court and the recitation of facts. Nevertheless, my hands were clammy, and I felt nauseated. I tried to focus by looking down at the pleadings on the desk in front of me and breathing in and out slowly.

We were called to order, and the judge indicated I would speak first. She actually called out my name. My name. How could I forget this personal intimate moment? I stood up and started to speak, but nothing came out. I stared at Judge Poe's face. Moments passed.

"Mr. Tutem?" She called my name again. Suddenly, I felt a ferocious painful pinch on the back of my knee from Heather who was sitting beside me. Wow, did that hurt! The sting and pain jolted me back to my purpose.

"Excuse me, judge, I just got distracted for a moment. I haven't been in the courtroom for a long time. I apologize," I said.

"Mr. Tutem, we are aware of your long absence, and we are so happy you have returned," she said.

Aware of my absence? Happy I've returned? These words were sweet vibrations to this shark's skin. Do I have my fins back?

I cleared my throat and began. I was back in the pool again, and this was my race to win. I had no competitors. I would win for Louise who had to be watching me from somewhere, no longer in a dream.

I was undistracted for the rest of my presentation and argument which lasted at least thirty minutes. I finally sat down faintly dizzy.

Judge Poe said, "Mr. Tutem, thank you so much for all your hard work, research, and conclusions. They are of great assistance to the court."

I hoped the record was clear to the court that Tammy, Louise's little sister, was the rightful heir. When I sat down, Heather squeezed my hand and whispered, "Well done. You had me worried for a moment." I squeezed her hand back.

I knew these other attorneys. Each side argued their respective positions, and, as I had expected, they argued equitable adoption of Louise by the Smiths supported by school records, affidavits, and tax records. Estate records from the Smiths also showed that Louise had inherited all their property at their deaths as their daughter. I had concluded that the doctrine of equitable adoption by the Smiths did not exist in South Carolina. Either you were legally adopted through proper legal proceeding or you were not. The other side had also failed to present an adoption decree by the Smiths.

These attorneys had been friends of mine once, but my reckless ways had driven them from me. They had been absorbed in lives of convention and fidelity, while my life had drifted—chasing a swimming pool of erotic adventure. Now, I was back in their pool at last. I was now a professional again. They looked stunned.

Their arguments finally ended. Then Judge Poe leaned toward the other attorneys and said, "If you have any further questions or objections, please state them now."

For once, the most of attorneys were speechless. One of them, looking around at the others, said, "Nothing more from the respondents, Your Honor."

Tammy's attorney rose and stated, "Mr. Tutem has properly stated my client's position in this case, Your Honor. I have nothing to add."

The courtroom was quiet, and everyone's attention was directed to Judge Poe. I was anxiously pondering whether or not she is going to rule from the bench.

She waited a judicial amount of time and then declared, "The record is now closed. I want to thank all sides for their arguments. The personal representative has done a great job, and each of the attorneys has done a fine job in representing their clients."

Next, she said, "I have thoroughly reviewed the record and evidence in this case. I am ready to make my decision. I hereby find that Louise Putnam was never properly and legally adopted by the Smiths. The tie to her biological family was never severed by law. I hereby find, therefore, that Tammy Gentry, the surviving sister and only sibling of Louise Putnam, is her sole and legal heir. Mr. Tutem, please prepare the final order. Thank you all."

"You may all be excused," she pronounced. Then we all stood as she exited the courtroom.

Once again, justice had been done, and the law had fulfilled its purposes.

A sudden emotion swelled up in me, but I couldn't cry.

We were all lawyers after all, and the romance of life is systematically beaten out of lawyers with the first lecture in law school. One professor had said, "There is no room for tenderness." But later, the dean warned us not to lose our abilities for empathy. He said it would make you a better lawyer. But the *way* leaves little room for feelings. There are two sides, and they argue it out every day everywhere—in offices, in courtrooms and record repository, in rule books, and in decisions and legislatures. Adversaries all. All of the time.

I just sat there. Heather beside me. The courtroom was empty.

Just then Judge Poe reentered the courtroom from behind the bench. She picked up her Probate Code Book. Seeing Heather and me still sitting there, Judge Poe dropped the book, walked down from her bench and over to the desk beside me, and asked with a worried look, "What's wrong? Do you need for me to call the bailiff?"

"Nothing," I said, "I'm not having a seizure." I reached out with both hands and patted her hands—which were both beautiful with elegant fingernails and polish that shone like mother of pearl. "Your Honor, you just made me feel like a Virginia gentleman again." Heather smiled beside me.

Then I got up and said, "But I'm in South Carolina now, and Heather and I have to get back to our office—is that all you need from us, Your Honor?"

"Yes, you are dismissed." Her eyes were wet.

PART V

CHAPTER SIXTY-THREE

When Heather and I got out of the courthouse, there she was—Eva in her glory, uniform shiny, creases like knife edges. Heather looked at me and looked at her and said, "Watch out, buddy, you may be a Virginia gentleman again, but you live in South Carolina now." She moved away fifteen or twenty paces, and I walked slowly up to Eva. We faced each other like gunslingers, except what we were slinging was the memory of old kisses and "stuff like that" as Travis had said the other night.

"You talked to Jason, didn't you?" Eva said.

"Yes."

"And he says you believe he didn't try to kill you."

"Yes, but . . ."

"You'll hear from me later," she said now as if she had seen another snake. She looked as mean as Butch.

"Eva, who is the baby's father?" I inquired.

"I put Jason on the birth certificate, and it's none of your damn business," she growled and then walked away.

For me that was one more down. The only one left was Butch.

Butch came by two days later, late in the day. I called Heather in because I wanted a witness.

That's something strange about the law. Everybody always wants a witness, but then there are standards for witnesses and funny little rules about which witness is better, obscure, and arcane arguments about why this witness doesn't apply in this or that case. Again, the rational man asserts himself, and usually the irrational man wants a witness. I didn't care about that. I wanted Heather to be there when I talked to Butch. People can drown in legal rules, like swimmers in a river that's too choked with water from recent rain.

He looked wilted. He had tried so hard. He hadn't polished his fingernails, and his hair was shaggy. His shoes weren't polished—he was, after all, in Greenville County. He was a provincial warlord forced to the capital. Pickens was the seat of his real power.

"So," Butch said, "is it over?"

"Butch, no, it's never over," I said firmly. "Technically, it's not over until the appeal time runs. You can appeal the results of the decision—except you are not really part of this, are you? I guess, practically speaking, you could say it's over. The sister takes all."

"No, actually I'm not a party to all this, but the relatives were counting on me to buy their land, and I was counting on it too. The Pickens County Development Authority had started talks with me last week."

"You are the head of that, aren't you?" I said. Heather giggled.

Butch replied, "Yes, of course, I am, but that doesn't matter. The other guys are with me."

"Well, Butch," I said, attempting to be conciliatory and a peacemaker, "your fortune isn't lost. You still don't know what's going to happen, and you, of all people, know things have ups and downs. As far as I can see, this isn't even a down yet. If we can, Heather and I will put in a good word with Tammy Gentry for you."

Heather jumped like she had been shocked with electricity. "You speak for yourself, Fred."

Butch said, "You guys calm down. You did what you had to do, I know that." He smiled weakly.

"I have one last question, Butch."

"And what is that?" he said, assuming a regal tone.

"Did you try to have me killed?"

"No, of course not. Don't be stupid. You are the only one who has ever helped me achieve my dreams. I know I am not a good man, but it balances out, and I would never try to kill you. Jason was mad, and Eva was hurt, and I wanted that land. You were on to this whole thing about the adoption papers the night you wrecked your car. I had invited you up to Dividing Water to see your cabin and to get a preliminary report, but then you wrecked that damn beemer. That was the end of your playboy days. Jason saved you—whether you know that or not. Anyway, maybe I can talk the cousins into appealing the decision. That equitable adoption thing sounded right to me."

"I don't know, Butch. That's between you and them." When I stood up, Butch slowly got up half-defeated. Heather was just watching.

"Do I need to walk you to the elevator?" I said.

"No, hell, no! I know my way around here as good as the Pickens County Courthouse," Butch said, and he was gone, some fire returning to his step.

I turned to Heather. "When do I tell him he is not a client of this firm any longer?" I said.

"Let's wait," she said, "I still don't trust him."

For me, that was the last peg to fall. Eva was only half down—I would hear more from her, but I thought after Butch left that I might never hear from him again.

My seizures remained under good control. Without the stress of this case and the philandering I had grown accustomed to, I was a different man. One day, after swimming, I realized how clean and fresh I felt. *In omnia paratus*. Ready for anything.

The appeal time passed without incident, so the case was over. Now my real job as the personal representative began—to probate the estate, meet with Tammy, dispose of the estate property, and close the estate—all in due time.

As things progressed, I sold some of the property as Tammy's request. I had a check for her that was too big to send to her, so I decided to deliver it to her personally. I called Tammy to get directions to her little house in the Judson Mill area.

"Well, Mr. Fred, do you not remember how to get here?" Tammy asked.

"Remember that knock in the head I got?" I replied. "Have I been to your house before?"

"Yes, just once. So sorry. I forgot about your accident, but here are the directions again."

As I walked up the porch steps to her house, I heard a dog growling and barking behind the door. It sounded big and ferocious, but I waited as patiently and calmly as I could for Tammy to answer the door. No doorbell or knock was needed.

Tammy came to the door and said to the protecting dog now behind her, "Sit and stay, Doc. Don't be a bad boy for Mr. Fred. He is my friend." It was the German shepherd, Louise's dog! He immediately obeyed and sat down behind her. "Come on in, Mr. Fred. Doc and I are so happy to see you again! I've got some tea ready and a piece of sweet potato pie just for you."

Doc began wagging his tail and licking my hand, just like Louise would have wanted in my dream.

CHAPTER SIXTY-FOUR

It was October now with the sumac turning bright red in slashes by the roadside. The poplars were golden yellow with a fringe of dry brown. Leaves adrift like little ballerinas in gold tutus. The oaks brown and orange and some green at the top. Pines green. Maples gold and red. Up at the cabin, the cool evenings demanded a fire, and I spent more and more time there. I tried out the pond for a swim—this time with my Speedo on. Wiley and I ate supper up there a lot. Smoke from the grill, and the fireplace made odors like perfumes. The frogs and crickets sounded like orchestras of Greek choruses. To a Virginia gentleman, even the crickets and tree frogs know Greek.

Then, as the fall slid into winter and dreary sunless days, Butch called.

"Buddy, Fred, buddy, I have to see you. You must come see me." He sounded drunk. It was not like him to be such an urgent beggar.

But I couldn't turn him down just flat. He was still full of mysteries, and I liked mysteries. Why call now?

"Butch, why? Why do you have to see me? You know I'm a stand-up lawyer now, and this wouldn't look good."

"Who cares?" he said.

"Well, I care!" I thought to myself, if I lie down with dogs again, I'm going to get up with fleas.

"What I meant was this doesn't have much to do with that. I have found a document that you must see. You'll want to see. So meet me at your cabin at eleven tomorrow." And he hung up.

He had given me no time to respond, and I had to wrestle with his demand all afternoon and into my session in the pool. Splash—should I splash, splash—should I not?

I called Heather and Travis and Wiley, and no one answered. I finally decided to go. It would be a beautiful day. The weather forecaster had prophesied, so I took that to be a good omen.

I got there just before eleven, and Butch was not outside or on the porch. Usually, he was punctual, but, oh well, I could sit and rock a bit . . .

Just then I heard a gun safety click off. I turned and faced Butch, red-faced, haggard, disheveled, drunk, and madder than I had ever seen him. He had a big pistol.

"Get back in your car, you slimy SOB," he said.

"But . . ."

"Shut up. We're going to Pretty Place."

Pretty Place—the outdoor chapel for Camp Greenville, up 276, past Caesars Head. It sits on the edge of the mountain looking into the Blue Ridge with hills and valleys and trees as far as you can see, right where North Carolina and South Carolina run together.

Butch was too drunk to reason, too drunk to talk straight. Between telling me to shut up and waving the pistol, he muttered about his dreams and how I had destroyed them. Anything I tried to say in my defense, he just pointed the pistol. I shut up to comply, and my mind just raced around in my head trying to come up with an escape.

"Slow down," he said as we passed Glassy Rock and hit all the sinuous parts of the road, curve upon curve. He saw me reach toward my car door and shouted, "Both hands on the wheel, snake ass!" And fired a bullet out of the window.

Now I was beginning to panic. It was like all the time I'd been given back since the fire was going to be taken again. Again, I'd dissolve into blackness and again . . . Again what? You only get one rescue like I had. Cats have nine lives, not people, even lawyers.

We passed Caesars Head then turned into the road to Camp Greenville. A mile or so of thick forest then a beautiful shallow valley basking in sunlight. Cows and barns and then the camp with signs to Pretty Place.

The weddings were over. All summer, almost every day, a wedding took place; the brides and grooms and wedding party gathered at the mountaintop to receive the blessings of the wilderness and the cool clean air there. "Let us pray for this couple . . ." I had been to three weddings there, all different, all the same in their pilgrimage to reach this high point. There were no weddings today.

Well, let us pray for this particular couple right now. I know we need it as much as newlyweds.

We stopped in the parking lot. Eva's ambulance was there.

"Get out. You too," he shouted at her. "Or I'll kill him." He had a manic look in his eyes. She had started the ambulance, and now she turned it off. She, too, had elemental fire in her eyes.

I was caught in a vortex of irrational force—a former lover and a jilted client! Any lawyer would beware.

I tried to be careful, move slowly, stay calm—but I truly did not know what to do.

"What's wrong, Uncle Butch?" Eva said.

Looking at me, he growled and spat, "You're getting married today, asshole!

I couldn't help myself. Butch smirked. "You fool—why do you think I set this all up? I wanted you to marry Eva. She's a queen, and she needs a lawyer husband."

"What if I don't want a lawyer husband?" she said, in full uniform glory, with all her passion showing. "I'm sick of you running my life."

"We're here for two things," Butch shouted at both of us. "I want to show you what you stole from me, you snake-tongued, slippery lawyer SOB, and y'all are going to get married!" He waved his gun at both of us. "I'm performin' the ceremony. C'mon now, neither one of you can get the other one off your mind. Remember the nekked swimmin', remember the kisses. Yep! You need to get married."

"But, Butch," I said.

"Then I'm gonna kill you," he said with a resolute drunken rage.

We started down the long sloping steps to the altar. Past the low wall there, the great ancient mountain range stretched out in the remains of autumn glory. Smoke from isolated cabins rose up and drifted in columns like ghosts over the treetops, still patchy red and green.

Butch was ahead of us, and he looked unsteady. He held the pistol on us, but his arm wavered as he tried to lecture, curse, and walk backward at the same drunken time.

"You took all this from me. I could have had it all. No more toothless moonshiners and boar hunters—we could have had real estate that the world envied! Sheiks, junk bonders, pirates, warlords, bankers, great world capitalists—safe here in North Greenville County in golden estates. Gated, graveled, they would have come from everywhere. Louise's land was the first step!

He looked at me, pointed the pistol, and pulled the trigger. I ducked fast and pulled Eva down too. He was off balance, and the recoil made him stumble. The pitch of the stairs was steep enough, so he continued to stumble and fall backward with momentum. His legs moved fast, but his fat head went faster. He fired two more shots wildly, and finally his body hit the wall and tumbled over. His voice was far away. Another shot, then silence. Another shot . . .

Eva and I crept slowly down to the altar once we realized we heard nothing. We peered carefully over the wall.

Butch was halfway down the mountain side, his head bloody and his clothes torn by the brush—blood all over his chest. Still clutching the pistol. He didn't move at all.

I looked at Eva.

"At last he's dead! His dreams have always ruined mine." She spat this out.

I reached for her hand, and she knocked it away. She brushed a tear off her cheek and stared down at Butch. "He deserved to die. My sweet baby son is his! I had the test done to find out. I thought the baby was yours. But no, he had raped me one last time after molesting me for years!

"No one else knows, not even Jason. Thank God he was my uncle by marriage. I put Jason down on James birth certificate. Jason is a good man and a father." She looked at me wistfully. "Sweetheart, we are from different worlds. It would never have worked."

Then her face hardened. "Now get out of here," she said. "When the police come, I will say that he called me and sounded drunk. By the time I got here, he'd already killed himself. That's the story . . . got it?" She looked at me fiercely, and I just looked away.

"Got it," I said as I moved swiftly back up the stairs and ran to my car.

My brain still swerved around the curves when I was good and down the mountain. Who was I going to tell about all this?

The answer to that was . . . nobody. I needed to go swimming.

EPILOGUE

A few days later, I went back to the cabin to make sure Butch left nothing. The ground was covered in golden leaves, and the sky was as clear as a vision. I felt Butch there, but no one can possess this gold and this light. He should have known that.

In the cabin, he'd taken out some paper and scrawled some kind of letter but had stopped in the first paragraph—"and I give, as my natural right, to Eva, as my last act on earth . . ." But there wasn't enough to make a will, and the document was worthless.

I'd give it to her, but it might just confuse things more. So be it. That's the way he ended it.

There was a bottle of whiskey, more than half empty, but nothing else.

Walking back through the carpet of golden leaves, the cool air, and the bright clear sky, I felt that it was, at last, all over.

Days and weeks and months passed. Travis and I made up to a degree, but Judge Alexandra Poe, with her lustrous waterfall of black hair—"my grandmother was a full-blooded Cherokee," she told me once, after we kissed awhile—and I had become very close.

Of course, I couldn't argue cases in front of her, but who cared? There was enough work to keep me busy elsewhere.

I'd run into Eva and Jason periodically. Always polite.

Wiley joined me swimming occasionally. We raced and he won. But I was better at the breaststroke.

I passed as much of my time as I could at the cabin. Alexandra liked it up there. The pond stayed fresh all year round, and in winter, we built a nice fire that stayed in the fireplace, the way they are supposed to, nowhere near my car.

What next I thought, how could all of this have happened? There is only one answer for that—the same answer I always gave myself when I couldn't remember anything after the wreck. I don't know.

It's a long swim.

"I swim, therefore I am."

Motto of the Washington and Lee University Swim Team